ANNA'

By

Areline Bolerjack
and
Barbara Wright Jones

Prairie Light Publishing
Tonya Holmes Shook, Publishing Coordinator

Anna's Song
Copyright © 2011
Areline Bolerjack and Barbara Wright Jones

Cover photo by Phyllis Ballew
Courtesy, Shattuck Windmill Park and Museum, Shattuck, OK

All rights reserved. No part of this publication may be reproduced, stored in a retrieval system, or transmitted in any form or by any means, electronic, mechanical, photocopying, microfilming, recording, or otherwise, without permission of the author.

All Scripture quotations are from the King James Version of the Bible.

ISBN-13   978-1466302464

ISBN-10   1466302461

Printed in the United States of America

Dedications

Areline dedicates this book to her great-grandchildren: Chloe and Alyssa, Caedmon and Iain.
Barbara dedicates this book to her grandchildren: Cullen, Blair, Christina, Alexander, Nathan, and Kenley.

Both grandmothers dedicate this book to their grandchildren, with the prayer that they will follow Jesus as have their parents and grandparents, and will pass along their faith to future generations.

Acknowledgments

To those who encouraged us to finish this book:
 Kenneth Jones, James and John Bolerjack.
And to those who supported us in many ways, including reading and advising:
Janice Estell, Vicky Wright, Carolee Briggs, Bari Meyer, and our PAWS writing group.
And to those who went the extra mile to review and edit the book Barbara would like to acknowledge her friend and inspiration, fellow 'storyteller', Molly Lemmons, and her friend and English professor, Dr. Maurine Dickerson. Without all of you, this book would still be in a box under the bed.

Oklahoma Cherokee Strip

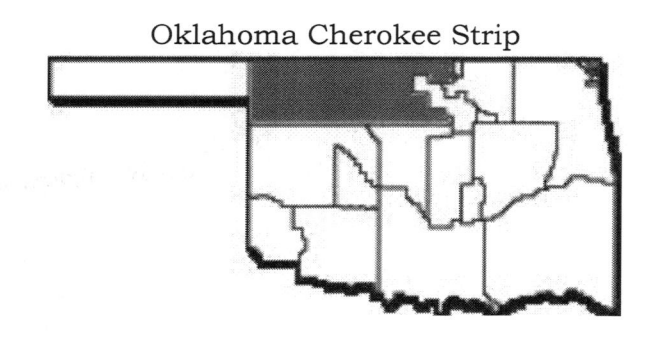

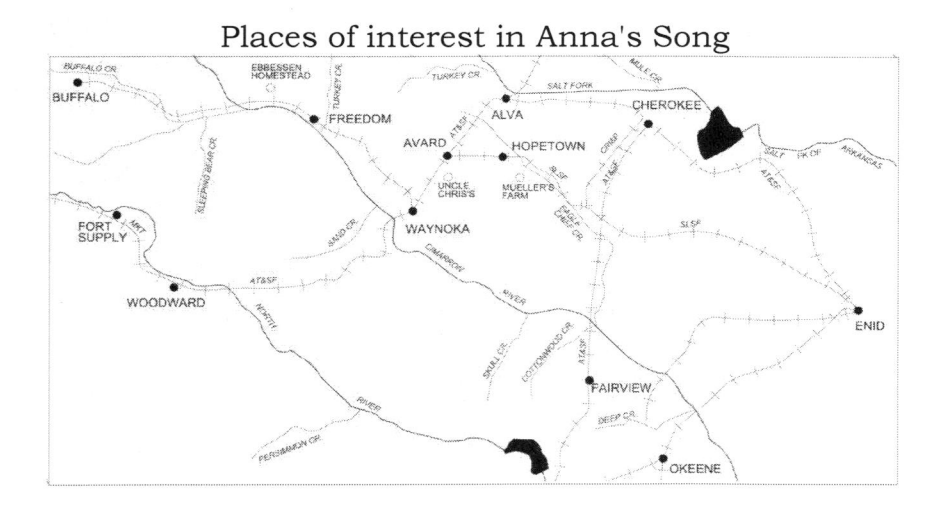

Places of interest in Anna's Song

The wedding picture of Anna Mary and Scottie Shroff, taken in the early 1900s. They were Areline Bolerjack's parents, and her inspiration for some of the experiences in *Anna's Song*.

ANNA'S SONG

Areline Bolerjack and Barbara Wright Jones

CHAPTER 1

Anna swept the dirt floor of the soddy making long swoops with her broom. It was a hapless task; still she felt almost happy. Maybe life would be better now that her brother had found a job working for their neighbors. Perhaps they could buy flour and she could make bread. M-m-m! She could almost smell its yeasty aroma.

A scream and then low animal-like moans shattered the quiet. Anna flew out of the house toward the barn from where the sound had come. She saw her mother crouched on the ground, covering her face with blood-soaked hands. Her father stood over her, clutching a monstrous bone. When he saw Anna coming, he turned and sauntered into the barn. Anna rushed to her mother's side.

"Ma, let's get you to the house." Anna, almost six feet tall and strong from working in the fields, easily lifted her mother and supported her as they walked to the house.

"Ma, what happened?" Anna asked. "Why did Pa hit you?"

"Oh, Anna, it's jist the same ol' story. I asked him if he were goin' ta town, and would brang us back a few victuals. He started mutterin' about not bein' made of money. Then he smacked me in the face with that thar bone." She paused, "He started drinkin' earlier today."

They entered the soddy and Anna helped her ma to the bed behind a curtain that separated her parents' room from the kitchen area.

"Ma, lie down. I need to get this blood washed off your face. This cut looks real bad." Anna eased her ma's frail, undernourished body onto her cot and covered her with a shabby quilt. The dark purple bruise on her cheek had begun to swell and blood surged from the gash on her forehead. Anna went into the kitchen and poured water from the tea kettle into a bowl and returned to the bedroom. She brushed her ma's reddish-gray hair from the wound and gently wiped away the blood.

"I'll go fix some dinner while you rest. Don't try to get up without help."

Mrs. Ebbessen rested a short time and then called, "Anna, I wanta talk ta ya."

Anna hurried to her mother's bed side. When she tried to sit up, Anna said, "Ma, lie still. We can talk after you're feeling better."

"No, I wanta talk ta ya now. I want ya ta pack a few things and leave. It ain't gonna git no better here." As Mrs. Ebbessen looked at her daughter's set, angry face, she added, "I want ya ta remember that yer Pa ain't always been like this. He useta be a good, hard workin' man, but things ain't been easy fur 'im, and he ain't made too much of a go with this here farm, what with the dry weather and all."

Anna gazed about their dwelling. It was nothing but a hole dug into the side of a hill, shored up with timber and blocks of dirt, divided into small rooms with shabby quilts. The front room, which they used as the kitchen, was built of sod. For most families the soddy-half-dugout would have been only a temporary shelter, but her pa had never bothered to build a proper home. She scowled.

Yeah, Pa's had a hard time of things, but how about his family? It hasn't been one long party for us, especially Ma. And all she does is excuse Pa's actions.

Go? Leave? Where? I'm barely seventeen.

Her lucent, blue eyes darkened with fury as she scrunched her forehead and tried to decide on a plan. What would be best for her and Ma in this situation? Maybe Ma was right; still it would not be easy to leave her with Pa as he was, drinking and using ma as an outlet for his temper.

Mrs. Ebbessen broke into her reflection.

"Anna, go git wanna them clean flour sacks and pack some things ta take with ya. And pack a jar of water an them left over vittles from breakfus'."

"Where shall I go, Ma?" Anna bit her bottom lip to keep it from trembling.

"I been thinkin' on that. The only place I know fer ya ta go is ta yer Uncle Chris's."

"But, Ma, that's thirty-five miles, at least. How am I going to get there?"

"You'll just have ta walk 'til a wagon comes along and picks ya up. Start out right after we eat, and Anna, take yer coat along; it might git cold or ya might hafta sleep along the road tonight."

Anna studied her ma. She looked so thin, so vulnerable. Worn out from birthing and raising nine children and living with an abusive husband, she seemed to have lost her will. Anna rubbed the back of her neck.

How could she leave her mother in this condition? Still she must obey her ma. Anna heaved a sigh and went to pack.

She found an empty flour sack, dropped in a work dress and her so-called Sunday dress, even though she seldom went any place on Sunday. After adding some underwear and long cotton stockings, she looked for a piece of string to tie around the top, tucked away the bag, and finished preparing the noon meal.

Anna shoved a pan of cornbread in the oven just as she heard her nineteen year old brother, Tom, drive the team of horses into the yard. That morning he left to plow for a neighbor and she hadn't expected him home this early.

The kitchen door banged as Tom entered the house. He had to stoop over to keep from hitting the top of the door and the beams that held up the sod roof. Anna turned and shook her head and put a finger over her lips to quiet him.

"Ma's resting," she whispered.

"What's the matter? Is she ailin'?" His cobalt, blue eyes held a puzzled look.

"Pa hit her and she's resting."

"Hit her? Why?" Without waiting for an answer, Tom stormed from the house to find his pa. Anna could hear Tom's irate yelling and ran out to the barn to prevent him from hurting Pa.

"You've hit Ma for the last time. You better be looking for trouble from me if you ever hit her again. Do you hear?"

Mr. Ebbessen hung a harness on a peg and turned to face Tom. His long, uncombed white hair and shaggy beard made him appear older than his fifty odd years. As he backed away from his young, muscular son, his short, stocky frame seemed to shrink. A look of fear clouded his faded blue eyes and he lowered his head. Tom stomped out of the barn.

"Pa, come on to the house and let's eat." Anna then hurried out of the barn, across the dusty, cluttered yard and into the house to check on the food. Mrs. Ebbessen was taking the cornbread from the oven. Anna dished up the bean soup and had the meal on the table before Pa got to the house.

Mr. Ebbessen came in and slumped down in his chair, a sullen, angry look on his face. He sulked during the meal and spoke only to ask for some food. Then, without a glance at his wife's bleeding and bruised face, he stomped out of the house, hitched the team to the wagon, and drove down the rutted lane to the road, and out of sight.

Anna helped her mother back to bed and began clearing the table. Before she had finished, her mother called, "Jist leave them dishes and I'll rest a bit, then wash 'em up. Ya best git out on the road so ya won't miss a ride."

Salty tears stung Anna's eyes and streamed down her cheeks as she gathered her belongings.

"Ma, there's some potatoes to fry for supper, if you feel like doing that. If you don't, then let Pa have leftover cornbread and milk." She clasped her ma's work worn hands.

"Ma, are you sure you want me to go? Let me stay until you're feeling better."

"No, chile, ya gotta git away now. I'll send Tom down to tell Esther and Lucy yer leavin' and they can pass the word on to Matt."

How could she leave? Only Esther and Lucy lived near enough to help ma, but they both had babies and small children. Matt and his wife, Katy, lived twenty miles north and her other siblings lived in Kansas and Oregon. That left only Tom, and what did he know about a woman's work?

Anna stroked her ma's furrowed cheek, and then fetched her sack and coat. With a determined step she crossed the yard to say her farewell to Tom. She found him in the barn mending a plow.

"Tom, Ma insists that I leave home today. I'm going to Uncle Chris's house. I don't know what will happen after that, or how long I'll be gone. Take care of Ma, will you? And send me a message as often as you can."

As Anna turned to walk out of the barn, she noticed tears in Tom's eyes. When she reached the end of the lane, she looked back and saw her ma in the door. Anna waved as she turned the corner to enter the dirt road that would take her away from her family and away from the only home she had ever known.

CHAPTER 2

Anna had walked about six miles when she thought she heard a horse coming. Could Pa have followed her? She slipped behind a scrub oak, close enough to the road to signal the rider, or remain hidden if it were Pa. By the time she realized it wasn't Pa, it was too late to stop the horseman.

She scrambled back on the road and continued her journey. As she trudged along, the dusty Oklahoma wind whipped at her skirt. Her cotton stockings inched down into her shoes, making them feel too tight. She hoped someone might ride by soon, but no one did. At last, when long shadows began to appear under the trees, she realized she must find a place to spend the night.

Anna had grown up in this area, but had never before been along this road. She was less than a year old when Pa moved the family to the dry, dirt farm where they now lived. The region had been a part of the Cherokee Outlet, which had been opened to white settlers in 1893. A year later, her father had traded a team of mules for a quarter section of land where they now lived. She loved Oklahoma, but often wondered if things would have been different if her pa had swapped for a better farm. She found a flat area, free of rocks and decaying logs, and tossed her bag on the ground and hunkered down.

"Hope snakes and other varmints are settled in for the night, or at least they don't know I am here," she muttered. Drooping with weariness, she ate the cold cornbread and drank part of the water. She then made a pillow of her sack and snuggled under her coat for the night. Never before had she been forced to sleep alone out in the open and a chill of horror tiptoed down her spine, but soon her weary body relaxed and she fell into a fitful sleep. Sometime later she was jerked awake by the howl of coyotes. Anna stifled a scream. No one would hear her out here if she did holler. Her good sense told her that coyotes didn't attack people, but her fear told her that they might. She huddled under her coat and tried to shut out the sound, and after a time the howling become weaker and Anna went back to sleep.

At the first light of morning, Anna woke up, stretched to remove the stiffness from her body, and brushed the dried leaves and grass from her clothing. She shook her long, brown hair, pulled a comb through it, and then braided it into one plait. She hated its mousy color. Why couldn't she have had golden, red hair as her ma's had been. Everyone said Ma had been a lovely woman when she married Pa.

Ma, I miss you already. Tears filled her eyes and she blinked them back. She wanted to return home, but still she felt she could not disobey Ma's wishes.

Anna looked around and decided Turkey Creek should be somewhere nearby. If it were, she could get some water from the creek and maybe find someone to give her something to eat. She picked up her belongings and resumed her journey along the rutted, dusty trail. By the time she reached Turkey Creek, she had walked more than fourteen miles. She filled her water jar and then looked for someone who might help her. When she found no one she marched on.

It was nearly noon before she saw a horse approaching. Her empty stomach growled and she did not bother to hide this time. She stepped to the side of the road and waved frantically, until the rider stopped. She recognized him as a neighbor of theirs.

"Anna, what are you doing out here?" the man asked.

"Ma thought I should go stay with Uncle Chris for awhile, and I'm on my way. Don't tell any of my family, except maybe Tom, that you saw me. Ma will feel bad about me not getting a ride, and I don't want Pa coming after me. Do you have anything to eat? I can't remember ever being this hungry."

The man drew a bag out of his pocket and handed it to her.

"I bought these in town for the children, but I think they would rather you have them."

She thanked him and popped two of the peppermint candies in her mouth. Turning his horse, the man rode on toward his home and she resumed her journey.

Anna pulled her sunbonnet forward to keep the scorching sun from her face. It felt quite hot for that time of year. The road, barely wide enough for two wagons to pass, wound through the trees and out along the open prairie. The rolling meadows were covered with tufts of fresh, green grass and the scattered colors of wildflowers, a pleasant contrast to the red-orange sandstones that littered the road side. The few trees that grew close to the road were covered with red dirt, making it difficult to tell if they were scrub oaks or sand plums. As she walked along, little puffs of dust whirled around her high topped shoes and up into her face. She took her handkerchief from her pocket and wiped the gritty sweat out of her eyes.

"I feel like a sparrow taking a dirt-bath," she mused. "Hope I can bathe as soon as I get there. Or maybe, I'll just wash my face and eat first."

Her shoes felt heavy and she yearned to stop and rest. The time dragged on and the road appeared endless. She longed to quench her thirst, but when she looked at her water jar only a few drops remained. It must be at least three more miles to her Uncle's house, and she could hardly take another step. Thinking she would rest a bit, she dropped to the ground, sat down and put her head in her hands and immediately fell asleep. By the time she awakened, the sun had dropped low and the western sky had changed from blue to orange tones. With a start she sprung to her feet.

"Oh! Oh! I'll never make it to Uncle Chris's before dark," she cried and began to half-jog as she continued her journey.

When she neared her uncle's house she saw her young cousin in a ruffled dress, golden curls bouncing as she pushed back and forth in the porch swing. When Betty Lou saw her she jumped up and called, "Mama, Mama, someone is coming down the road."

Aunt Nettie came out onto the porch.

"Betty Lou, what's all the yelling about?" With her plump hands she tucked up the curls that had escaped the loose twist of blond hair fastened on top of her head.

"My lands, I believe that's Anna! I wonder how she got here and why."

Betty Lou skipped up the road to meet her favorite cousin. When they neared the porch Aunt Nettie cried, "Sakes alive, girl! You look like something the cat dragged up."

Anna replied, "I feel like that too, or maybe even worse." She half fell as she dropped onto the porch step. "Could I please have a drink of water? And maybe a wet cloth to wash my face?"

She unlaced her shoes, pulled them off and removed her long stockings as well. Her feet were red and swollen with broken blisters on both heels.

"I knew my feet hurt but I thought they were just tired. If I'd looked at them earlier, I probably wouldn't have taken another step."

By then Uncle Chris had joined them. He buttoned his shirt sleeves as he came through the door. His hair, still wet from the washing up before supper, lay slicked down on his head. His long face, with a strong determined jaw line, appeared even longer as his mouth fell open at the sight of Anna.

"My dear, how far did you walk?" he asked.

"Every step of the way. Every blessed step." And to everyone's surprise, especially her own, Anna started crying.

An American Soddy-Half-Dugout House.

In 1904 Alex Ehrlich built a soddy-half-dugout for his family on his land in Ellis County. This soddy has been reconstructed with the original stones, felling local cedar for the roof, and cutting sod behind a pair of mules, and is located in Shattuck Windmill Park, Shattuck, Oklahoma.

CHAPTER 3

Several days later as they were cleaning up the kitchen, Anna said, "Aunt Nettie, your Frikadeller was delicious. It tasted just like Ma's." Anna's parents, who were born in Denmark, shared their love of Danish foods and when times were better Anna's ma had often made dishes she learned from her ancestors.

"Thank you. I try to fix a few recipes that Chris and your pa ate when they were growing up. We usually have on hand the sausage, potatoes, and pickled beets used in making it." Aunt Nettie set the clean milk bucket and separator parts on the table.

"Anna, what are your plans for the future? Have you decided what you want to do?" She looked at Anna and drew a deep breath. "I don't think you should go home yet. Your ma seemed all right last time we saw her, and maybe if you aren't home, your pa will behave himself. I don't think he's going to do anything else to make Chris or Tom angry at him for a while."

"It's hard to believe that Uncle Chris and Pa are brothers; they're so different. I love living in a house with a wooden floor and papered walls, instead of sod walls and dirt floors. In our house, it was dirt everywhere. If anyone bumped the wall accidentally at night, sand and dirt fell into the bed.

"As for deciding what I am going to do, I don't know." Anna picked up a glass and began polishing it until she saw her image reflected.

"I don't know any man I want to marry or one who would have a big, ugly girl like me for a wife. I'm taller than most men. I'm not trained to do anything except work in the fields or keep house." She turned her head away to keep Aunt Nettie from seeing her tears. Suddenly, a feeling of home-sickness washed over her. She wanted to see her mother and Tom, even Pa.

"Do you mind if I stay here a little longer? Maybe Ma will send for me. I'll help with the work all I can."

"Anna, you're welcome to stay as long as you want."

In the following days, Anna helped her uncle sow seed corn while Betty Lou tagged along the rows with her.

"Want to hear a story about when I was a little girl like you, helping my brother Donald plant corn? Donald's the one that lives in Oregon. You probably don't remember him." Anna said.

"I love stories." Betty Lou jumped up and down.

"Lucy was still home then and Tom was there also, but he wasn't much more help than I was. Pa gave us this big sack of seed corn to plant. We planted and planted and it seemed as if we would never run out of seed. We had planted the entire field and still had at least a quart of seeds left." Anna set her sack down and pushed back a loose strand of hair that had escaped her braid and wiped the sweat from her brow and continued.

"A small stream ran alongside the field when it rained. It was dry then and Donald suggested that we dig a hole in the stream bed and bury the rest of the corn. That seemed like a good idea at the time and we thought Pa would never find out, so that's what we did. It wasn't long before it rained and water filled the stream for about a week. Pa went out to check on the corn field and found corn plants in the stream bed. The seeds we'd hidden there had sprouted and were growing. Pa was furious. We didn't try that trick again."

"I like that story. I'm glad you came to visit us Anna," Betty Lou said.

"I'm glad too, but I really miss Ma," Anna said.

~~~~~~~~

Anna had about decided to go back home when one afternoon her aunt's neighbor, Mrs. Mandy Beckner, came to visit.

"Anna, my sister needs help for a few months," she said. "She had a fall and injured her back. She has two little children, and is expecting another in about four months. The doctor insists she stay in bed, maybe until the baby is born." Mrs. Beckner knitted her brows together.

"I don't know how a doctor expects a woman with small children to stay in bed. If she does, the kids will be crawling all over her." She smiled at Anna. "I heard you were visiting your aunt, and I thought of you when my brother-in-law sent me word of Ellen's accident. She has no one who can help her full time. I wondered if you'd like the work. They live about ten miles from here."

If she went, she would be almost fifty miles from home and that seemed a very long way. She breathed deeply and said, "I'll go, but I don't have a way to get there and I am not walking again."

"My husband and I will take you. Can you be ready to leave today?"

"If it's okay with Aunt Nettie," she said.

"Anna, this is a good opportunity for you, and perhaps you could help your pa and ma out at the same time," her aunt said.

Anna knew that it would difficult to live with strangers and the distance would prevent her from seeing her family, still it would give her a chance to earn her own money and even send some home to Ma. After Anna gathered her clothes and stuffed them into her sack, she went out to the Beckner's wagon.

"Thanks Aunt Nettie for everything. Tell Uncle Chris good-by for me," she said. She gave her little cousin a hug.

"Bye, Betty Lou." She would certainly miss them. Mr. Beckner helped her and his wife into the wagon. Anna turned and waved at her aunt and little cousin and they rode away.

Anna felt anxious. This was her first job and she had no experience working for other people. Could she meet their expectations?

"Mrs. Beckner, what's your sister like?" she asked.

"Please, just call me Mandy. My sister Ellen is a hard worker, and being put to bed near harvest time tries her patience. She'll be thankful to have help." Mrs. Beckner continued chatting for most of the trip and didn't seem to notice that neither her husband nor Anna said much.

As they bumped along, strong wind whipped at Anna's dress and she grabbed her bonnet to keep it from flying off. Sometimes she grew tired of the relentless Oklahoma wind; still, she knew without it the heat would be unbearable.

Anna had never before traveled in this area, and as they rambled on she studied the scenery. The country was mostly flat prairie, covered with stubby buffalo grass, and dotted with colorful Indian blankets and other wild flowers. As they traveled east, lush fields of wheat filled the countryside.

It was nearly dark when the wagon pulled into the Mueller's farm yard. As they drove up the driveway, Anna could see the outline of several buildings scattered about the area. At sight of the house, her eyes widened with awe. It was a two-storied structure, painted snowy white. A concrete porch went across the front and west side of the house. Several gables made up the roof which extended down to cover the porches. A cistern had been built at the side of the house. Ruffled white curtains showed at the windows where light was shining. It looked like a fairytale castle to Anna.

"This is the most beautiful house I've ever seen, and the largest one."

Mr. Becker helped his wife and Anna from the wagon and then unhitched and cared for the horses. The group entered the house through a screened-in back porch that also had a concrete floor. Near the screen door stood a work table and benches. At the other end of the porch two wash tubs were turned upside down on top of a table.

Sam Mueller, a tall man with large hands, opened the kitchen door. His sandy hair just touched his collar and his fair skin was sprinkled with copper colored freckles. Smile lines around his hazel eyes deepened at the sight of his guests.

"Come right in. I was afraid you couldn't get here tonight and Ellen has been fretting to get out of bed."

Mandy left Anna with Mr. Mueller and his daughters and hurried to the bedroom where her sister lay flat on her back with a pillow under her knees. Her face showed signs of pain and her chin quivered as she told Mandy how glad she was to see her.

"It's been so hard on Sam to have the care of the children and the outside work also. The girls have been into everything today and I didn't feel like correcting them. I hope you brought us is a good worker."

"Have you had supper yet?" Mandy asked.

"No. I just haven't felt like getting up."

"Let me make you a bit more comfortable and then we will see about supper," Mandy said. She hastened about to sponge Ellen's face and tidy the crumpled bed. When she finished she said, "Now I will see about a meal. Everyone feels better after they have eaten. Then we will put the babies to bed and Sam and Frank can do any outside work. Ellen, stay here and rest now."

When Mandy returned to the kitchen, she found that Anna had already stoked the fire in the large, black cook stove set at the back wall of the kitchen and had a ham in the oven and a pot of coffee ready. She was bent over the sink peeling potatoes. The men and the children waited in the living room.

"M-m-m that ham sure smells good. Glad to see you've got supper going. I'm hungry as a bear," Mandy said.

"Mr. Mueller brought a ham in from the smokehouse to go with the pot of beans, and I'm fixing some potatoes. Is that all right?" Anna said.

"Indeed. Do you think you could work until Ellen's baby is born and she is able to be up and do her own work?" Mandy asked.

"Yes, I'll stay." Anna set the potatoes on the

burner and looked at Mrs. Beckner. "I've never used a sink. And this little pitcher pump at the sink is going to be a joy. We always carried water from a pump outside into the house."

When the meal was ready, Mandy took a plate to Mrs. Mueller while Anna served the others. After supper and the kitchen cleaned up, Mandy took Anna to meet Mrs. Mueller.

"Ellen this is Anna. She has agreed to help out for a while."

Mrs. Mueller sat up and extended her small hand to Anna. It felt warm, but rough from working on the farm. Even though her face showed signs of pain, and her blond braids untidy, she was still lovely, with cream colored skin, touched with pink at the cheeks, and green eyes, framed by dark lashes. She smiled at Anna.

"It's a blessing to have you with us." The kind words set Anna at ease and she felt more confident.

After they had visited awhile, Mandy said, "It's time we put the girls to bed."

Mr. Mueller had made up a cot for Anna in the children's room. He said, "Anna, I hope you don't mind sleeping in the room with Martha and Sarah. It will be more convenient for you there and also you can hear Ellen if she needs help in the night."

Mr. Mueller's thoughtful suggestion surprised Anna. She knew she would like working for the Muellers.

CHAPTER 4

Early the next morning Anna awoke to the clinking of crockery in the kitchen. She slipped into her clothes, trying not to wake Martha. Anna glanced at the child, sleeping peacefully, her golden curls spread across her pillow. She looked about five or six years old. Last night Anna had observed how independent the little girl was when she wanted to undress herself and get into bed without help. Sarah was the younger sister and her bed was empty. Anna wondered where she could be. She smiled when she thought about Sarah wanting her to tuck her into bed and hug her good night.

When she entered the kitchen, Anna found that someone had already started the fire in the cook-stove, made coffee, and left it on the back burner to keep warm. She tiptoed into Mrs. Mueller's bedroom, and saw Sarah nestled in bed beside her mother. Both were still asleep. Quietly she went out the front door and stood on the porch to get her bearings.

Outside the front door she saw a neat yard enclosed by a white picket fence. The grass inside the area was turning green and tulip blossoms lined the pathway. The charming scene was quite unlike Anna's home, which had no enclosed yard and no grass, only red clay that turned to gumbo when it rained. The Mueller's house faced the south, and to the west, straight across the yard, she saw a large barn. Anna heard sounds near the barn and walked over to investigate. Mr. Mueller and his brother-in-law stood at the door holding empty milk buckets. Suddenly she heard a rumble and had to jump out of the path as the cows trotted into their stalls, eager to eat the grain and hay that had been placed in the mangers. After she got her breath she said, "Do you want me to help milk?"

"Good morning, Anna," Mr. Mueller said. "No, not this morning. Sometimes you may have to help, but today, just go ahead with breakfast."

"What do you usually eat for breakfast?"

"Today you'll have to make pancakes or biscuits. We used all the bread last night. If Mandy's up, she'll show you where things are. If she isn't, and you can't find things, just wait until I finish milking." Mr. Mueller set his stool beside a cow and began squeezing the cow's teats, pulling down in even little jerks. Streams of white foamy milk made pinging sounds as they hit the pail.

"Mandy set the sponge for bread last night. Do you know how to make bread?" When she nodded he continued, "You could start the bread, if you like."

Anna made a circle around the outhouse then entered the house by the back door. Her head had been turning back and forth trying to see everything at once. Later she would explore all the buildings, but now she must hurry and prepare breakfast.

"Good morning," Mandy said when Anna entered the kitchen. "I hope you slept well. I've started the biscuits and if you would slice some bacon and start it cooking, we'll get breakfast going.

"Ellen's awake and I've helped her to the chamber pot. She's drinking a cup of coffee and entertaining Sarah until the breakfast is ready."

As she talked, Mandy deftly mixed the biscuits in the largest wooden bowl Anna had ever seen. It must hold at least ten pounds of flour. How many biscuits was this woman making? Anna grabbed a sharp knife from the shelf over the sink and began slicing the bacon. She removed the rinds, placed the bacon strips in a large iron skillet, and set it on the front of the stove. The bacon sizzled and popped as it fried, and its smell made her mouth water. When it looked ready she pushed the skillet to the back of the stove to stay warm and walked over to watch the biscuit making again. By now, Mandy was pinching the biscuits off smoothly and nearly all the same size, dipping them in melted lard in the baking pan and arranging them in neat rows. Anna wondered if she would ever learn how to make biscuits like Mandy's.

After the men finished milking they carried the milk to a building behind the house and by the time they entered the kitchen breakfast was almost ready. Mr. Mueller filled a wash basin at the sink pump and carried the pan to the back porch where the men washed up. Martha came into the kitchen, yawning and rubbing the sleepies out of her eyes. Her dad picked her up and hugged her.

"Good morning, sweetheart. How's Daddy's little lady this morning?"

Anna had never seen people so well mannered and kind and loving to each other. She thought perhaps they were just putting on a show that morning and would behave differently when no one was watching.

Mr. Mueller settled the girls in their chairs and fixed their plates while Anna poured the coffee. When everything was ready, Anna slid into her chair and after she lifted her coffee to take a drink, she heard Mr. Mueller speak. Looking up, she realized the others had bowed their heads.

"Lord, we thank Thee for the good night's rest," Mr. Mueller prayed. "We thank Thee for sending Anna to help us. We pray for Ellen and ask that she might have grace and patience to accept this problem as being Thy will for her at this time. Thank Thee for this food. In Jesus' name, Amen."

Anna had never heard anyone talk to God the way Mr. Mueller did. She began eating, careful to mimic their table manners. As the family ate they laughed and talked, leaving her a bit bewildered. Her family never talked and joked, and certainly not at meal time!

After breakfast Anna cleaned the kitchen and set the bread to rise. Mandy then offered to show her around and explain things. First they went to the building where the fresh milk was stored in lard cans. Mandy picked up one of the cans and said, "Put an empty cream can under this small spout, and then slowly pour the milk into this big bowl at the top of the strainer and turn the crank. The machine will separate the cream from the milk. After you're finished we will take the cream and milk to the springhouse to keep it cool."

The springhouse floor and walls, up to the bottom of the windows, were made of rocks set in concrete. A stream of crystal clear water flowed through a deep concrete trough built against the back wall. Mandy poured the cream into a small bucket and the milk into the larger buckets and she covered them with lids; then set them into the water.

"The windmill pumps the water into the depression and then it flows out into the horse tank to water the animals."

"This is a very modern farm. Mrs. Mueller has many things to make her work easier," Anna said.

"While we're outside, I'll show you the other buildings," Mandy said. "This is the smokehouse."

Anna saw two hams and two sides of bacon hanging from the rafters.

"Sam butchered late this winter so there would be meat left for harvest."

As they went back outside, Anna looked around. Golden colored wheat fields filled with plump heads of grain surrounded the farm yard.

"I've never seen so much wheat. Pa didn't plant any nor did many other farmers in our area. I haven't seen a harvest either. When will it begin?"

"In about four or five weeks, I think," Mandy replied. "That's why Ellen wants to get out of bed. Getting ready for harvest's a lot of work. Some of the neighbor women will help you all they can."

They returned to the springhouse and Mandy picked up a bucket of skim milk and asked Anna to bring the other one.

"We might as well give this milk to the chickens and pigs as we look around," she explained. "Fill these pans with milk from your pail."

They poured the milk into pans and the chickens came running. They set their buckets down and entered the chicken house.

"It looks like Sam just recently cleaned it," Mandy said.

Anna looked around the well-organized chicken house with nests filled with fresh hay.

"During harvest, you will clean the chicken house at least once a week."

Anna noted several eggs already in the nest.

At least, we will have plenty of eggs. I don't think in my whole life I have ever eaten as many eggs as I would like.

Mandy picked up her bucket and they started walking toward a pig pen, which stood a good distance away from the house. The pig pen was built with straight boards and log posts, and not in the haphazard way Pa had built theirs. She saw four hogs, two large sows with bulging stomachs that looked like they would farrow soon and two smaller pigs. They rooted around in a muddy ground making grunting sounds. Anna wrinkled her nose at the putrid smell.

"These shoats are being fattened up for the fall butchering time. They are such gross, ugly animals to taste so good," Mandy commented.

As she poured her bucket of milk into a trough, she said, "Use all the extra milk and grain and kitchen scraps to feed the hogs."

"We have time to look at the barn, and then the bread dough will probably be ready to make into loaves."

As they walked through the barn, Anna noticed a hen's nest filled with eggs. She reached out to pick up the eggs and a large, red hen flew at her.

"Ay!" she yelled, and nearly fell backwards.

"Are you okay, Anna?" Mandy reached out and took Anna's hand to steady her. "Hens like to lay eggs in the barn and can get quite protective if they're setting," she said as she picked up the eggs. "Can you milk?"

"Yes."

"You may not have to milk except during harvest.

Sam says with the extra work of caring for Ellen you'll have all you can do."

Mandy then showed Anna the water pipe that brought fresh water to the barn.

"I've never seen anything like this."

"The men have already mucked out the barn. Sam believes everything should be clean and the work as easy as possible," Mandy said. "Still, in spite of all these modern conveniences, Ellen and Sam work very hard. Our farm is fairly well up-to-date, but this one is way ahead of ours. I'm thankful that Ellen has it so good. We better get to the house. I'll show you the cellars and the garden after lunch, and then we must head for home. Walter's mother is caring for our children and she tires easily."

The yeasty smell of the bread dough greeted them as they entered the kitchen. The dough had already begun to droop over the sides of the mixing bowl and Anna washed her hands and punched it down, and then shaped it into loaves and put them aside to rise again.

Mandy suggested that Anna whistle for the dog and send the children outside to play.

"I imagine Ellen has read to the girls about as long as she can. They play with the dog and he also watches over them when they are outside. Try to keep them in sight all the time."

The house-keeping duties still needed attention and it was already after nine. The separator and milk utensils had to be washed and the parts scaled and then she would have to remember how to put them back together. Still the work would be easier because she could pump the water in the kitchen rather than fetching it from the windmill and carrying it inside to be heated. She completed the dreaded job and then prepared the noon meal.

"Well, we'll be off now," Mandy said soon after dinner. "We'll be back around Thanksgiving."

Anna waved good-by to them. She would miss the verbose woman and looked forward to her return.

After she had tucked the girls in bed for their afternoon naps, Ellen called to her.

"Anna, come and rest while we discuss your work."

CHAPTER 5

Anna sat down with a sigh.

"I am dead-dog tired, and the day's just half over."

"Sam and I both are pleased with what you've done, and it should be easier as you become familiar with everything and learn where things are." Mrs. Mueller picked up a note pad. "I've made some lists, not because I think you will forget to do some things, but rather, they will make your work simpler. We'll help you anytime you need it, and don't be afraid to ask questions." She handed the lists to Anna.

"Tack these up where you can see them. Put them high enough so the girls won't take them down."

Anna looked at the heading of the first list: All the daily tasks. Her eyes widened as she studied the length of the list.

Mrs. Mueller laughed.

"Don't worry. Some of those things can be done almost as fast as you can read them. You can read, can't you?"

"Yes."

"I assumed you could read since you use good grammar. Tell me a little about yourself."

"I turned seventeen in April. Since I'm the youngest child and my brother, Tom, is close to me in age, there were no children at home for me to care for, so when I wasn't needed at home Pa let me go to school. He complained that all that learning would ruin me, but Ma insisted." Anna's eyes brightened as she remembered how her mother had stood up to Pa on her behalf.

"I was the oldest one in school but the teacher

didn't mind. She seemed glad to have someone that wanted to learn and I helped her some. She gave me extra books to take home, but Pa thought reading was a waste of time. I didn't get to attend all year because of the planting and any other excuse Pa could think of."

Anna stopped for a bit, dipped her head, then continued, "My pa drinks a lot and is real mean when he's drunk. That's why Ma wanted me to leave home. I'm worried about Ma, but she thought maybe Pa would be better if I wasn't there for him to blame. He's never hit me, only Ma." Anna gripped the seat of her chair until her knuckles hurt.

"I hope Ma's all right. My Uncle Chris, who lives near your sister, told Pa if he ever hurt Ma again he would be sorry. I just hope Pa remembers."

She had never before shared her life with a stranger and feared that Mrs. Mueller would think ill of her for being so open about her troubles. Anna lowered her gaze.

"Two of my sisters live about five miles from Ma, but they both have young children. My oldest brother lives about twenty miles from us. My brother Tom's at home. He'll do his best to take care of Ma, but he's got all he can handle with the outside work. I must write to Ma and Lucy and Esther so they will know where I am now. I've been gone from home almost three weeks and it seems a lifetime." Anna's shoulders hunched and she closed her eyes to squeeze back the tears.

Mrs. Mueller, sensing Anna's homesickness, suggested they look at the lists again. On the next one, she had written the work schedule for each day except Sunday. Anna read, "Straighten up the cellar where the canned goods are stored. Check the root cellar and organize it, if necessary." She had not been shown these two places. She said, "While the girls are asleep why don't I go look at the cellar?"

"The entry door is on the east side of the house," Mrs. Mueller said. "It is under the kitchen section."

Anna left Mrs. Mueller and located the cellar, lifted the heavy wooden door, and carefully moved down the steep steps hoping there were no snakes or mice below. A lantern she carried lit her way as she descended into the dark cavern. Shining the light around, she discovered all sorts of canned fruits and vegetables: corn, beans, sweet potatoes, pumpkin, berries, peaches, even dried nuts. On the shelf across the room she saw jars of canned, fried, and stewed chicken as well as sausage.

Goodness! I've never seen this much food in one place. She hurried round to the root cellar and found potatoes and turnips in wooden bins, and bunches of onions hanging from the rafters.

All this food leftover from last year's season. I've got to see the garden that produced this much food.

She found the garden between the house and orchard. The neat rows were already lined with small plants that promised a rich harvest. Anna clapped her hands. In a few weeks these vegetables would be ready to pick. Green beans, peas, potatoes.

I can hardly wait! Fresh lettuce and spinach. And rhubarb. And tomatoes. I'll be able to eat tomatoes every meal. When she compared the Mueller's garden with the little patch that was all Pa ever plowed, it made her want to laugh and cry at the same time.

The May sunshine felt welcome on her cool skin.

She wished she could stay outside the rest of the day, but work waited. She found the little girls in their mother's room laughing and talking. Anna was surprised at the patience Mrs. Mueller had with the children.

"Girls, put away your toys and go with Anna."

"I have some crackers and milk for you and then you may play in the yard."

After the girls finished their snack, Anna whistled for the dog, and he came running. Martha grabbed him and said, "Ben, have you been chasing rabbits? He loves to chase rabbits better than anything," she told Anna.

Ben, a handsome, golden collie, was a willing slave of the girls as they tossed a ball for him to chase. He even allowed Sarah to put her bonnet on him and pretend he was her baby.

When Anna returned to the house Mrs. Mueller asked, "Would you please help me up to the chamber pot? It's really hard for me to depend on others for such a small thing, but Doctor Harris said I can only get up with help. I am so tired of the bed already." Still, after she had finished Anna could see that she was more than glad to be back in bed.

"Except when the girls were born, I've never been waited on. Mama helped then but she isn't well now, and with harvest being so near and all the canning and other things that have to be done in the summer, we didn't feel she should come this time." Mrs. Mueller rubbed her forehead and sighed.

"It's hard to accept someone else doing things for me." Shifting a little under the sheet she continued, "Do you know how to make noodles, Anna?"

"Yes, Ma taught me."

"In the cellar are some jars of stewed chicken. Bring up two of those and make some chicken noodle soup for supper. You will need to get an onion from the root cellar, also bring a jar of carrots and mash some of those and put them in the soup for color." The woman shifted position, trying to get comfortable. "A bread pudding would be good for supper, also. A notebook should be on one of the shelves to the left of the stove. I have written down some recipes you might want to use. Fix what you can, Anna. I think I will rest now."

Anna started the chicken broth simmering and made the bread pudding. When Mrs. Mueller rang her bell she went to check on her.

"If Sam isn't back from town by five o'clock, tell Ben to go get the cows. Sam is going to try to find a man to hire to help through harvest. You will have as much, or more, as you can do without having to do outside work."

Anna made the noodles, and then after making sure the children were all right, she went to gather the eggs. It wasn't long before she heard a wagon drive into the yard. By the time she set the bucket of eggs on the back porch, Mr. Mueller and a young man had entered the house.

"Anna, I want you to meet Carl Hunter. He's going to work for us until after harvest. Carl, this is Anna Ebbessen. She's helping while my wife is sick."

Carl brushed his straw colored hair off his forehead and stared at Anna with sullen, pale blue eyes. He didn't offer a greeting and neither did Anna. He was small framed, with long arms and large hands, and looked about two inches shorter than Anna. She judged that he was about her age.

"Carl's the nephew of our nearest neighbor, Tom Hunter." Mr. Mueller said. "He came from Arkansas to visit and find work. He'll help with some of your outdoor chores. This will free you up a bit to spend more time with Ellen and the children."

Mr. Mueller's consideration surprised Anna. She glanced at Carl and noted his sour expression and heard him mumble, "I ain't doin' no woman's work."

CHAPTER 6

Several days later, Carl came into the kitchen where Anna was drying dishes and said, "Mr. Mueller said the chicken house needs to be cleaned." His upper lip twisted in a smirk and he turned and sauntered out of the house. Anna watched as he strolled leisurely toward the orchard, but didn't think anything more about it. She glanced at the list tacked to the back porch wall. Her responsibility for the day did indeed include cleaning out the chicken house. She would have to hurry to finish and get cleaned up in time to prepare the noon meal.

Anna checked to make sure Mrs. Mueller didn't need anything and found her sleeping. She left the children playing inside the fenced yard with the dog and after tying a cloth over her head she walked to the tool shed for the rake and shovels, loaded them on the wheelbarrow and headed for the henhouse.

"I hate this smelly, dirty job," she grumbled. "But I do enjoy fried chicken and fresh eggs. Guess you can't have one without the other."

An hour later she looked with pride at the pile of waste she had dumped on the compost heap.

"Well, that's done for this week. Now it's time to get cleaned up." She wiped her smelly hands on her apron and went to pump a bucket of water, and then carried it to a sheltered corner between the back porch and bedroom where she could wash-up. She unpinned her long hair, shook it and her clothing to remove as much dust as possible, and rolled up her sleeves, and washed her face and arms. After taking off her shoes and stockings, Anna poured the rest of the water over her hair and let it run down over her dress. She wrung out as much water as possible from her hair and dress and went to her bedroom to change clothes hurrying about because she knew that dinner should have been underway before this. She wound her wet hair up into a knot, put on a clean dress and arrived in the kitchen just as Carl entered.

"Guess dinner's late again," he said. Before Anna could say anything he ducked out the back door.

At dinner, Mr. Mueller said to the hired man, "Carl, the chicken house looks nice. You did a good job on it."

Carl just grunted and said, "Yeah," and went on eating.

Anna gasped and nearly choked on her food, but no one took note of her discomfort. When the meal ended, Carl excused himself and sauntered out the back door. With a set jaw and lips pressed together, Anna began clearing the table. Rage at the insolence of the man got her to thinking of how she could get revenge. Her chance came that night at supper. It was almost dark when the men rode their horses into the yard. Anna heard Mr. Mueller say, "Carl, it's late. Why don't you stay for supper tonight?" Carl agreed to stay.

When she dished up his soup, she added about a tablespoon of salt. She didn't see his reaction when he tasted the soup because she had taken supper to Mrs. Mueller. Still, she could imagine his shock when he realized something was wrong and could hardly keep from laughing just thinking about it. *Serves him right,* she thought as she got ready for bed that night.

~~~~~~~~

The next few days the conflict between the two

became obvious to the Muellers. Anna continued to ruin Carl's food at every opportunity. Once he exchanged plates with her when she wasn't looking. He frequently made rude remarks about Anna's cooking, her size, and her clothes, even in front of the girls.

"Carl talks ugly to you Anna. Why don't you tell Mama?" Sarah said.

"I'm no tattle tale," Anna told her.

One afternoon Carl came into the kitchen where Anna was sweeping.

"You're the slowest person I've ever met." He sneered as he grabbed the broom handle. "Weren't for your pokey ways I wouldn't have to be doing a woman's work."

Anna's eyes narrowed and she gritted her teeth, but before she had a chance to respond Mr. Mueller entered the room.

"What is going on in here?" he asked.

When no one answered, Martha said, "Carl's talking ugly to Anna. He's just a mean old bully and I don't like him."

"Martha, you go see if Mommy needs some help. Sarah, go with her." The man looked at the two.

"All right, let's settle this problem right now and I do not want to hear another thing about it. What started the trouble?"

Anna sat with a stoic look on her face. She did not answer, and neither did Carl.

"What started this trouble?" Mr. Mueller asked again.

Neither of them said a word.

"Carl, I don't remember having trouble before you

came. Did you do something that made Anna angry?"

Carl closed his lips, and turned his eyes away from Mr. Mueller's penetrating gaze.

Mr. Mueller looked at Anna. "Did you start this problem, Anna?"

She turned tear filled eyes toward Mr. Mueller and shook her head.

"What did Carl do to you, Anna? You must tell me the truth so that we can settle this now."

"I'm not a tattle tale." She straightened her shoulders. "I can take care of this situation. And I can get revenge for anything he does to me. And maybe more."

"That doesn't solve the problem." Mr. Mueller looked sternly at Anna then turned to Carl, "Tell me what Anna has done to you."

"Well, first she put salt in my food," he complained. "And some other stuff that I don't know what it was. She put sand in my bed the night I stayed here. She put molasses in my boots, and other stuff I don't remember right now."

Anna hated the sound of his whiny, peevish voice and wanted to respond, "Poor little me," but instead she kept silent and tried not to smile.

"Anna, did you do those things?" When she nodded, he turned to Carl. "What did you do in return?"

"I didn't do nothing to her."

Anna looked at him, eyes wide and mouth open. Still, she did not accuse him of anything. Mr. Mueller looked from one to the other. He turned and started for the door. "Let's get to work, Carl."

As Carl left the room his mouth curled into a

smirk, and he tossed his head like a thorough-bred horse and swaggered out the door.

"I'll get him yet," Anna promised herself. She had just finished cleaning the kitchen when Sarah came in.

"Time for your nap," she said as she picked up the little girl and carried her to her room.

"I don't like that mean old Carl for making you cry," Sarah said. She put her arms around Anna's neck and hugged her tight.

"Mommy said I can't say I hate him no more. She said God wants us to love everyone, but I don't love Carl, but just a little bit. I love you the most, Anna."

Had anyone ever told her that they loved her? Surely, Ma had loved her, but she never expressed her feelings much.

"Sarah, I love you too." She hugged the little girl. This was the first time Anna had ever told anyone that she loved them. It felt strange, yet good. As she thought about these things, she couldn't remember anyone hugging her, either. Still, Ma must have hugged her when she was little. Anna tucked Sarah into bed and went in to visit with Mrs. Mueller. After a while, she spoke to Anna about the trouble between her and Carl.

"We've tried to have harmony in our home. Early in our marriage we discovered that dissension between Sam and me made us both feel bad. We began to imagine slights and hurts and the situation grew until we had to deal with it. Do you think you and Carl could solve your difficulties? This hostile atmosphere is beginning to affect the children."

Anna twisted her hands together and scooted

back in her chair.

"I can drop the whole thing if Carl will leave me alone and keep his mouth shut about how I do my work."

Martha was lying on the bed with her mother, looking at a book. She sat up and said, "I wish Carl would keep his mouth shut, too."

Her mother looked at the child, "Martha, we don't like for you to talk like that."

"But Anna said that and Carl talks like that too. And he says mean things to Anna."

"Take your book and go read it at the kitchen table, Martha." When the little girl was out of the room, Mrs. Mueller turned to Anna and said, "We have had enough evasion and silence, Anna. I want to know what started this quarrel and I want to know now."

Anna sighed and wiped her sweaty hands on her apron.

"When Mr. Mueller introduced Carl to me, he said Carl would help do some of my outside chores. After Mr. Mueller left the room, Carl mumbled to me, 'I ain't doin' no woman's work.' Those are his words, not mine."

"Is that all?"

"No. A few days later he came into the house and told me Mr. Mueller said the chicken house needed to be cleaned. I hurried to get it done before fixing dinner. Then I had to take time to clean up some before I could come into the house and get dinner ready. Carl complained about the meal being late." Anna looked down.

"During the meal, Mr. Mueller told Carl he'd done a good job on the chicken house. Carl grunted and didn't say that I'd done the work." Anna paused then remembers, "After telling me I was to clean out the chicken house, I'd seen him walking toward the orchard, so I guess he just hid out while I worked."

"I believe that would have made me angry, also. But, the name calling and dissension must stop. It makes me tense, which isn't helping my back, and it upsets the children, also. Yesterday, I heard Sarah call Martha a 'stinkin' polecat.' Does that sound familiar?"

Anna twisted her hands together and looked at her lap.

"Please promise me, Anna, not to take revenge for what Carl does to you. Sam will deal with Carl. You tell me what he does and I will tell Sam."

Anna frowned and said, "I'll try. But it's not going to be easy. I'll probably forget and call him names sometimes."

~~~~~~~~

That night a gentle rain, that didn't harm the wheat, fell. The next morning Anna scrubbed the kitchen linoleum and while it was still wet Carl came into the house to get a drink. He tracked across the clean, wet floor with muddy boots. He was at the sink, drinking some water, when Anna saw the dirty floor.

"Why you stinking little weasel, you low down, dirty, conniving little dried up..." She broke her tirade as Carl threw a dipper of water at her. Anna was standing with clenched fists and angry face, breathing deeply and heavily, when Mr. Mueller entered the kitchen.

He stood looking from one to the other.

"What's wrong now?"

Anna sputtered, "Just look at my clean floor."

The man looked at Carl. "Did you track in this mud?"

Carl shrugged his shoulders as he answered, "Well, what did you expect me to do? It's muddy out."

"What I expect you to do is clean the floor. Show him where the mop is, Anna, and take the girls outside to play while I watch Carl."

Before going outside, Anna stopped at Mrs. Mueller's door and said, "I'm sorry I forgot my promise to you when I saw that dirty floor. I am going outside with the girls while Carl cleans the floor." With a grin, she added, "I would rather stay and watch."

Outside with the girls, Anna suggested going for a walk.

"Maybe we can find some wild flowers blooming and pick your mommy a bouquet."

As they walked along the sandy road, the two girls chattered cheerfully. The sun shone bright, and a light breeze ruffled Anna's skirt. She felt glad to be outside. The dog scurried along beside the girls, making occasional side trips to chase a rabbit or small animal. After picking flowers from a locust tree and a few wild roses, they started back to the house. A buggy was parked in the yard when they got home.

CHAPTER 7

"Anna I would like you to meet, Alice and Roy Peterson," Mrs. Mueller said.

An enormous woman with camel-colored hair pulled back into a loose bun, greeted Anna. She wore a blue, vee-necked dress trimmed with a lace collar that drew attention away from her round cheeks and plump neck and to her sparkling blue eyes and open smile. The woman's body spread over the sides of her chair, reminding Anna of bread dough. Mr. Peterson, a tall, thin man with carrot red hair and a multitude of freckles, stood beside his wife's chair. Anna could hardly keep from staring at such an odd couple.

"Anna, please get our guests some grape juice from the cellar and bring along some of the cookies you baked this morning."

After the refreshments were served Mrs. Peterson said, "We must be going. Thanks for the delicious cookies and juice."

They left the house and Anna watched as Mr. Peterson gently helped his wife into the buggy. After seeing them off, Anna returned to Mrs. Mueller's room. "She is the biggest woman I've ever seen. I don't know how she gets around. Her husband's really kind and helpful with her, though."

"Please don't judge her by appearance. She's one of the most warmhearted, helpful neighbors we have. She will be helping while the harvesters are here and you'll find that she's a fast worker, and you will be thankful for her assistance.

"Anna, the Bible tells us that man judges by outward appearances, but God judges the heart. We have to be careful how we judge people."

"I've never read a Bible. We didn't have any at home, but my teacher might have read from it, I'm not sure." Anna bit her upper lip and fidgeted with her hands.

"As for God, I've only heard His name as a swear word, mostly by Pa, so I guess I could say I don't know anything about Him. I never thought of Him as a person or someone that talks or judges."

"Anna, God is our heavenly Father. He loves us very much. And we love Him. That may be hard for you to understand because of your pa."

"It is God Mr. Mueller talks to when he says whatever he says before we eat, isn't it? I don't understand much, but, Mr. Mueller speaks in a kind way. I noticed that."

"Our heavenly Father wants what's best for his children and He only allows things to happen that help them become strong and mature Christians." After a pause Mrs. Mueller added, "Do you know what a Christian is?"

"I have never heard of one. What is it?"

"A Christian is a person, Anna, not an it. A Christian believes that the Lord Jesus Christ is the Son of God and that He died for their sins. An important verse in the Bible, John 3:16, says, 'For God so loved the world that He gave His only begotten Son, that whosoever believeth in Him should not perish but have everlasting life.' It is by trusting Christ to take away our sin that we become a Christian. We cannot do enough good to save ourselves."

"I don't understand," Anna said, her eyes clouded with confusion.

"I have been a Christian for many years and I don't understand it all either. There are many things I don't understand, but I still believe and accept them. I don't understand how my body takes the food I eat and digests it and sends the nourishment from it to every part of my body. I eat the food and it happens whether I believe it or not."

Anna tried to listen politely but she felt that this God talk was not something she needed. Mrs. Mueller saw her blank expression and changed the subject.

"What do you plan for the supper?"

"This morning I picked some greens. I'm going to cook those and some fried potatoes. I also picked some radishes and green onions. Mr. Mueller suggested canned sausages with gravy. Sometimes, I think I ought to pay you for letting me stay here because of all I eat. If I had any money, that is." They laughed together as Anna left to prepare the evening meal.

After supper, Anna went outside to sit on the front porch. The window to Mr. and Mrs. Mueller's bedroom was open and she could hear Mr. Mueller reading a story to the children.

I can't imagine my pa reading any of us kids a story. As she listened, the words, "Ye thought evil against me; but God meant it unto good," caught her attention.

She heard Mr. Mueller continue telling a story about a man called Joseph. He said, "Joseph's brothers saw that their father was dead and were afraid that Joseph would harm them for what they had done to him when he was a young boy. Remember they had sold Joseph to their enemies for money. Now that their father had died they were afraid Joseph would get revenge. You know what that means?" Mr. Mueller asked.

"Yes, that means to do something mean to get back."

"That's right, girls. They said that it had been their father's wish that Joseph forgive them. He told them not to be afraid because, while they had done a bad thing to him, God had changed it into something good. He said only God had the right to judge them and even though they had meant to harm him, God had used it to save his people. Remember Joseph's words?"

They repeated with their father, "Ye thought evil against me; but God meant it unto good."

Anna stopped listening and repeated what she heard, *"Ye thought evil against me; but God meant it unto good."* She wondered what this could mean. For the rest of the evening she kept hearing these words over and over in her head. What did they have to do with her? Why did they keep clanging around in her mind? It was time to put the girls to bed, maybe that would shut off the echo of the strange words.

She went inside and after she tucked the children in for the night, even though it was early, she decided to turn in, also. Maybe then she could shut out the haunting words. She blew out the lamp and climbed into her little cot and tried to sleep, but pictures of her pa standing over her ma clutching that monstrous bone rumbled around in her head. Good come from her pa's abusive behavior. Never! Forgive him? Never! She needed to go home, but she had given her word to stay and work for the Muellers until the baby was born. What should she do? Anna fell into a restless

CHAPTER 8

The next day Anna received two letters, one from Esther, and the other one from her oldest brother, Matt, the first she had ever received from him. She eagerly ripped it open and began reading. As she read his gentle rebuke the smile left her face.

"Anna, I think Ma would have been better off if you had stayed. She just lies in bed most of the time, won't hardly eat anything. She won't talk to Pa at all, and speaks to Tom only when he asks her a question." He continued telling her something about his family but the words about her mother were all she remembered.

Wouldn't eat? Probably, because she didn't feel like cooking. And Tom was no cook. Why did she leave anyway?

She folded Matt's letter, put it in her pocket, and went to her room. She sat on the side of the bed looking off into space. Did she have the right to live in this lovely home with people that were kind to her? Yes, she worked hard, but still she felt guilty about her life being pleasant when her mother needed her. Until now she had almost forgotten about the problems at home. Tears ran down her face. She opened Esther's letter.

"Ma seems to be gettin weaker every day. Most time she jist stays in bed. Tom does Ma's work and his own outdoor work both. Pa is drinkin more. Ther don't seem to be hardly no money..." Bits of Esther's words bounced against Anna's consciousness. Tears filled her eyes and made it difficult to continue reading. "Tom growed up fast ... Workin hard ... Ma weak ...

Worried ... Ma could die ..."

By then Anna could not see to finish reading the letter. Rushing from the house, and grabbing a hoe on her way, she dashed to the garden. As she hoed along the rows of showy green plants, she began to feel a little better. Later, Mr. Mueller found her chopping away at the stubborn weeds.

"Anna, Ellen said she heard you running out of the house. What's troubling you?" he asked.

"I am all right now." She stopped her frantic hacking and looked up. "I had some news from home that upset me and I needed time to think." Fingering Matt's letter in her pocket, she continued.

"I ought to go home, but I promised to stay until the baby comes. I don't know what to do. Ma's getting weaker and Pa's drinking more. I can't do anything about Pa, but maybe I can make things easier for Tom and Ma."

"Come on back to the house and cool off with something to drink. You can visit with Ellen," Mr. Mueller said as they walked back toward the house.

At the sink Anna splashed her face and arms in the cool stream, and then filled a glass with water and went to talk with Mrs. Mueller. Mr. Mueller had left in the wagon with the girls, leaving Anna and Mrs. Mueller free to talk without interruption.

Anna put the drinks on the side table and sat down next to Mrs. Mueller's bed. She twisted her hands together.

"Tell me what's troubling you Anna. I heard you running out the door and knew something must have happened to upset you. Has Carl done something?" Mrs. Muller asked.

"No, not, Carl. I got a letter from my brother today. He thinks I shouldn't have left. He says Ma just lies in bed most of the time, won't eat anything. She won't talk to Pa at all and speaks to Tom only when he asks her a question." Tears filled Anna eyes and she put her head in her hands.

"Come over here and stand by my bed, Anna," Mrs. Mueller said. "I want to say a prayer for you and your family. Is that OK with you?"

Anna agreed.

"Lord," Mrs. Mueller began, "We know that you love Anna's mother more than she does. We put her in your hands and trust you to care for her. Thank you. In Jesus name we pray. Amen."

Anna relaxed her shoulders. She didn't understand why but she felt some of the burden lift from her troubled spirit.

"Mrs. Mueller, thank you," she said.

The next day the doctor came to see Ellen. After he had examined her she asked, "Do you think I can be back on my feet in time for harvest?"

"I know you too well, Ellen," he laughed. "If I say you can get up, you would stay up until all the work was done. You may sit on the side of the bed for fifteen minutes at a time, and no longer. If your back tires, or begins to hurt sooner than that, you get back in bed. You may sit propped up in bed with your head as high as you want, but put a pillow under your knees. You may do any work you want to in that position until you get tired."

"Doctor, you know perfectly well I'll be no help at all if I follow those directions," Mrs. Mueller said.

"The week after harvest is over, you may begin

getting out of bed," Doctor Harris said. "Walk short distances when you feel like it. Even go outside on the porch. But not before."

Turning to Anna, he added. "You tell Sam what I told Ellen."

Anna walked out to the buggy with the doctor.

"Could I please ask you about my mother?"

"Indeed."

"She just lies in bed most of the time, eating very little. She doesn't talk to Pa at all and speaks to my brother only when he asks her a question. I can't go home and I don't know what to do."

"Sounds like your mother has lost the will to live. Has she had a hard life?"

"Yes."

"I don't think there is anything you could do about her condition if you were there. I'm sorry Anna." The doctor patted her on the shoulder, got into his buggy and drove off.

Tears pooled in Anna's eyes and ran down her cheeks as she watched him drive away. Still, she had no time for self-pity. She gathered the eggs and then checked the position of the sun. It looked like she would have time to pick the peas before starting supper.

The green plants swayed in the hot afternoon wind. She adjusted her bonnet and tied the strings securely to shield her face from the sun and then bent over to see if the peas were ready. Soon she had filled her bucket with more than she expected to pick and stopped to look with longing toward her favorite thinking spot, down by the stream where the towering shade trees grew. No time for resting now; Carl had already started milking and she had to get the separator put together before she started supper so that he would not yell at her. Anna had avoided the man as much as possible, but still, at every chance, he made nasty remarks about her being slow and lazy and complained that he had to do her 'woman's work.' The sly man took care that no one else heard him. Anna felt proud that she had been able to ignore his snide comments and to keep her temper under control.

After the evening work was finished and the kitchen cleaned, Anna took the peas to the front porch to shell. Mr. Mueller's voice drifted out through the open bedroom window as he was telling the girls a bedtime story. Anna listened as he read.

"What man of you, having a hundred sheep, if he loses one of them, doth not leave the ninety and nine ..., and go after that one that is lost, until he finds it? And when he found it, he layeth it on his shoulders, rejoicing. I say unto you, that likewise, joy shall be in heaven over one sinner that repenteth, more than over ninety and nine just persons, which need no repentance." Luke 15:4-7

"Girls, this story is about God's love. Each night, when the shepherd brought his sheep into the sheep pen he would count them. One night as he counted he found that a little lamb was missing. He had one hundred but that one missing lamb was important; he had to find it, even though he put his own life in danger. The shepherd searched and searched and when he found it, he was filled with joy. Can one of you girls remember a Bible verse that tells about a sheep or shepherd?"

"I can! I can!" Sarah cried. "The Lord is my

Shepherd."

"Do you remember one, Martha?"

"I only remember a little of the verse," Martha answered.

"Say what you remember, Sweetheart."

Martha slowly quoted, "All we like sheep have gone astray." That's all I can remember."

"That's the verse I wanted you to say. The verse goes like this: 'All we like sheep have gone astray and the Lord hath laid on Him the iniquity of us all.' This verse means that we are all lost like that lost sheep in the story. Our shepherd is Jesus. When a sheep is lost, it can never find its way home. Ben could find his way home. One of our horses could as well, but not a sheep. People are lost like that sheep. They can't find their way back to God, either. That's why God sent Jesus from his home in heaven. Jesus came to earth to lay down His life for His sheep, to show them the way to God. Some bad men killed Him. ...."

Mr. Mueller continued talking but Anna was no longer listening. She grasped a few of Mr. Mueller's' words, but not as many as the little girls. Truthfully, she didn't understand at all.

CHAPTER 9

"Sam thinks the wheat will be ready to cut next week," Mrs. Mueller told Anna a few days later. "It will probably be the busiest time of your life and you'll need to prepare as much as you can before the crew arrives. We'll have only two days' notice." Mrs. Mueller picked up a cardboard and began fanning.

"The Peterson's will help during the day. I've asked Mrs. Hunter to watch the girls, but they will be here for the last day." She sighed and pushed her pillow up a little. "Tomorrow when Doctor Harris comes, I'll ask him how much I can be up and what I can do."

"If Mrs. Peterson works as fast as you say, surely we can handle things."

"We'll see, Anna."

As harvest approached, it seemed to Anna as if everyone were spinning around in a frantic whirl that reminded her of the little girls' top. Mrs. Mueller gave Anna orders from her bed, but chafed under her confinement, itching to get up and do the work herself. Anna gave the house a thorough cleaning and also tidied the out buildings. The children tried to help but mostly just slowed her down. Carl cleaned the henhouse. He grumbled about doing a *woman's* work, but he didn't dare leave it undone. Everything except the cooking seemed in order for the coming harvesters.

Saturday evening Ellen said, "Sam's going to speak at church in the morning. He said you could go with them. Sarah will stay with me."

"I don't think I'll go," Anna said. "I've never been to church. I wouldn't know what to wear or how to act."

"Anna, anything you have is suitable. As to how to act, just act normal. Bow your head when someone prays. Pay attention when someone's speaking. Don't allow Martha to whisper and she's not to take any toys with her. She's been told to stay with you except when she goes to her class. Between Sunday school and church, take her to get a drink and to the outhouse. During service, don't allow her to get out of her seat for any reason."

Anna twisted in her chair and frowned. All these directions sounded like a lot to remember.

"Other than this, greet the people you know," Mrs. Mueller continued. "The ones you haven't met will be friendly. I don't think you need to be concerned with anything else."

It seemed that Anna would be going to church in spite of how she felt. She had nothing proper to wear, and didn't look forward to meeting strangers. Still, she could not refuse to go when her employer made it clear that it was expected of her.

~~~~~~~~

Sunday morning the sun filled the horizon like a golden fireball, and Anna felt grateful for the swirling wind that cooled her skin as they rode along. This was the first time she had been away from the Muellers' farm except for short walks down to the stream. She adjusted her bonnet and studied the countryside dotted with various patterns and shapes of wheat.

"Why do all fields look different?" she asked.

"In some fields the wheat's been cut and placed in shocks, waiting for the thrashing crew," Mr. Mueller said. "To prevent mold, it's piled into shocks so that if it rains between cutting and threshing the water will drain off. When the thrashing crew comes they'll separate the grain from the stalks." He paused, "I don't know what we would have done without you, Anna. I'm afraid it would have been impossible to keep Ellen in bed."

"Mrs. Mueller doesn't feel as well as she wants us to believe. When she gets up to go to the commode, she never asks to stay up longer. She often asks for aspirins."

"Ellen's always been a fast, competent worker, and staying in bed doesn't suit her," Mr. Mueller said.

The horses slowed and turned into the school yard where church services were held. Mr. Mueller helped Anna and Martha from the buggy and then drove the horses over to a shaded area and tied them to a tree. Since they were early, no one else was about.

The school house was a wooden building, badly in need of paint, surrounded by a sandy field. A silver colored bell stood beside the front door, ready to call the children to class. The front door opened to a large room with rows of student desks at the center and a large, oak teacher's desk facing them. A blackboard filled the wall behind the teacher's desk. Backless benches were pushed against the outer walls. The room smelled of chalk dust and musty books. At the back of the room Anna saw a door that led into a smaller room. She imagined that this room was used as the cloak-room. The building felt stifling and Mr. Mueller opened the few windows to let in some air.

"Let's move these desks over there and pull the benches into the center." Mr. Mueller pointed to the back wall.

"Can you give me a hand? Just give them a shove and guide as I move them." After they had the benches in place, Anna began dusting while Mr. Mueller tuned his guitar.

A short time later, Anna heard the neighing of horses and the rumble of wagon wheels as the school yard filled up with buggies and wagons. As people gathered to visit before they entered the building, Anna recognized a few who had visited the Mueller house, and they smiled or spoke to her. Anna took Martha outside to get a drink and go to the outhouse. When they returned she found a seat near the back.

Mr. Mueller opened the meeting by playing his guitar and singing and the people followed along. She looked around as they sang, faces upturned and eyes sparkling with joy. They seemed happy, even carefree; something Anna did not share. How could she sing when her heart felt heavy with worry about her ma? The songs ended and the children filed out into the smaller room. A man in a pair of overalls, clean but work-worn, stood up and began speaking to the adults who had remained in the larger room. He held a small book and began reading, and then explaining the words. She guessed this must be what Mrs. Mueller called 'Sunday School.'

The still air and slow speech and unfamiliar words didn't hold Anna's attention and she fidgeted and tried to stay awake. After the teaching ended the children returned. Anna was glad to escape and hurried to take Martha to the outhouse again. When they came back it seemed as if the program repeated itself. More singing and more speaking. Mr. Mueller stood up, and in his clear baritone he began to sing.

"In shady, green pastures, so rich and so sweet, God leads His dear children along. Where the water's cool flow bathes the weary one's feet; God leads His dear children along. Sometimes on the mount where the sun shines so bright, God leads His dear children along; Sometimes in the valley, in darkest of night, God leads His dear children along. Some thru the waters, some thru the flood, some thru the fire, but all thru the blood. Some thru great sorrow, but God gives a song. In the night season and all the day long."

When he finished singing many people shouted, "Amen." That seemed strange to Anna, but she loved the song. She wished she had some cool water in which to dip her weary feet. As for a song, she didn't have a song in her heart, but wished she did. And how was God leading her along when she had left her ma at home with only Tom to look after her?

Ma, I miss you so. Tears ran down her cheeks and into her mouth. She quickly wiped them away. What would these people think of her?

Mr. Mueller opened his Bible and began to speak. Occasionally, Anna recognized some of the message from the stories she had heard him tell his daughters. Still, it was a struggle for her to concentrate. Maybe a little air would help. She took out her fan and pushed it back and forth. Truly, however, it wasn't just the hot air that distracted her; it was the presence of a handsome young man that sat across the aisle from her. Soon after she and Martha had returned to the school building, she had noticed him. How could she help but notice? She liked what she saw. By turning her head just slightly and shifting a little in her seat, she could catch an occasional glance, and each peek gave her a fluttering sensation in her mid-section. She hoped someone would introduce her to this good looking stranger.

After the service Anna hurried Martha toward the door, keeping an eye on the handsome man and hoping she would be able to speak to him before he left. Disappointment choked her as she watched a petite young woman, with hair the color of sunlight, reached out a dainty gloved hand and touched the stranger's sleeve. The girl wore a pink dotted-swiss dress, with ruffles from waist to the hem. The man halted in his tracks, and gave the girl a heart-thumping smile. She returned the smile, dimples dancing at the corner of her mouth. Anna heard her say.

"Good morning John. I'm so glad to see you're back. I can't say how much I missed you." The young woman pushed a strand of golden hair away from her face and fluttered her long, dark lashes.

As Anna watched them, a knot formed in her throat. I believe she's flirting with him and he looks as if he loves it. She felt relieved when she saw Mr. Peterson walk over and interrupt the couple. The young man followed Mr. Peterson and as he moved along Anna observed that he walked with a limp. When Mr. Peterson spotted Anna he drew the stranger toward her. Her heart began to race as they strolled in her direction.

"Good morning, Anna. I want you to meet my nephew, John Edward Davis," Mr. Peterson said. "He's come to visit us and help out for a while."

John acknowledged the introduction and smiled at Anna. He then spoke to his uncle.

"Auntie said she was ready to go home."

He turned to Anna and asked, "Do you live around these parts?"

"Anna works for Muellers," answered Mr. Peterson.

John ran his hand through his dark hair and said, "Then I guess we'll be seeing each other soon. I'll be helping Mr. Mueller with his harvest."

Anna's throat seemed to close and she could only nod in response. He must think she was a little daft, but looking into those smoky gray eyes, surrounded by thick, dark lashes took her breath away. Surely those eyes were wasted on a man. His mahogany brown hair, was combed straight back from a wide forehead. His nose was straight and maybe just a bit wide. Well shaped mouth. Sun tanned from working outside, probably. About two inches taller than she. Anna's eyes traveled down to John's wide shoulders, small waist and hips, and on down his long legs.

His arms and legs are longer than mine. Hands and feet bigger than mine, also. Looking up, she realized that he was smiling at her and Mr. Peterson was grinning. She felt heat creep up her neck and face. What must they think of her forward behavior? She said, "It's nice to see someone, especially a man, taller than I am."

When Martha grabbed her hand, Anna was glad for the excuse to escape her uncomfortable situation.

"Daddy says it's time to go."

On the way home Mr. Mueller asked what she thought of the service but she just stared off into space. All she could remember was her encounter with John. And he would be working at the Mueller's farm.

That meant she would really get to see him again!

CHAPTER 10

Harvest started with a bang, clatter, and roar as a neighbor, Mr. Stewart drove his team of three horses, towing his enormous binder, into the Muellers' yard. Mr. Peterson's buggy pulled in behind the binder and several men on horseback followed. Anna peeked out the window to see if that, "entirely satisfactory" young man was with them. He was. Tingles tiptoed down her spine as she saw him slide off his horse and glance toward the house. Fearful that he would see her observing him, she rushed back to the stove to finish breakfast preparations.

The men washed up on the back porch, and then strolled into the kitchen. Mr. Mueller showed them where to sit and Mrs. Peterson and Anna filled their bowls with oatmeal and set out generous servings of biscuits, bacon, sausage, eggs and gravy. After Mr. Mueller gave thanks for the food and asked for God's protection as the men worked, they began eating and quickly, as if by magic, all the food disappeared.

At the first sign of light the men finished their coffee and excused themselves from the table. Several expressed their thanks as they headed out the door, but Carl puckered his mouth in disgust and marched out without a word. As he left, John smiled at Anna and said, "Mighty fine food." Her heart started thumping and skipping and it was several minutes before she could breathe normally. How was she to keep her head around the man when he caused her usually sober, sane behavior to go all amiss?

She wiped her hands on her apron and fixed a plate for Mrs. Mueller and took it to her.

"Would you like me stay until you finish eating?"

"Thank you. I'm fine. You have much to do today."

Anna returned to the kitchen and was sipping the last of her coffee when Mrs. Peterson said, "Time to plan meals for the rest of the day."

"After all the food they ate for breakfast, surely the men won't be hungry until supper time," Anna said.

Mrs. Peterson laughed, "They'll be hungry, all right. We must be prepared."

They reviewed the list that Anna and Mrs. Mueller had made.

Mrs. Peterson said, "Doughnuts and coffee sound good for the ten o'clock feed. Now for dinner. Ham. Is that already cooked?"

"Yes, it's ready to slice."

Mrs. Peterson continued, "Chicken and noodles. Are the noodles made?"

"Yes."

"Candied sweet potatoes, green beans, bread and pie. Is there enough bread for today, or do we need to bake some?"

"I baked bread last week, but I don't think it will last for two days like we planned. I made four pies yesterday, also, and an applesauce cake and a chocolate cake. Do you think that will be enough for dinner and supper? I didn't have time to make the cookies for the afternoon snack today. Maybe we can do that after dinner."

Anna groaned as she thought about how long it had taken her to do all the baking and how fast it would disappear.

"I'll clean up the kitchen while you help Ellen get dressed. By then Roy and Carl should be finished with the milking and we can take care of the milk things. Roy will slice the ham and that will save us some time," said Mrs. Peterson as she stacked dishes.

The woman seemed to be doing and thinking about three things at once. Anna remembered what Mrs. Mueller said about her being glad to have Mrs. Peterson help her. It was more like Anna helping Mrs. Peterson. When Anna returned to the kitchen, Mrs. Peterson had almost finished.

"I'll go feed and water the chickens," Anna said, anxious to get out into the fresh air of the bright, balmy June morning. A cooling breeze touched her skin and fluttered her skirt, making her thankful to be out of the stuffy house. She looked about with pleasure, inhaling the scent of apple blossoms that promised juicy, red fruit in the fall. Beyond the orchard were fields filled with wheat, tall and straight, their ripened heads dancing in the sun waiting for the harvesters. Anna had never seen the ocean but she imagined that the waving wheat looked something like the ocean waves. She gazed with longing toward her favorite resting spot down by the stream under the towering, shady trees.

No time for such today. She rubbed her neck and moved it back and forth as she anticipated the duties that lay ahead. First, she must feed the chickens. When she entered the chicken yard the hungry fowls circled her, flapping their wings and squawking as she flung corn from her basket. By the time she had finished, she saw Mr. Peterson carrying the milk to the milk house.

"I'll do the separating while you go have another cup of coffee," Anna told him.

"As soon as I carry up the rest of the milk, I'll be glad to sit on something besides a milk stool," he said rubbing his back. He handed the buckets to Anna and she began pouring the foamy, white liquid into the separator.

Anna finished the task and then washed the separator and buckets while Mrs. Peterson made batter for the doughnuts. Anna helped her roll them out, cut them into shape, and had them cooking in hot lard when Mr. Peterson came into the kitchen.

Mr. Peterson handed his wife the platter of ham and said, "Alice, I'll take the doughnuts and coffee out to the men in the field. Save you two from the long walk so you can get on with your other tasks."

Anna knew that Mr. Peterson was not physically able to farm his land, and that most of his land had been rented out to a family member. She didn't think he should be walking all that way carrying a heavy pan of doughnuts, as well as the heavy pot of coffee. Besides, she longed to get out in the sunshine. She said, "I'll go with you and carry the dish pan full of doughnuts; otherwise, you might eat too many before the men see them."

"You seem to know him pretty well, Anna. He's kinda known as a 'champeen doughnut eater.' This morning with his coffee he ate three. And that, after eating five biscuits, four eggs, and I don't know how much gravy and jelly and oatmeal." Mrs. Peterson sugared the last of the doughnuts.

Mr. Peterson's eyes widened and his mouth gaped open. When the women laughed, he realized that they were teasing him and he smiled at their joke.

Anna grabbed the pan of doughnuts and Mr. Peterson hoisted the pot with the coffee in his hands, and they headed out to the field. As they walked along, the breeze tousled her hair and cooled her cheeks. The massive binder, pulled by the team of horses clattered and clanked across the field, breaking the stillness of the morning, as it cut the wheat and tossed it onto a belt. The pulley then carried the wheat into the machine that tied it into bundles and tossed them out into the field again. Several men, walking some distance behind the binder, stacked the pile of wheat into shocks, with the heads of grain toward the top.

Anna watched as the men set up the heavy shocks and then scurried to keep up with the binder. Anna saw John and her heart quickened as she noted the breadth of his shoulders and the way his khaki shirt stretched across the width of his chest and arms. She watched as he lifted the bundles with his strong shoulders and his bulging, muscular arms, and observed that while he had an uneven gait, he kept up with the other men just fine. What, she wondered, had caused his limp?

When the men saw Anna and Mr. Peterson, all activity stopped, and they jogged over to get their snacks.

Where did they get their energy after working hours out in the hot sun? Surely they must be tired, but apparently the possibility of a break overcame their fatigue.

When the men returned to the field all but two doughnuts had disappeared. After seeing how hard the men worked, Anna understood why it took so much to feed them.

Mr. Peterson and Anna gathered up the cups, empty coffee pot, and dishpan, and returned to the house. Sweat ran down Anna's neck and the glaring sun sucked the energy from her. She hurried to the water well, pumped cool water into the wash pan, carried it out to the back porch, and splashed it on her face, allowing the water to stream down her neck and arms, washing off the dirt and sweat that covered her skin after the walk out to the field. She felt refreshed and ready to return to work by the time she returned to the kitchen. She and Mrs. Peterson finished preparing dinner and had it ready by the time the clock struck twelve.

Mrs. Peterson said, "Roy, please set up some tables on the side porch. You'll find the empty barrels and boards you need on the porch. Anna would you help Roy set them up?"

They placed the tables in rows and set out the dishes of food and then Mr. Peterson rang the dinner bell. The workers hurried in from the fields and gathered around the horse tank, where Mr. Peters had placed soap and towels so they could wash.

The hungry harvesters woofed down the abundant supply of food, and after they had finished eating Mr. Mueller said, "Take a break men. Don't want anyone to get a heat stroke in this sun."

Some of the men sprawled out to rest in the shade of the porch roof or under a tree, but Mr. Mueller spent the time with his wife, helping her with her meal. Anna and Mrs. Peterson sat a spell, giving them a chance to catch their breath and then they set the washtub on a table.

Mrs. Peterson said, "You wash since you are tall enough to reach the bottom of the tub. I'll rinse and put them to drain. It's hot enough in here to dry anything in no time." Mrs. Peterson only came to Anna's shoulder, and she seemed as broad as she was high.

The task flew by as the two women chatted and laughed about the hearty appetites of the workers. Without even taking a break Mrs. Peterson dried her hands on her apron and said, "We need to start preparing the afternoon snack. Will you go out to the water trough and get some eggs to boil for sandwiches?"

Anna agreed but as she was leaving, Mrs. Peterson grabbed the back of a chair, leaned on it and sighed so deeply Anna thought she might be having a heart attack.

"Are, you all right?" Anna asked.

Mrs. Peterson shook her head and said, "Ju-u- st need to catch my wind." After a time she continued, "Do you have mayonnaise made?"

"Please, Mrs. Peterson sit and rest until I return," Anna said. The woman sank her bulk into a chair and closed her eyes.

When Anna returned Mrs. Peterson had bread sliced and they made sandwiches and lemonade for the afternoon snack. When they finished Mr. Peterson came in and said, "Everything ready? Anna, want to help take the sandwiches out to the men?"

She agreed and they took the workers their refreshments.

When they returned Mrs. Peterson said, "It's time to think about supper. One pie was left over from dinner and you have the two cakes. That should be enough for dessert."

When the day ended, every limb ached and Anna's feet felt like festered boils ready to burst. Would she ever feel rested again?

~~~~~~~~~

That day set the pattern for harvest. It took most of five days to bind the wheat; after that the threshing crew, more than twenty men, came and stayed until all the grain was stored in the granary. Anna and Mrs. Peterson had the last meal prepared for the crew and almost ready to serve when Anna hurried to the milk house to get some food cooling in the water trough. Nearby the hired hands stood around the water tank washing up for supper. In the milk house, through the open window, Anna could hear the men's voices. She recognized Carl's whining tone.

"Well, she's as big as a giant. She ain't much to look at either. She can't cook very good and she's lazy. I have to do a lot of her work. I don't think anyone else will marry her. Guess I'll have to. I'll tell her after har..."

Suddenly, Carl realized that the men no longer looked at him. He turned and saw Anna marching toward him. Her lips were compressed into a flat line; jaws drawn and fists clenched. Carl's eyes began to twitch and alarm showed on his face. He backed away from her, hit the edge of the water tank and, feet flying in the air, he fell into the water head first. Anna stopped, then turned and strolled into the house. As she entered she could still hear the men laughing.

When it appeared that Carl could not lift himself up, John offered him a hand. Carl climbed out of the tank, face beet-red and eyes shooting fire. Clothes dripping and shoes squishing, he stomped into the kitchen.

Mr. Mueller looked at him, brows scrunched together. "What happened, Carl?"

"That wild girl, Anna, pushed me into the water tank. I ain't done nothing to her!" Hearing Carl's complaint the men outside began laughing again.

Mr. Mueller looked at Anna. She glared at Carl, mouth curled down showing her disgust.

That sniveling little toad. It's whine, whine, whine, with him. I wish I had pushed him in and held him under for awhile. But I'm glad I didn't.

John stepped into the kitchen and came to Anna's aid.

"It was an accident," he said. "She didn't touch him."

Anna's look softened as she heard his words. He had defended her. She smiled her thanks and he returned the smile.

After the other men had gone home, Mr. Mueller had a talk with Carl.

"Carl, you had your warning. I'll let you stay on until after the threshing crew has finished or you can quit right now. Either way, you will not have a job here after harvest is over."

"Guess I'll just take my pay and find me another job. Work here's too hard for the little money I'm getting anyway."

CHAPTER 11

Harvest ended as it had begun, with a bang, clatter and roar as Mr. Stewart pulled his team of horses and the gigantic binder from the Muellers' yard and down the road to the next wheat field waiting to be harvested. Anna's work settled back into a routine of cleaning, cooking, washing, and ironing. One afternoon as she shelled peas in the kitchen, she heard the door bang.

"Anna, you have a letter. Looks like it's from your sister, Esther," Mr. Mueller said. He laid the letter on the table and headed in to see his wife.

Anna wiped her hands down her apron then snatched up the letter, ripped it open and read a few lines. Hooking her foot on one of the chairs, she pulled it up and sat down. She read through the first page quickly skimming the words. On the second page her eyes froze and her brows shot up.

"Ma's real sic," she read. "Doc sez there werent nothin wrong with her body 'cept overwork and she were under nourished, or some thin like that. Ma is sic in her head. She jist got to settin thar and staring off into space. She dont talk no more neither and doc sid she had to be put in the insane asilum at Fort Supply so someone cud take keer of her. Pa taken her yisterday."

"Tom cum and got me the day before. Ma didnt talk to me. I guess Pa cum home likkered up agin. Ma hada blue place on her cheek and a cut there. When I looked her over mor blue spots wer on her body and around. She aint nothin but skin and bones. Pa wont answer no questions even when doc asked him what happen. Tom dont know neither. Doc said we caint see Ma for awhile. We ar as well as common. You shoulda stayed............"

Anna threw the letter down, "No! No!" She jumped up from the table, turning her chair over with a crash. Harsh, wracking sobs were shaking her body as she ran out of the house. Letting the door slam behind her, she ran through the gate heading for her favorite spot on the farm. As she ran across the yard toward the wooded area by the stream, the words of the letter and her thoughts churned around.

Insane...Committed...you should have stayed..... Poor Ma. I hate Pa. I think I'm going to be sick. Her heart beat fast and hard in her throat: She thought she would choke. Gasping, she paused, panting and sucking in air until her lungs burned. Running until she had a stitch in her side she stumbled, but caught herself before she fell, and then she trudged the remaining distance to the stream, shoulders hunched and feet dragging. She fell on the grass, pulled up her knees, and rested her head on them and began to cry softly. A short time later she dozed off. When she awakened, she saw Mr. Mueller sitting nearby. The sun was low in the sky and Anna realized that it was late. She started to jump up, but Mr. Mueller laid a hand on her shoulder.

"Anna, what's troubling you?" He sat down beside her.

"The letter from Esther. They put Ma in the insane asylum. It's all Pa's fault. I hate him." Anna began to sob. "I should have stayed home." Mr. Mueller listened as Anna recounted parts of Esther's letter.

"I know this is hard to hear but you need to forgive your pa," he said,

"I'll never forgive him for what he's done to Ma. Never!" Anna gripped her hands into a fist.

Only the whispering wind sounded as the two sat in silence. Then Mr. Mueller said, "I need to do chores. And it's time to begin supper."

As they approached the farm yard, Anna saw a team of horses and a buggy. When she entered the house, she could hear voices and laughter coming from Mrs. Mueller's room.

My ma's in an insane asylum and my heart's breaking. And no one cares. She wiped at the tears forming in her eyes. After clearing the table and washing up the dishes, Anna went into Mrs. Mueller's room.

For a while they sat in silence then she said, "I read the rest of Esther's letter. The doctor doesn't want any of us to go see Ma for a while. How can I stand not knowing what's going on? The doctor thinks this probably happened to Ma because of Pa's treatment." She gripped her seat.

"Mr. Mueller said I had to forgive Pa. How can I? I hate him for what he's done!"

"Anna, the Bible tells us that God gives us a song in the night. This may seem like the darkest time in your life. God isn't limited by tough problems."

Anna said, "Mr. Mueller said if I didn't forgive Pa, I'll become bitter and angry. I am angry. It feels good to be mad at Pa. I don't want to forgive him."

"Anna, the Bible says that God forgives us as we forgive others."

Anna looked at the woman in amazement.

"Why would God need to forgive me? I haven't done anything that He needs to forgive me for. I don't know anything about God, anyway. So I guess I can hate Pa as long as I want to."

She jumped up out of her chair and said, "I'm going outside while there's still a little light."

In the following days, Anna seldom spoke, and her shoulders remained slumped as if she were weighted down with more than she could bear. The Muellers' concern for her and her family took them to their knees. They prayed that God would begin a softening process in Anna's spirit and that He would give her a heart and mind to know Him, and to accept his love and forgiveness so that she might experience peace in her soul. Still, Anna continued to build a wall of self-pity and bitterness between herself and everyone around her, and nothing seemed able to penetrate that barrier. Her emotions sapped her strength. She took no pleasure in her work and at night she felt exhausted, but her restless sleep failed to refresh her.

One day as Anna chopped weeds in the garden, the burden of her grief and anger overcame her. In desperation, she flung the hoe aside and sank down on the carpet of grass beside the garden and prayed.

"Oh, God, I'm so tired, I just want to die. Are you there? Do you care what's happening to my family? To me? The Muellers said I have to forgive Pa. I don't want to, but I can't stand this pain any longer. Can you help me? Will you?"

As Anna opened her heart to God, the heaviness lifted. She raised her face toward the sky and it seemed as if the wind gently kissed her checks and wrapped its arms around her, drawing her into the presence of God. She sucked in the fresh air and breathed deeply. She didn't understand what had happened, but she knew God had heard her cry. As she returned to the house she felt as if the oppressive bitterness and anger had gone; replaced by peace and patience.

That evening as she talked with Mrs. Mueller, she wanted to tell her about her prayer in the garden but she felt shy and tongue tied. As she meditated on what to say, Mrs. Mueller said, "We so appreciate all you did during harvest, Anna. The way you worked with so little supervision. You haven't had any time off since you came, so tomorrow Sam's going to take you and Sarah to Alva. We want to buy you new shoes. If you have any money left over you might want to buy material for a new dress. Maybe we can get some sewing done before fall vegetables are ready to can. Soon we'll need to make some things for the baby, also.

~~~~~~~~

Anna's parents lived about thirty miles from Alva. She had never been there, but her neighbors back home told stories about its fancy stores and wide, smooth roads filled with wagons, buggies and horses. When she thought about the upcoming trip, she felt like skipping and singing, and would have if she dared. New shoes! Never in her life had she had anything but hand-me-downs that pinched her toes because her big feet were larger than the secondhand shoes.

The next day Mrs. Peterson came to stay with Mrs. Mueller and Martha. When Anna had finished her morning work Mr. Mueller helped Sarah and her up onto the wagon seat and their journey began.

"How far is Alva, Mr. Mueller?"

"Only about fifteen miles from our farm."

The horses pounded the earth, their hoofs kicking up the sandy soil as they trotted along. The wagon bumped up and down but Anna hardly noticed. The air smelled sweet with the scent of sunflowers and freshly cut hay and the call of the bobwhite echoed across the prairie. Sarah chatted merrily while Anna enjoyed the view and being outside. When they had gone about four miles they came to the township of Hopetown. The railroad track ran alongside the road. As they passed through, Anna studied the town. The main street boasted a grain elevator, a bank, a small store, and a doctor's home that also served as his office where he cared for his patients as well. Anna thought hope and town both were lacking in spite of the name.

When they arrived in Alva, Anna's eyes widened as she scanned the tall buildings, crowded together around a large square plaza. As Mr. Mueller pulled to a stop in front of the mercantile store, a horse and his rider galloped past making Anna cringe in fear that he would run smack into their wagon. Mr. Mueller helped Anna and Sarah out of the wagon.

"Anna, don't worry about getting lost here," he said. "The city square is only two blocks long and one block wide. The city and county buildings are inside this area." He pointed toward some trees that lined the square.

"Over there are some benches. When you and Sarah finish shopping, find a bench and wait for me."

"What time should we look for you, Mr.

Mueller?"

"Meet me here around noon. I'll buy you ladies some lunch. The stores you might want to look in are over that way and about two doors from here there's an eating place we like."

Sarah and Anna walked to a store that Mr. Mueller had shown them, and entered. The door gave a little tinkle as they closed it. Inside it was dark except for the light that came from the glass windows at the front. Anna gazed around in wonder at all the merchandise: tools for farming, saddles, dry goods, calicos and silks, material of all colors and patterns. She had never been shopping and many of the items she saw she could not identify, and was too shy to ask. She located the shoe department and went over to find a pair of shoes. A few minutes later she had chosen a pair of sturdy, practical shoes and took them over to the clerk. The clerk showed her another pair.

"You should try these on. They're the latest style."

"I'm sure I couldn't afford them."

"They cost no more than the ones you chose. Try them on. See what you think."

Anna yielded to temptation and slipped on the dainty, soft leather shoes.

"My goodness, these seem more comfortable than the other shoes. I'll take them." She gave the clerk her money before her better judgment stepped in; however, after paying for the shoes she counted her money and was happy to find that she had enough left to buy fabric.

She went to look at the piece goods, something practical that didn't show dirt. She had never picked out her own cloth. Her mother usually made their clothes from flour sacks or brown fabric that her pa bought in Freedom and Anna, being the youngest, always wore whatever her sisters out-grew. She practically danced with excitement as she fingered the bolts of cloth and pondered what to buy. Finally, she chose a soft, blue cotton fabric with pink and yellow flowers and a rose colored chambray. After she paid for her purchases, she looked for Sarah. She found the child on the floor near a wooden barrel filled with penny nails, holding a gray and white kitten in her lap, and petting it gently.

"What a lovely kitten," Anna said when she saw them.

"I've always wanted a kitten to play with but my Pa would never allow us to have pets."

The little girl said, "Wish I could take you home with me." She set the kitten back on the floor and gave it a final pat.

When they left the store they strolled around the square and looked in the windows and even went into a few, but purchased nothing. When it was near time to meet Mr. Mueller, they walked back to the square and found a bench under a spreading elm and sat down. The warm air made Anna feel drowsy and her eyelids had just begun to close when someone walked up to the bench.

"Why, Anna, what a surprise."

She looked up and recognized Fern Stephens, a near neighbor of her sister Lucy.

"Hello, Fern. I am so glad to see you. Can you give me any news from home?"

"You know that your ma's been put in an insane

asylum?" she asked.

"Yes, Esther wrote me," she said. "Have they heard how she's doing?"

"I'm not sure. The doctor still does not want your family to see her. I don't think there has been any change. At least, Lucy hasn't told me, if there is."

"What about Tom?" Anna asked.

"Tom's working for a neighbor. Lucy takes meals to your pa when she can."

Poor Pa. Poor Tom. Poor Ma. Anna dabbed tears from her eyes.

"How are you doing?" Mrs. Stephens asked. "You look good. Do you like your job?"

"I love working for the Muellers. This is Sarah, their youngest child. Sarah, this is Mrs. Stephens, my sister's neighbor." The little girl smiled and Mrs. Stephens returned the smile.

"They have another girl who's nearly six and Mrs. Mueller's expecting a baby in two or three months. She's been in bed since before I went to work for them. We just finished harvest, and I didn't know I could work that hard." Anna laughed, and Mrs. Stevens joined her.

'They've been kind to me and even gave me money to buy shoes as well as material for a dress. That's why I'm in Alva today." Delight sparkled in her sea blue eyes.

"Mrs. Stephens, would you take some money to Lucy to give to Tom? I have a little left from my salary." Anna dug into her pocket and brought out a dollar and handed it to Mrs. Stephens.

"Tell Lucy I'm all right and I'll come home when the Muellers can do without me." Anna looked up and saw Mr. Mueller coming toward them. She made the introductions.

Mr. Mueller said, "We're headed to the café for dinner. Would you like to join us?"

"Thank you, but my husband's probably waiting for me at the creamery."

Anna waved good-by. Seeing someone from home had made a great day even better.

CHAPTER 12

Just before they arrived back at the Muellers, Anna said, "I don't think I would have been this tired if I had pulled weeds in the garden, dug the potatoes, and canned all the small ones."

"I believe I could have mucked out the barn and plowed two fields. At least I would feel like I'd accomplished something by being this worn-out." Mr. Mueller's mouth turned up and his eyes danced.

By the time they turned off onto the road to the Mueller farm, Anna's back was aching and her bones felt broken, some of which she had never been aware.

"These wagons should be called 'bone bruisers' instead of spring wagons. I would laugh but it might hurt."

Sarah was asleep, leaning on Anna, so it was difficult for her to shift around into a more comfortable position. The rutted road made it impossible for the wheels to miss all the ruts.

"How can Sarah sleep with this wagon jerking back and forth and bouncing up and down over this road?"

Mr. Mueller said, "We'll be home soon. I bought a stick of bologna and a chunk of cheese in town. We can have sandwiches for supper and you won't have to cook anything."

Anna dipped her chin, feeling embarrassed that her comments had sounded like a complaint. She said, "Truly this has been one of the best days of my life. Thank you for taking me."

"Help me with the milking tonight and we'll get finished up and go to bed early," Mr. Mueller said.

The fragrance of chocolate cake welcomed them as they entered the house.

"Oh, Mrs. Peterson, you dear person," Anna cried. "Chocolate cake is just the thing to make me forget how tired I am. Seeing the stores and new sights was a treat, still I don't think I'd want to go again, especially in a wagon." She rubbed her back as she slipped into her apron.

"Well, I'll probably forget if I get another invite." Anna, snatched the egg basket and said, "I must see about my duties."

Mrs. Peterson cut a generous slice of the cake and handed it to Anna.

"Sit a spell and then take care of the egg gathering."

At that moment Mr. Peterson entered the kitchen with a bucket of eggs. When she saw him, Anna's eyes pooled with tears of gratitude. No, it was more than gratitude she felt; it was love, and this new emotion surprised her. She had never learned to express love. The only emotions demonstrated in her home were anger and bitterness. Pa *didn't* love anyone, probably not even Ma. Perhaps Ma loved her children but she never told them, nor showed it. Mr. and Mrs. Peterson had become dear to her and she wanted them to know her feelings, but how? Feeling clumsy and shy she said, "Mr. Peterson, I would give you a kiss for doing my chores, but somehow you don't quite look like the prince I pictured giving my first kiss."

Mrs. Peterson said, "Well now Sweetie, he's my prince and you better get my permission before you go kissing my man." She laughed and patted Anna's arm.

Anna gave Mrs. Peterson's hand a squeeze and said, "You're both very fortunate. I only wish my ma and pa were like the two of you. I don't know why I'm being so emotional; just tired, I guess."

Later Anna stuck her head in the door of Mrs. Mueller's room where she and Mrs. Peterson chatted. "Do you need anything?" Anna asked.

"Why don't you bring your new things in and show Alice and me?"

Anna brought in her packages and removed the wrapping from the shoes.

"These seemed too frivolous to me, but the clerk thought I should have the latest style. My old shoes are about finished. I can wear them around the house and save these for Sunday best. They don't look as sturdy as my old ones and probably won't last as long." Her mouth turned up and a smile filled her eyes.

"I like my new ones, though." She handed Mrs. Mueller her other parcel.

Mrs. Mueller lifted the rose colored, chambray fabric from the bag and said, "This will make a lovely dress for church. The color will bring out the golden tones in your chestnut colored hair."

Chestnut colored hair? Anna had always thought of it as mousey brown. Then Mrs. Mueller saw the soft blue cotton fabric.

"This lovely blue will complement your eyes," she said.

Anna dipped her head, feeling embarrassed. She had never before received a compliment and didn't know what to say.

Mrs. Mueller continued, "I like this. I'm glad you

didn't buy brown fabric. Surely, you must be tired of wearing brown all the time."

"That's what Pa bought when he went to town. I guess he thought it wouldn't show dirt as plain as other colors. Maybe it was the only choice in the little store in Freedom."

After the evening meal and the Petersons had gone home, Anna cleaned the kitchen and then went to tell Mrs. Mueller good night.

"Anna, see that parcel on the dresser? It's for you. The shoes and dress goods were from Sam, but I wanted you to have this also."

Anna picked up the box and opened it. Inside was a leather-bound, black book like the one Mr. Mueller read in the mornings and when he told the children stories at night. She opened its pages carefully.

"It's a Bible, Anna. Have you ever had one?"

"The first time I remember seeing one is here, or maybe that's what my teacher read from in school. She didn't say it was a Bible, or if she did, I don't remember."

"When you start reading, begin with Genesis, the first book. Genesis means beginning and it speaks of the beginning of the world and the human race, and of the nation Israel. If you have questions, I will try to answer them."

~~~~~~~~

After harvest, Mrs. Mueller occasionally felt able to get out of bed to help with inside tasks, giving Anna a bit of spare time. On Sundays she often went to church with Mr. Mueller and in the afternoons she took her Bible to her special place by the stream and read. As Mrs. Mueller had suggested, she began reading the book of Genesis. When she came to the story about Abram and Sarai in Genesis 15 she felt bewildered. Why would God promise them a child and still they remained childless? It seemed as if God didn't treat them right, making a promise that he didn't keep. Abram had everything he wanted except a child. Why would anyone want to know God if He didn't give them what they wanted? She decided to discuss this puzzle with Mrs. Mueller.

After the children were in bed, Anna went to Mrs. Mueller's room. They visited for awhile then Anna asked, "I have a question. If God doesn't give a person everything he wants, why would anyone trust Him? What's the advantage of it?"

"That is a hard question, Anna, and I don't know if I can answer it for you." After a long silence, she asked, "Do you think we have everything we want? What do you want that you don't have?"

"You have a lot more than anyone else I know, certainly a lot more than my family. As for me, I would like to have been born into a family that was kind and successful. If God knows everything like you say, why didn't He know that I would like to be better looking and blond, and not big boned and clumsy?" Anna hunched over and lowered her eyes. Did she have the right to question God?

"Anna, I don't know why God made us as He did. He created us all different and it was His choice. When we complain about physical appearances that we cannot change, we accuse God of bad judgment. Find Psalm 139 in your Bible. The book of Psalms is about in the middle of the Bible."

Anna began thumbing through the pages until she found the place and Mrs. Mueller continued, "David, who wrote this Psalm, said that we should praise God because we are fearfully and wonderfully made. Let's read verses 13 and 14. "Thou hast covered me in my mother's womb. I will praise thee; for I am fearfully and wonderfully made: marvelous are thy works: and that my soul knoweth right well." Verse 13 is a little easier to understand if we say, Thou, and this means God, has created me, and formed me in my mother's womb.

"But I thought a baby came about when a man and woman... well, you know what I mean. Now you're saying that God... uh... I don't understand this." She fidgeted with her hands and then dug them into her pockets.

"I'm saying that when certain conditions are met a baby is started, but God takes care of the process. He created the first man and woman and placed in their bodies the ability to reproduce. Why don't you study this Psalm to see what it tells of God's part in how life begins?

"Now, for the rest of your questions. Yes, Sam and I have been blessed and to the best of our ability we have been faithful stewards. We've worked hard and spent our money carefully and prayerfully. I'm not saying that everyone who does not have as much as we have has not worked hard or made unwise choices, nor am I saying that God loves us more. God doesn't express His love by giving us things." Mrs. Mueller scooted around under the sheet, moistened her lips and pulled her brows together.

"Next year our crops might fail, or disaster may

strike. If this happens, and it has, I will say, like the prophet Habakkuk, in good times and bad, I will praise the Lord.

"This has been a long speech, but before we stop talking, I want to also tell you that God, as our Creator has the right to choose into which family one is born. He's the Supreme Ruler and has the right to make that decision, but He always acts in love. We believe this whether it seems this way or not. I'd like for my back to be well and normal so I could do my own work. Still, I try to remember this has come from God for a purpose."

Anna yawned and struggled to listen, but she was finding it hard to follow this long speech.

"Now, Anna, I think it's time for bed, don't you?"

Horse and buggy - Oklahoma, 1910.

CHAPTER 13

The air smelled pungent with fresh turned soil. The early crops had been harvested and the ground tilled for new planting. Anna surveyed the garden. The remaining bean vines looked shriveled and only a few pods were left. The long rows of corn swayed with the weight of heavy heads, plump and ripe for picking. She snapped off the bean pods and threw them, along with a few ears of corn into her basket. Then she strolled over to the orchard. Perhaps she would find some windfall apples to make a cobbler tonight.

The peaches looked almost ripe. What a variety of foods she had prepared since working for the Muellers, many she had never before heard of, let alone eaten. She walked among the trees thinking how God sent the rain and sunshine and made all these things grow. The Muellers planted them, but she had cared for them this summer, so they all had shared the bounty. She scooped up a few apples and dropped them in her basket.

I wish Ma had some of this good food. That would help her get well faster than anything. Guilt and grief consumed her soul. *I wish I knew how to pray for Ma. Would praying make any difference? Maybe I'll try.* She closed her eyes.

"God, can you hear me? Help Ma? Help me bear all this pain?" She opened her eyes and looked around. She felt no different. Nothing had changed. Her ma was still in an insane asylum and she had no way to help, not even able to go see her. Anna glanced up and squinted at the ball of golden light floating overhead and realized that she had wasted too much time walking around the garden and orchard. Now she must hurry or dinner would be late.

~~~~~~~~

July brought hot, dry weather with strong winds. Most days the temperature climbed above 100 degrees. Damp towels were hung in the windows to cool the house from the scorching air. Time seemed to move leisurely now that harvest had ended. Anna didn't have to watch the girls as closely since Mrs. Mueller was out of bed some. On his last visit the doctor assured everyone that all seemed well with the patient and the baby. Mrs. Mueller had only five or six weeks before her due date, and everything had been knitted, crocheted, or sewn, ready for the arrival of the baby. Anna had no experience with infants and was caught up in the excitement of the family.

August came and the blistering heat continued. Dust from the plowed field flew in clouds, covering everything. Still it was too hot to close the windows against the suffocating dust. The apple trees sagged with the weight of ripe apples, which demanded to be picked and then canned or dried. All meals seemed to include apples, baked, fried, stewed, or applesauce. Even apple pie and fresh apple cake no longer tasted good. Anna felt if she never saw another apple, it would be all right. The pears were ripening now and they would make a welcome change.

One evening Mr. Mueller drove into the yard after a visit to town with an unusual package. "Girls, come see what we have," he called as he entered the house. The little girls skipped into the kitchen where Anna was preparing the evening meal. Mr. Mueller held a large object, wrapped in an old quilt and newspapers. The girls jumped up and down as they stripped off the wrappings, "Oh! Papa! It's ice," Martha cried. "Can we have some?"

"Anna, bring me the ice pick and we'll give these little ladies a chip to suck on. Then we'll use the rest for cool drinks tonight."

That night they enjoyed glasses of lemonade with sparkling ice. What an unexpected treat. Anna had never before tasted ice. Usually, they cooled drinks with a wet cloth tied around the containers, and then placed them on the front porch to catch the South breeze. The wind blowing on the wet cloth cooled the liquid a bit. The ice made the lemonade a special treat after the hot July weather.

The heat drained their energy, and Mrs. Mueller especially seemed listless and tired. Her clumsy, swollen body made even simple tasks, such as putting on her shoes, difficult. The scorching heat did not ease up, even in early morning or late evenings when Mrs. Mueller took short walks.

After harvest Mr. Mueller had asked John Davis to help with the plowing. They worked from sun up to sun down and only had time to unhitch the horses and care for them before night fell. The plow was hitched to a horse and a man guided it up and down the field. As they followed the plow, the red earth covered their clothes and any exposed skin. Earlier in the summer, Mr. Mueller had installed a bath tub on the back porch. He attached a drain hose to the tub that carried the water out to the flower bed after the last person bathed. By the time both of the men had bathed, the water looked like mud. Anna felt they added about as much dirt as water to the flower bed.

As Anna was never sure what time the men would be ready to eat, she prepared simple suppers. Tonight the meal, made mostly of leftovers from dinner, seemed unusually plain. After the meal she looked up, surprised when John turned to her and said, "You're a mighty fine cook, Anna. After that tasty food and the cool bath I feel like a different person."

A different person? But I don't want you to be a different person. I like you just fine as you are. Her heart hammered in her chest so hard she could hardly speak.

"Th..thank you," she stammered. He must think she was a little slow. Fire shot to her cheeks and she turned away so he couldn't see her flushed face.

Mrs. Mueller hardly ate anything that evening. After supper she walked around outside and then she tried sitting in a comfortable chair, lying on the bed, and walking around in the house. Nothing helped. She read part of a story to the children, but they made her nervous and she gave up. Finally, she said, "Anna will you help me take a bath? I think if you put a chair in the tub, I can pour some cool water over me and that might help me relax."

After the bath she said, "Thank you Anna, but I'm afraid I still feel miserable and restless. It may be getting near my time of confinement, but the doctor says I have two more weeks. I hate to sound a false alarm. Help me to bed. I'm too tired to stay up any longer."

Once she settled Mrs. Mueller in bed, Anna fell on her cot and tried to sleep, but the night felt oppressive. No air stirred. August in western Oklahoma was always stifling, hot almost beyond endurance. Anna tossed and turned, trying to sleep. She had just settled into an uneasy slumber when she heard Mr. Mueller tap on her door.

"Anna," he called. "Are you awake? I think I'd better go get the doctor. Ellen thinks the baby's ready."

Anna sprang out of bed, tied her apron on over her night gown, and scurried into Mrs. Mueller's room. Mrs. Mueller looked up as Anna entered.

"He'll stop at the Petersons and ask them to come while he goes on for the doc ..... Oh!" She turned pale and caught her breath. A few minutes later she said, "These pains are getting closer.. an...and... harder." She clutched the bed covers and gasped, "I hope they make it back in time. My back! I feel as if an ax just hit it."

Anna had never been with a woman in labor and prayed that Mrs. Peterson would indeed get there. And soon!

"There now, that pain's over." Mrs. Mueller relaxed her grip. "Why don't you get dressed and make some coffee? The doctor can drink coffee anytime of the day or night."

Anna went to her room felt around in the dark to find her dress and slipped it over her head. She moved as quietly as she could trying not to wake the sleeping girls. Anna hoped they would remain asleep throughout the night.

In the kitchen she filled the coffee pot with water and coffee grounds and stirred up the coals in the stove and set the coffee pot on the front burner to boil. She could hear Mrs. Mueller turning about and moaning. She got a pan of water and a wash cloth and went back to her bedroom.

"Mrs. Mueller, would it help if I sponged your face with a wet cloth?"

The contractions began coming faster and harder and when they eased Mrs. Mueller said, "Anna, get the linens in the bottom drawer of the chest. You will find the things we need for the birth there."

Mrs. Mueller stood up while Anna placed a large rubber sheet on the bed and covered it with another folded sheet. Mrs. Mueller gasped and clutched the bedstead as another pain gripped her body.

"Oh! Mrs. Mueller, hold on, please. The doctor should be here soon." Anna had never helped with a birth and she had no idea what to do.

"I'll be all right Anna. Don't let me scare you," Mrs. Mueller said.

"I think I hear a buggy coming," Anna peeked out the window and saw Mr. Mueller pull his buggy to a stop and Mrs. Peterson stepped down and rushed into the house.

"Roy's going for the doctor. I was afraid.... we.... might... be too late," Mrs. Peterson panted as she gasped for air.

"I don't think it will be long. I hope the doctor gets here in time," Mrs. Mueller said.

"Anna," Mr. Mueller said, "Why don't we leave these two to get on with their business? We'll have that cup of coffee, and you'll have time to turn your dress right side out."

She looked down at her dress and laughed. "I guess I was a bit hurried."

Mr. Mueller walked over to the bed. "Sweetheart, I want to pray with you before we leave the room." He took Ellen's hand in his and bowed his head. "O heavenly Father, comfort Ellen in this time of giving birth. May everything go well for her and the baby. Thank you, Jesus. Amen."

Anna changed her dress and went to the kitchen where Mr. Mueller sat drinking his coffee.

"You people pray about everything," she said.

"Anna, the Bible says to *Cast all our care on Him*, meaning God, *because He cares for us*. Our thinking is that if something is a problem big enough for us to be concerned, it's big enough to pray about. I certainly am concerned about Ellen and the baby. Many things can go wrong with a birth, and Ellen isn't in the best condition after her fall."

In a short time Mr. Peterson and the doctor arrived and joined Mrs. Peterson in Mrs. Mueller's bedroom. Mr. Mueller appeared calm, even though as they waited he paced about the kitchen while Anna sat on the duo fold at one end of the kitchen. The day had been especially stressful and in spite of the discomfort of that hard, horsehair stuffed piece of furniture, her head jerked frequently as she dozed off. It seemed as if she had just closed her eyes when she was awakened by the cry of a baby and a voice.

"Sam, it's the cutest little boy," Mrs. Peterson said as she came to the kitchen door. "Ellen's all right."

Samuel David Mueller Jr., was born at 3:15 a.m. on August 10, 1910. After the doctor had eaten a sandwich and some cookies and had drunk several cups of coffee, he left. When he had gone, the family settled down to get a bit of sleep while Mrs. Peterson looked after the new mother and infant."

~~~~~~~~

Anna would look back on that night as the best night's sleep she could remember. In the nights to follow, the fretful baby kept them all awake. Even the little girls complained about their noisy little brother.

Baby Davy frequently threw up his food and then cried with hunger. A new born often takes a bit of time to adjust but Davy's colic strung out over the days and months. He wailed night and day. Someone had to carry him about or rock him or he screamed in anguish. They tried peppermint drops and even tincture of anise, but nothing seemed to help. Mrs. Mueller cared for the baby as long as she could and then Mrs. Peterson or Anna relieved her. All the women felt exhausted. Thankfully his symptoms settled down after two months, and he began to sleep and eat at more regular times. The household went back to normal, but Ellen's strength did not return. She appeared listless and disinterested in everything around her. When she wasn't caring for the baby, she lay on the bed, eyes closed, yet not really sleeping. She did not complain, but still something seemed amiss.

Mrs. Peterson said, "Mr. Mueller, your wife isn't herself. Some women have what I call, 'the baby blues' but Ellen seems more than blue."

"I'm worried, also. I just don't know how to help her," Mr. Mueller said. "I'm going to see the doctor next week when I go to town for supplies."

Mr. Mueller consulted Doctor Harris. "You know, Doctor, this isn't like Ellen. She doesn't seem to care about anything as she had before the baby came. What am I going to do?"

"I'm puzzled also, Sam." The doctor flipped through his notes and sighed. "I hate to admit this, but her condition has me baffled. I thought when the baby came and the pressure was off her back, she would be all right. When I examined her last, her spine still had some tender areas, but I think it is more than that. I think Ellen should go see a doctor in Enid. I don't want to give you any false hope, though, because he may not be able to help her at all."

"Doctor, that's about seventy miles away. How would she get there?" Mr. Mueller asked. "It would be hard for her to travel that far in a wagon, even if we made a bed for her."

"She will have to go on the train and since she's nursing the baby, he would have to go, also. With cold weather almost here, she should leave as soon as possible. Anna seems a sensible girl; could she go with your wife?"

"I'll go talk to the Petersons on the way home. See if Mrs. Peterson can come see to the girls," Mr. Mueller said. "I'll try to have them ready to leave tomorrow. That way Ellen won't have time to think up an argument."

"You might stop at the store and check out the train schedule and, Sam, I hope this works, but try not to get your hopes too high." As the doctor started for the door, he added, "You might say a little prayer. I know how big a store you set by prayer. I think this is more than just the blues that some women get after they have a baby."

"We've prayed. We've prayed long prayers and short prayers. I think I breathe a prayer with every breath. I'm to the place where I don't know what else to pray. Still, I know I can trust God to do right by us.

"Why, Doctor Harris, I'm surprised you

suggested prayer. You say you're a man of science and have no need for God. That's like a person depending on a spider web; everything he trusts in will come to nothing. It's God that created nature, not the other way around. I say this because you have been a true friend."

The doctor merely looked at his hands and made no comment.

"Thank you, Doctor. I'll go make arrangements," Mr. Mueller said and left the office.

CHAPTER 14

On the way home, Mr. Mueller stopped by the Petersons' and told them he had decided to send his wife to see a doctor in Enid.

"Roy and I'll come over and stay with the girls," Mrs. Peterson said. "Tell Anna to get their things ready and not worry about the dirty laundry. We ain't never run one of them newfangled washers, but we can learn. When Roy gets tired of movin' that dasher thing and turnin' the wringer, we can set down and rest," Mrs. Peterson laughed at her own joke. "We'll get our things together and be there early in the morning."

"Thank you Alice, Roy. You have no idea how much your kindness means."

As Sam rode toward home he mulled over his decision. How could he send his wife off to a strange place and an unknown doctor? Ellen had never been away from the girls and since their wedding they had never been separated.

"Lord, give me courage to deal with this. Give this doctor wisdom to find the problem. Lord, thank you for sending Anna to help us. Protect them in the city. In Jesus' name, Amen." When the horse stopped at the gate entering his farm yard, Sam realized he was home.

"Now for the hard part," he muttered.

Sam entered the house quietly and went into the bedroom where he found his wife on the bed, shoulders shaking with silent sobs. He hurried to her and gathered her into his arms.

"Oh, my dear, what's wrong? What's happened?" He held her and stroked her hair.

When she could speak, she said, "I'm so tired of feeling bad. I want to get up; to be myself again. Suddenly, everything seemed too much. I'm sorry I'm so weak." She caught her breath and began to sob again.

"Oh, Love, you aren't weak. I must tell you something before the baby and the girls wake up. I stopped to see Doctor Harris on my way to town and he…"

"Are you sick, Sam, and I didn't even notice?"

He shook his head. "Nothing's wrong with me. I talked to him about you. He wants you to take the baby and Anna and go by train to Enid and see a doctor there. He thought maybe that doctor could help you."

"I can't do that, Sam. I can't leave you and the girls."

"Mrs. Peterson's agreed to stay with the girls. You know how they love her. Dr. Harris wants you to see a Doctor O'Brien. He has special training and he may be able to help you. Hope it won't take long." He hugged his wife again and went to find Anna. She was locking up the chicken coop.

"Anna, come to the house. We need to talk." She hurried into the kitchen, afraid of bad news concerning her ma's condition and felt relieved when he said, "Anna, I need you to go with Ellen to see a doctor in Enid." He explained about the trip and then gave her instructions regarding the items to pack.

"You can't manage a lot of luggage. We're not wasteful, but I want you to pack only enough diapers to last until you can buy more. Probably there won't be a place to wash up the dirty ones." Mr. Mueller rubbed the back of his neck and pinched his brows together. "Just throw them away in spite of anything Ellen may say. Take enough clothing for you and Ellen for one week. If you must stay longer, buy whatever you need. I'll give you extra money and Ellen will have some more if you need it."

Anna's head was spinning, trying to keep all the information straight in her mind. A trip to Enid! She could hardly wait.

"The train leaves Hopetown at 11:30 tomorrow morning. We'll leave home around ten o'clock. Can you be ready by then?"

"Yes."

"Roy and Alice will stay while you're gone. She said not to worry about food or laundry. Just get the things ready that you'll need."

Anna set out the food for a light supper, and after cleaning the kitchen, milk pans and buckets, she began to sort her clothing. I'll have to wash out some underwear and stockings and my nightgown. At least I have more things to wear than when I came here. I guess we'd better take coats along and blankets for the baby and a pillow for Mrs. Mueller on the train. She folded the items and packed them into a travel case Mr. Mueller gave her. Then she went to Mrs. Mueller's room to pack for her and the baby. Diapers, shirts, bands, shoes, socks, gowns, blankets, undershirts; the list seemed endless.

Suddenly, Anna stopped and asked, "What will Davy sleep in?"

"I imagine the hotel will provide something," Mrs. Mueller said. "Don't worry about it now. We can hold him on the train. Sam said it should take about two hours to get to Enid."

"Have you ever been there?" Anna asked.

"No, but I've heard it's a large city."

The next morning the air felt brisk as Mr. Mueller loaded their baggage onto the wagon. Even with the steps he had built for her, Mrs. Mueller had difficulty getting into her seat. He helped her as gently as he could. As he watched her struggle, he had to bite his lower lip to keep from crying.

The train had not yet arrived when they arrived in Hopetown, and as they waited, Mr. Mueller said, "When you get off the train there will be buggies lined up to take the passengers to their destinations. One of them will take you to the hotel. The next day you can take another buggy to the doctor."

They looked up at the sound of Doctor Harris's boots as he sprinted over carrying a small bottle. "Ellen, I brought you two pain pills. Will you be nursing Davy soon?" She nodded and he continued, "After you nurse him, take one pill. It will reduce the pain while you're traveling. After you take it, give yourself some time before nursing again. The medicine might be secreted into your milk and affect the baby. Tonight, if you have pain, take the other pill to help you rest." He handed Mrs. Mueller the bottle.

"Tell Dr. O'Brian I gave you some codeine. And ladies, behave yourselves in the big city." He smiled, touched his hat and walked back to his office.

The train depot stood higher than ground level with a ramp up to the platform which made it easier for Ellen to board the train. The train arrived and Sam took them to their seats, with the little girls following along. Ellen and Anna had just sat down, when the conductor called, "All aboard." Sam and the little girls said a tearful good-by and scurried off the train.

As the train left the station it gave a loud whistle and little Davy began to wail. Anna handed him over to his mother, and she nestled him in her arms and began to feed him. He made contented sounds as he nursed vigorously at his mother's breast. When he finished Mrs. Mueller said, "Anna, Davy's gone to sleep. Lay him on the seat and make a bed for him with this rolled up blanket." When Davy was settled, Mrs. Mueller took a pain pill and in a short time both she and Davy slept soundly.

Anna had never been on a train and this was a great adventure. She listened to the wheels as they rolled along the track, clackety, clack, clackety, clack. The sound comforted her. She looked out the window, but everything appeared a blur as the train raced along. How fast did this train go anyway? People were now getting out of their seats and walking down the aisle, but Anna's legs would never hold her up. She felt a little dizzy just sitting there. Thieves sometimes boarded trains pretending to be passengers, and then later pulled on masks and roamed the train, robbing the people. They then jump off the train and ride away with their gangs who wait with horses alongside the tracks. She remembered stories her pa and brothers told about the Rock Island train robbery by the Doolin Gang and Zip Wyatt. She studied the people near her.

The woman across the aisle wore a white shirt waist, navy jacket and skirt that touched the top of her fancy leather boots. Her hat matched the navy suit with a wide brim and a showy plume. She must be at least as old as Mrs. Mueller but she appeared to have never scrubbed a floor or cleaned out a chicken coop. Surely she must be a city woman.

Anna looked at the man in the seat facing the sophisticated lady. He wore a brown pin stripe sack coat and trousers, with a leather valise on the seat beside him. Nothing seemed suspicious about either one of them.

If she turned just a bit she could see a few other people but only one man appeared suspicious. He had a hard look, swarthy skin tone, with a deep scar across his cheek. His eyes darted about and he could not keep his hands still. He wore tight blue jeans and a blue plaid shirt with a red bandana around his neck.

That would make a quick face mask. Goodness, my imagination is running away from me. I must stop this nonsense.

What would Enid be like? Would she get lost? Clackety, Clack, Clackety, Clack. Anna's head began to bob. Soon she was asleep. When she awakened the train was slowing down and pulling into the station. She picked up the baby and helped Mrs. Mueller gather their things.

"Sam said we could catch a buggy to take us to the hotel," Mrs. Mueller said. "When we get off, look around to see if you can locate one."

When the women stepped off the train, however, a tall, wiry man with a bushy white beard strode up to them.

"Are you Mrs. Mueller?"

"Yes, I am. Do I know you?"

"I am Doctor O'Brian. Doctor Harris sent me a telegram to say you were on this train and asked if I could meet you. My automobile's right over here." He held his arm out for Mrs. Mueller to take.

"Automobile?" both women chorused.

"Yes, I finally bought one since my practice is growing. Now I can make my rounds in less time."

"I haven't even seen an automobile, let alone ridden in one," Mrs. Mueller told the man.

"Have you, Anna?"

"Indeed, I haven't."

Just then Davy began to stir and she shifted him into a more comfortable position. The doctor led the way to a large, black vehicle parked nearby. The porter carrying the luggage and other items tagged along behind. Doctor O'Brian helped Mrs. Mueller into the front seat, and then held the baby while Anna climbed into the back seat. He handed them scarves to tie over their hats.

"Cover the baby's face. We're ready to go," the doctor said. He then leaned into the automobile on the driver's side and did something, then went to the front of the vehicle and turned something.

POP. Chug. Chug. POP. The sound exploded from under the hood of the automobile. Anna covered her mouth to keep from screaming in terror. The baby began to wail. The doctor hopped over the door and settled into the seat. The automobile jumped into action and sped down the road. The doctor, his hands clutching the wheel and his beard blowing in the wind, drove with complete abandonment. People ran to the side of the road as they saw him coming. As they rolled along, the vehicle made loud popping noises, and dogs followed along barking. Poor Mrs. Mueller gripped her seat for dear life, squeezed her eyes tight and gritted her teeth to keep from screaming. The baby howled and Anna thought *she* might start yelling any minute, but the doctor paid no attention to the commotion he and his automobile were causing.

When they reached the hotel, he threw on the breaks and screeched to a stop. He laughed and said, "That was some ride, wasn't it?"

Anna could not even answer. She just wanted to get her feet back on solid ground.

"My office is in the next block west. In the morning, shall I come for you in my auto, or can you find your way?"

"Thank you, we will find our way, I'm sure," Mrs. Mueller gasped. "What time should we be there?"

"Well, we're not too strict about appointments; just come in early. Around eight o'clock, all right?"

When they found their room, the baby was still crying, and Ellen drooped with fatigue and pain.

"Anna I'll feed Davy, and then I must rest."

"If you don't mind I would like to walk around town before it gets dark." Anna had not seen much of the city because her eyes were tightly closed on the ride from the station.

"I'll never complain about riding in a wagon again. And I'll walk everywhere I go while we're here!" Mrs. Mueller agreed with her.

CHAPTER 15

While Mrs. Mueller and Davy dozed, Anna slipped from the room and out of the hotel. She looked around in awe at the tall buildings and activity. People strolled along the boardwalk, in groups or alone, buying and selling their goods or just enjoying an evening walk. On the dusty road beside the boardwalk horses, carrying riders with grace and aplomb, trotted back and forth. Buggies, carriages, wagons, and a few automobiles also made their way along the crowded street. The noise was deafening and she felt like putting her hands over her ears. She had never seen this many people in one place. Where did they all come from and where could they be going?

The business section was laid out in a square, about six blocks around. She ambled about, gazing in the shop windows. Surely, one could find anything they desired to buy in these shops.

By the position of the sun, Anna realized she had been out longer than she had intended and she hurried back to the hotel. She could hear Davy crying as she neared their quarters. When she entered the room, Mrs. Mueller was just getting up. Anna said, "I'm sorry to be so long. The time slipped up on me." She picked up the baby, changed his diaper, and tried to quiet him.

"Don't fret, Anna. We've both been asleep until just now," Mrs. Mueller said. "Did you see many interesting things?"

"Oh, you wouldn't believe it. I don't understand how anybody survives in this city. I felt like I had to run for my life every time I crossed a road." She laid the baby back in his bed. "I didn't take time to buy anything this time, but some time tomorrow, I'll have to buy diapers. I only brought enough to last through the morning."

"That was poor planning, Anna. Did you not think to bring more, or did you plan to wash them out every day? Maybe I can help with that."

"Mr. Mueller threatened me within an inch of my life if I tried to wash out anything, especially diapers. He said to throw them away."

"We can't be that wasteful, but it really is a problem. Maybe we can ask the girl who cleans the room where we can wash them."

"When we go down to eat, I'll check with her," Anna said. "But, regardless of what she says, please don't do any laundry. Mr. Mueller will be upset if I don't follow his instructions."

They ate a light meal in the hotel restaurant and after they finished Mrs. Mueller and the baby went back to the room. Anna stayed to look for the cleaning woman. When she returned to the room, Mrs. Mueller was still awake.

"The problem is solved," Anna said. "Mrs. Barnes, the woman who cleans our room, said she will take our laundry home with her. I told her that when we leave to go home, any baby things that are soiled she can discard or keep them. She told me her sister is expecting a baby soon and will welcome whatever is left. Still, we must buy some things because I brought only enough diapers for one day."

The next morning Anna started out early to shop for the baby and by eight o'clock she had returned to the hotel in time to go with Mrs. Mueller to the doctor's office. Anna watched Davy while the doctor checked Mrs. Mueller. After the exam, she looked exhausted. The doctor came into the waiting room with her.

"Now, Missus, you go back to your room and rest until this afternoon, and then go see the woman who makes corsets. Do you want me to drive you back to the hotel?"

Both Anna and Mrs. Mueller quickly said, "No, thanks!" After they arrived at the hotel room, Mrs. Mueller told Anna what the doctor had said.

"It seems doctors don't know much about what goes on in our backs. He thought I had bruised the big muscle when I fell, and that it takes a long time to heal. Being pregnant with Davy seemed to stretch that muscle which made it worse. He recommends that I be fitted with a tight corset to wear when I am out of bed. And he showed me an exercise to do very gently. This was all he knew for me to do except take pain medicine, but that would affect Davy, and it takes a short time to become addicted. I can't take that risk."

"Do you want to rest until noon?"

"Thank you Anna, I believe I will."

Anna took the sleeping baby, placed him on her bed, and lay down beside him.

"I never sleep this time of day. This big city exhausts me more than working on the farm." She stretched and yawned and was soon fast asleep.

After they had eaten dinner, they walked to the corset shop where Mrs. Mueller was to be measured. The shop was near the hotel, still Mrs. Mueller felt enervated when they arrived. The owner, Mrs. Sanders, greeted them warmly, and seeing how pale Mrs. Mueller looked she said, "Ma'am,' please have a seat. How can I help you?"

"Thank you. I do need to catch my breath before we get started."

After Mrs. Sanders completed her measurements and fitting, she said, "It should be ready in about three days."

"Three days! We must get back home," Mrs. Mueller said. "Couldn't you just mail it to me?"

"Oh, no, Madam, the stays have to be fitted to your body so that the corset fits properly. I'll also have to show you how to lace it up. Some adjustment in the garment itself may have to be made, also."

"Very well. I see nothing else can be done. We will do as you say."

As they walked back to the hotel, they passed a store displaying some baby items. Mrs. Mueller stopped and said, "Anna, let's go look at that little buggy thing there. We can use it to push Davy while we're here. Later he could use it to sit in at church; if I ever get well enough to go."

After they purchased the carriage Mrs. Mueller said, "I need to sit a spell before we continue to the hotel, Anna. This day has been quite exhausting."

Three days turned into six as Mrs. Sanders and the doctor worked at getting the corset adjusted. Mrs. Mueller rested as much as possible during this time and Anna pushed Davy around town. After a particularly difficult trip Anna said, "Cars, wagons and horses come at me from every direction. I'll never get used to these busy streets. Crossing them on my own is difficult, but crossing with a baby carriage, unnerves me." Big towns might be interesting to visit, but Anna would never want to live in one. Both women felt quite anxious to return to the farm.

CHAPTER 16

The day to return home arrived, but not too soon for the women. Mrs. Mueller was eager to see her husband and girls. Anna had missed cooking and even her other work; however, she especially looked forward to seeing John. As the train chugged along her heart skipped and raced at the thought of his winsome face and strong, muscular body. Still, sadness settled over her as she realized that she had no claim to him. He had never given her a reason to think she was more than just a friend. She looked at baby Davy as he sat in his buggy and played with his hands. Would she ever have children of her own? The thought filled her with longing.

In the seat beside her Mrs. Mueller rested quietly. The doctor had given her a pain pill and she had relaxed enough to doze. Anna sincerely hoped the fitted corset was the remedy for Mrs. Mueller's pain and she would soon be back on her feet; however, she also knew that when that time came they would no longer need her. She would be free to go see her ma and return home. *Home?* She felt that she had no home. The train blew its whistle and jerked to a stop. Were they already in Hopetown? Anna helped Mrs. Mueller gather their bags and disembark. Doctor O'Brian had sent a telegram ahead to say they were coming and when they arrived at the station Mr. Mueller met them.

"I'm happy to have you home," Mr. Mueller said as he helped his wife off the train. "We missed you and little Davy. When we're settled tell me all about it." He gave her a careful hug and gathered their bags and loaded them into the wagon.

"It seems like we've been gone for weeks," Mrs. Mueller said. "I can't wait to see my little girls."

When the wagon pulled into the farmyard, Martha and Sarah ran out to meet them.

"Mama, Mama, you're home. Don't ever leave us again." Sarah grabbed her mama around the legs when she stepped to the ground.

"Take care, little one," her father cautioned. Still, he understood how they felt. He also had prayed his wife would never be parted from them again.

When they pulled into the farm yard Anna said, "Everything looks fresh and green. I'm happy to be away from that noisy town." She changed into a work dress, and bustled about putting things in order, and then went out to renew her acquaintance with the chickens, cats, and Ben. The girls tagged along everywhere she went.

The days following their return Mrs. Mueller was able to be up and helped with light housework, but the outside work and canning were Anna's responsibility. Anna had received no news from home, and she longed to go see her ma, but how would she get there? She decided to write to Matt.

Summer passed quickly; soon cool weather arrived and with it came time for butchering. First they slaughtered a large hog and hung the ham, chops, and bacon sections in the smokehouse to cure. They threw some parts into large crocks filled with brine while other pieces were cooked, then canned. Meat from the head was made into head-cheese and others portions were put through the grinder and seasoned for sausage. The feet and tongue were pickled. Nothing was wasted.

When they finished with the pork, Mr. Mueller butchered a steer and the work began all over again. Anna canned the various kinds of meat until they filled the cellar shelves. She counted the different meals she could fix with all this meat: roast beef, meatballs, soup, beef and noodles; and she felt thankful for the bounty of food the Muellers enjoyed. However, she wondered about her ma. What did she have to eat these days? And Tom? And Pa? With no one to cook for Pa he must be living from one drink to the next.

I'm the one who should be doing for them and here am I, living like a queen.

Matt's letter had arrived but the news was discouraging. Ma still refused to talk and neither the doctor nor the hospital administrator would permit her to have company until her condition improved. Anna bowed her head and covered it with her hands.

Ma. Ma. I'm sorry. I should have never left.

~~~~~~~~

A few weeks before Thanksgiving Mr. Mueller caught a wild turkey and penned it up to fatten for their Thanksgiving dinner. The day before, he came into the kitchen and found Anna rolling out a crust for sweet potato pie and said, "Anna, finish up there and come with me out to the barnyard. The turkey's been dipped in boiling water and is ready to pluck."

She wiped flour off her hands and said, "I've picked many chickens but this is the first turkey."

"Not much difference, just bigger."

Anna pulled the giant bird out of the boiling water, made a face and said, "Smells like rotten potatoes. If it tastes as bad, I don't want any."

She sat on a box and began removing feathers. By late afternoon, when the turkey looked clean of all its fluff, Anna's back felt as if she could never sit straight again.

"You better be tasty, after all this work," she said to the naked creature. She carried it onto the back porch where she covered it with a clean cloth to wait for the next day's preparations.

Before dawn Thanksgiving morning, the women began preparing tasty dishes. Mrs. Mueller's sister Mandy and her family had arrived the evening before. She said, "I'll make pumpkin pudding. It's a tradition in our family." Mrs. Mueller used a favorite dressing recipe, handed down from her grandmother to stuff the turkey.

"Anna," Mrs. Mueller said, "Would you like to make that Danish dish you said your family loved? What was it called?"

"Frikadeller," she said. "Both my parents were born in Denmark and before times got hard, Ma often made recipes passed down from the old country." The thought of making the traditional family favorite filled Anna with a longing to see her mother.

Would Ma have anything special on this holiday?

Thanksgiving Day broke beautiful with a clear sky and brisk temperatures. The air tasted of snow, which at this time of year could quickly bring about a raging blizzard. Anna hoped the weather would hold.

She knew that John, along with his aunt and uncle were invited for dinner. Would she be fortunate enough to sit beside him at the table? It seemed anytime he was at the house she hardly had a moment to speak to him, let alone sit and visit. She yearned to learn more about him. Well, perhaps this would be the day. Maybe he would seek her out and they could have time alone. Just imagining the possibility gave her chills along her spine.

The pies waited in the pie saver on the porch. The turkey was stuffed and baking in the oven when the Peterson's buggy drove into the farmyard. Mrs. Peterson walked into the kitchen carrying a corn casserole. Anna saw Mr. Peterson join the men in the barn, but John wasn't with him. What could have happened?

Anna was frantic to know, but too shy to ask. Her day didn't feel as bright as it had and she struggled to keep her disappointment from showing. She listened as Mrs. Peterson chatted with the other women, hoping she would say what had happened to John, but she said nothing. It had been almost a month since Anna had seen him. Had he returned to his grandmother's house, and she had not even been able to tell him good-by? Oh! She could hardly bear the thought.

Around two o'clock Mr. Mueller came into the kitchen.

"Sure hope dinner's ready, Ellen," he said. "The smell of your turkey and dressing makes my stomach growl."

"Come in. It's ready to carve and then we can to eat."

Just as Mr. Mueller began cutting, Anna heard horses' hoofs pounding into the yard. Who would be coming at this time of day she wondered? Mr. Peterson came into the porch.

"John, you made it just in time for dinner," he

said. "Did you get that ornery calf back into the corral?"

John! He wasn't gone after all. Anna's heart started skipping and pounding. The men came into the kitchen as she was carrying a large steaming bowl of mashed potatoes into the dining room. John brushed against her arm as he eased around her. At his touch she felt as if she had been shocked with a bolt of lightning.

They both stopped and stood gazing into each other's eyes. John looked confused and full of wonder. Anna thought her legs would not hold her weight. The moment passed and John said, "Oh, excuse me Anna. Here let me help you with that dish."

Her hands trembled as she handed him the bowl and without a word she turned away to hide her nervousness.

What is happening? John pays no more attention to me than he does the little girls; maybe not as much.

The family and guests sat waiting around the long dining table when Mrs. Mueller and Anna brought in the last of the food.

"Come sit by me, Anna," Martha called.

Realizing that John sat on the other side of that empty chair, Anna hesitated. She wasn't sure she could sit that close to John and eat. The decision was made, however, when John stood up and pulled out the chair for her.

"Sit right here, Anna. Seems like you're always busy and I never get a chance to talk to you," His mouth curved into a lopsided smile and his smoky, gray eyes beamed.

She wasn't sure she could breathe, much less

speak and sit that close to him. Still, there seemed to be no other choice, so she sat down.

After Mr. Mueller said a prayer of thanks and they had filled their plates, everyone began to eat. To Anna's relief, Martha kept up a happy chatter so that she need not talk. John must have sensed her discomfort and began telling amusing stories.

"Anna, have you ever heard the story about my cousin's amazing horse?"

"Certainly not. But it sounds interesting."

"Tell us, please," Martha cried.

"All right. In the summers, when I was little, I always went to stay with my cousin. We called my cousin, Buttercup."

"Why did you call him Buttercup?" Martha asked. "That's a strange name for a boy."

"We called him that because his hair was the color of churned butter. He hated that nickname. Thought it was a sissy name. Anyway, he had the smartest horse you ever saw. He named his horse, Mule, because he was as stubborn as a mule, as they say. That animal hated to work. Didn't mind taking trips to town as long as you only went once a day. He loved to run wild in the field, but saddle him up to work and he'd balk, just sit down or lie on his side. Don't know how he knew where you were headed, but somehow he did.

"Buttercup's Pa would get mad at that horse and threaten him with a razor strap. 'Course he never hit Mule, but all the same he made him think he would. Still, didn't do any good. Buttercup tried everything to get Mule headed out in the field to work. Nothing succeeded. One day Buttercup decided to trick 'ol

Mule. He figured if he could back him out of the yard and into the field he could get him to go where he wanted. It worked but sure looked strange, making a horse go backward to get him to go anywhere."

Everyone at the table had been listening as John told his story and they began laughing. Anna laughed until the tears rolled down her checks.

"John you just made up that story. That couldn't have been true," Anna said before she caught herself. "I... I... mean..." She thought, *He must think I'm calling him a liar.*

"It's true, but sure sounds made up, doesn't it," John said.

After dinner, while the women cleaned up the kitchen, the men hitched up a wagon and took the children to look for a Christmas tree. Western Oklahoma didn't have many pine trees, but cedar trees grew wild throughout the area. By the time they returned with a tree, the kitchen was clean and the leftovers put away.

Anna had gone to help Ellen get ready for bed, and when she returned everyone had gone. She felt a tinge of disappointment that she didn't have the opportunity for a private talk with John. Still, remembering his story at the table brought joy to her heart.

~~~~~~~~

That night John couldn't sleep. Pictures of Anna danced around in his head. The way she laughed. The way she looked at him when he talked. He wished she had come along as they looked for Christmas trees. Maybe they would have been able to walk about together and get better acquainted. Still, what would a lovely girl like Anna see in a man with a handicap? Moreover, he had nothing to offer a woman. Besides she didn't know his Savior. No, he could not consider Anna as more than a friend.

CHAPTER 17

Mrs. Mueller grew stronger each day, but she was not able to return to all of her duties. With Christmas holidays near, Anna was needed to help with preparations. The tree had been set up in a corner of the kitchen, and Anna had baked pies, cookies, and fruitcakes. The girls made colorful paper cutouts, and strung shiny, scarlet cranberries together. Mrs. Mueller popped corn, and the fluffy white puffs were threaded onto a string. The cranberry and lacy popcorn chains, and paper cutouts became decoration for the Christmas tree. Several times a day the children would rearrange the decorations that hung on the lower part of the tree. Since the girls already had dolls, Mrs. Mueller decided to make them new velvet dresses with matching dresses for their dolls. Anna knitted stocking hats and mittens for the children.

On Christmas Eve they went to the school house for the special program. In Anna's home Christmas was no different from any other day. They never had money for gifts, and they had never attended a Christmas service. But here everyone sang carols and the children recited Scripture and then acted out the nativity story. As she watched the children portray Jesus' birth, it became real and she understood its meaning.

After the nativity drama, a visiting minister went to the pulpit to speak. Anna's mind began to drift and she looked around to see who was present. She had not seen the Petersons come in. She wasn't sure if they had come as the cold night air made it hard for them to travel. She didn't think John had come either. There was some talk that for the holidays he might go back to Kansas where his relatives lived. She didn't know much about his family. Just across the aisle from her she saw the beautiful young woman she had seen that first Sunday. Again, Anna wondered why she could not have been petite and dainty, with golden curls, like that lovely lady rather than big boned and plain. Perhaps then John would notice her. She was jolted out of her day dreaming when she heard the preacher say, "Since we do not know what day Jesus was born, we have taken this time of the year to celebrate His birth."

With a start Anna heard him say, "Without Jesus' death and resurrection from the grave, His birth has no meaning. His one purpose for coming to Earth was to die for our sins. God cannot die, so Jesus, God's Son, took upon Himself the body of a man and gave his life so that we could be freed from the curse of sin."

Anna felt a tremor run through her.

I'm that sinner. He died for me.

The preacher continued, "The Bible tells us that Jesus Christ stood as a Lamb slain from the foundation of the world. All we can do is say from the bottom of our hearts, Thank you, Father God, for sending Your Son to save us from our sin."

Anna repeated, "Thank you Father God for sending your Son to save me from my sins." *Father God? He's my Father? I have a heavenly Father that loves me. Me!*

She could hardly contain the joy it gave her when she realized she was truly loved by God, so much so that He gave His Son to die for her sins. She continued her prayer, "Forgive me for hating my Pa. Forgive my anger. Forgive me." It felt as if a weight had lifted from her chest.

I'm forgiven. My anger is gone. Thank you, Father God. Thank you, Jesus. I'm free! Anna's heart sang with a new song; a song of pure joy. *I'm free. I'm forgiven.*

The preacher closed his message with a prayer and then the children's choir sang, *Away in the Manger*. After the music Sarah Mueller stepped to the center of the stage and began to recite a poem. The audience sat in perfect quiet as she spoke.

"What can I give Him poor as I am?
What can I give Him, I have no lamb?
What can I give Him? I'll do my part.
What can I give Him? I'll give him my heart."

Anna listened carefully to the poem and thought,
I'm poor. I have nothing to give you, who gave your all to free me from my burden of hate and anger. But I **can** *give you my heart.*

Suddenly, Anna realized everyone was making their way out of the church. She quickly stood and joined the crowd.

As she stepped into the brisk night air she saw the petite young woman that had been with John the first time she saw him. As she watched them chatting happily she felt a jolt of pain, not jealously she prayed, but pain and perhaps, a sense of loss. She lifted her spirit upward and whispered a prayer, "Jesus, even John doesn't mean as much to me as pleasing you. I know you love and accept me, big, ugly, and poor as I am. That's all I need."

"Anna, I couldn't find you," Sarah caught Anna's hand. "Tell me, did you like my poem?"

"Sweetie, it was the most beautiful part of the program." Anna hugged the little girl and they started toward the Mueller's wagon together.

John walked toward Anna with a light step. He had watched her as the preacher told the story of Jesus and could see that she had been touched. He decided to invite her to ride home with him and find out the reason.

"Anna, may I have a word with you?"

Anna stopped and looked at John with surprise.

"Good evening, John. Yes, of course, but the Muellers are waiting so I must be quick."

"Well, I was wondering if you would like to join me in my buggy for a ride home."

Ride home with John? She must not have heard correctly.

"I....I... why yes, I suppose so. I must first speak with Mrs. Mueller."

"Of course. I'll walk over with you."

~~~~~~~~

The star-spangled basket of stars and half-grown moon broke through the cobalt night sky above them as John helped Anna into his buggy. They sat quietly, comfortable with the silence, as John drove the horses out onto the road and began their journey homeward. The sound of the horses' hoofs, clip, clop, clip, clop, kept up a steady rhythm as they moved along the rutted road, but Anna's heart was skipping and jumping, and pounding.

She wanted to ask him about his family but

wouldn't he think her forward if she did? She wondered why he never spoke of them. She had only heard him mention his grandparents. That seemed odd. The buggy bumped along with John trying to avoid the deep ruts left by the heavy traffic after the snow had melted. As they rounded a sharp curve the buggy jogged too far to the left. Anna could not keep her balance and fell against John's arm.

"Are you all right, Anna? It's a bit hard to see and I must have pulled a little too much to the left on that curve."

She righted herself and said, "I'm fine. It's a beautiful night."

"It's true. God seems very near on this night, especially as we're reminded of the birth of His Son."

Anna just could not hold back her questions. She said, "John you never talk about your parents. Won't they feel a little sad that you're not going to be with them on Christmas?" She trembled a little. What would he think about her bold question?

"Anna, my parents are dead."

"Oh, forgive me. I had no right to pry."

"My ma and pa were killed in a wagon accident." The words came tumbling out as if he needed to tell the story. "I was only a little boy, but I remember it as if it were yesterday. We were traveling quite fast and the horses were spooked by a rattler crossing the road and reared up, or something. Somehow, the wagon spun around and turned over. Ma and Pa were thrown under the wagon. Dad died at the scene.

"My legs were pinned under the wagon for what seemed like hours until a rider came along and found us. Ma died a few days later. I lived, but my legs were broken, and the left one was crushed and mangled. For a time they thought it would have to be amputated to save my life. But my grandma said, "No, leave it be." She was – is - a woman of prayer. My leg never grew as it should. That's why I limp, but because of her prayers I'm alive today."

Anna remained frozen to her seat. She could think of nothing to say.

After a time John went on. "After my parents died I went to live with my grandparents. I've had a good life, but always felt I missed something other boys had. For a time I blamed God for what had happened. My grandparents prayed for me, and loved me, and I finally made peace with God. I know that someday I will see my parents in heaven."

Anna wanted so to comfort John but didn't know how. They sat without speaking, listening to the night sounds.

"Anna, you see why I don't speak of this. It brings back so much pain and sadness. Still, I'm glad I talked to you about it." John fussed with the reins.

Anna looked around and realized they were nearing the Muellers' farm. She wanted to share what God had done for her that night before they parted.

"John, thank you for telling me. Tonight is now even more special." She shifted in her seat. "You see tonight I felt something in the service I've never felt before. I realized I was a sinner; that Jesus gave his life for me. I prayed with the preacher and asked Father God to forgive my sins. I want to know God the way the Muellers do. I have a lot to learn."

"Well, praise the Lord. We've all been praying that you would come to realize your need of salvation."

They had arrived in the farm yard and John pulled the horses to a stop.

"It's been my pleasure to escort you home tonight," John said as he hopped down and came around to help Anna to the ground.

"Would you like to come in? I'll fix you a cup of cocoa."

"Thanks. I'll be getting on as it's late. I'll see you tomorrow. I'm bringing Uncle and Aunt over for dinner."

"Good night, John,"

"Good night, Anna." John jogged back to the buggy, hopped in and left.

When Anna entered the kitchen Mrs. Mueller was sitting at the table.

"Anna, would you like to help me fill the stockings," Mrs. Mueller asked. "Fill each stocking with one of these little gifts, and then put an orange and some candy in it. After we finish we'll hang them on the wall where the girls can reach them."

"I've never seen this done," said Anna.

"For fun we tell the girls that Santa brings the stockings, but we make sure they know Santa's not a real person, just an imaginary one. We never let them think that he has special powers to know things about us; only God knows about us." Mrs. Mueller stopped and looked up.

"They know the true meaning of Christmas and Martha has memorized the Scriptures about the birth of Jesus in Luke chapter two. Sarah knows some of it by memory. They know that we fill their stockings, but we let them have a little fun about Santa."

After they hung the stockings, Mr. Mueller came

into the room and said, "Ladies, I think you have forgotten that morning comes earlier on Christmas than any other day of the year, and if we want any sleep at all, we had better go to bed."

Anna felt that she had just closed her eyes, when one of the girls tried to awaken her.

"Wake up, Anna. It's dark. We can't see anything," Sarah said.

"Please, get up and light us a lamp," Martha said.

The girls pulled at her as she sat up on the side of the bed. Anna knew it was useless to try to go back to sleep. Yawning, she stood up and stumbled her way over to the dresser. Groping for the matches, she knocked them to the floor. Finally she lit the lamp and she and the girls went into the kitchen.

"Look Martha, Santa filled our stocking while we were asleep," Sarah said.

"Silly, you know it's Ma that filled them. Never mind, let's see what's in them," Martha said.

They lifted their stockings down from the hooks and rummaged through them. Anna returned to the bedroom to find each of them warm clothes. Soon the rest of the household was awake and the kitchen came alive with the excitement of the day ahead.

Mr. Mueller said, "Look at this. Here's a stocking with Anna's name on it."

Anna took the stocking and began pulling little packages from it. Unwrapping them, she found a hair brush, a pair of stockings, a pair of scissors, and a picture of the three Mueller children and Ben, along with an orange and some candy and nuts. Tears welled up in her eyes. She said, "Thank you. I've never had a

Christmas gift before."

"Since it is too dark yet to do the milking, why don't we have some pancakes for breakfast? Then after that we'll open our other gifts and read the Christmas story."

Rather than read the Christmas story, the girls asked to recite what they had memorized. Martha began with the words of Luke 2:1. When she got to verse eight, Sarah began to recite with her. Both of them quoted the Scriptures to verse twenty.

"I don't even know one of those verses by memory. I haven't heard this story over and over like these girls," Anna said.

"Why don't you teach Sarah the verses she doesn't know and that will help you learn them also?" Mrs. Mueller said.

After morning prayers, Mr. Mueller asked Anna to help him outside while Ellen cleaned the kitchen.

"The girls can help me," Mrs. Mueller said. "We need to be ready when the Petersons come."

When Anna and Mr. Mueller returned to the kitchen the smell of the goose baking in the oven filled the house. Mr. Mueller said, "M-m-m, that baking goose makes my mouth water."

Anna brought the mince and pumpkin pies and the fruitcake in from the screened-in porch to warm up. It wasn't long before the Peterson's buggy pulled into the yard. John helped Mrs. Peterson down from the wagon seat and hurried over to greet Anna. In his hand he carried a small, neatly wrapped package.

"Anna, I have a little gift for you. Something I hope will mean as much to you as it has to me."

"Oh, John, I can't take this. I don't have

anything for you."

"It doesn't matter. I want you to have it."

He handed her the gift and said, "Go ahead and open it."

When she carefully removed the wrapping she found a small book.

"Thank you John. Have you read this book?"

"Yes, I read it along with my Bible. Look! I've underlined some of the readings that helped me when times were tough."

Anna hugged the book to her heart and said, "Thank you John. I'll read it every day I can."

Time slipped by quickly and by the end of the day, Anna had many precious Christmas memories, especially finding Jesus as her personal Savior. She felt light hearted as she remembered she now knew the true meaning of Christmas, and that she was forgiven and free of her burden of anger and resentment toward her father. She longed to see Ma and share her new faith. Somehow she would find a way, and soon.

CHAPTER 18

John read the letter again. "Your grandma fell and broke her hip. She needs you and we think you should come home." Aunt Ethel.

Certainly, he must go, but before he left he needed to chop enough wood and stack it near the house to last through the winter. The cattle needed to be rounded up and brought into the corral so that his uncle could take care of them. That would take a day or two; then he should be ready to leave. Leave? How could he leave when his friendship with Anna had just begun? Still he thought it better that she forget him. What did he have to offer a fine young lady such as Anna? He had no money. No house. Nothing. She deserved someone better than a cripple. The next day he saddled up his horse and rode away, leaving behind all of his hopes for what might have been.

~~~~~~~~~

The Friday after New Year's it snowed, not the light dusting they had had in December, but a deep blanket of white that came halfway up to the windows. That Sunday no one was able to go to church. By the second week after New Year's the snow had almost melted when it turned desperately cold, and without warning a freezing wind shook the house. The doors and windows began to rattle and a blinding snow storm struck. Anna ran outside to gather as much fuel as she could; praying it would outlast the blizzard. Mr. Mueller hurried to give the stock more feed lest he wouldn't be able to get out the next morning. They tied ropes from the house to important buildings so that no one would be lost in the snow as they took care of outside duties. The snow fell for days and before it stopped, drifts stood as high as the roof.

The bad weather continued throughout the month of January, with a succession of storms: hail, snow, sleet, and wind, everything dreadful in Oklahoma weather, except tornados. The roads were impassable, the track devastated by the wind and drifting snow, and when at last the snow melted, the deep ruts left in the roads, made travel beyond their farmhouse impossible.

The people in the community had been practically house bound for almost two months before they were able to journey beyond their farm yards. Mr. Mueller was concerned about his neighbors and as soon as he could, he ventured out to see how they had fared. When he returned from his visit he said, "The Petersons made it through the storm in good shape. They had enough fuel stacked near the house to last them. John had moved the animals into the corral before he left. He returned to Kansas right before the New Year. It seems that his grandma broke her hip. With the bad weather and all, they haven't heard how she is. They have no idea when he will be coming back."

Anna prayed that his journey had been a safe one and that he would not forget her while he was away.

~~~~~~~~

Davy was now six months old and Mrs. Mueller was up and able to do the house work and most of the outside work. Anna knew that she was no longer needed at the Muellers and must think about her future. She was now free to go home, but how would she adjust to life she had known before? Could she leave without knowing if her friendship with John had a chance of growing into more? Still, she knew she had to make plans for her future. It was time to leave.

One day early in March, Mr. Mueller brought Anna two letters from home. She opened the one from Tom first.

"Dear Anna," she read, "Can you come home and take care of Pa? I've met this girl and her dad has a big farm east of here and wants me to work for him. Pa needs someone to watch after him and I guess it will have to be you.

"Janie is a real pretty girl. She has big brown eyes and long, black hair. She isn't very tall: she can stand under my arm. I think she likes me and I know I like her. She sure is pretty. When can you come home? Love, Tom."

Anna sat in her chair with her shoulders slumped and gave a big sigh. "Father God, how can I go back to a place where not a soul knows you? How can I live in that house of dirt when I have known how wonderful it is to live in a clean house?" Tears streamed down her face.

Mrs. Mueller came into the room and asked, "Anna, what happened? Is your ma worse?"

Anna sat and shuffled the letters around, trying to get her tears under control before she spoke. "I had a letter from Tom and he wants to leave home to work for someone who has a cute daughter. He says I have to come home to take care of Pa. How can I go?"

"Why don't you read your other letter? Maybe it will give you the answer."

Anna picked up the letter from Esther. *I can*

hardly stand to read a letter from Esther. I'm already upset. She's so negative and bossy. She tore open the envelope.

"Well, I guess ya have to cum home and live like the rest of us fur a change. Guess that will help ya get rid of some of them thar high and mighty ways ya learned. Ya better hurry since Tom is gonna leave next Monday. Uncle Chris said if ya rod the train ta Avard, he would brang ya the rest of the way in his wagon. I guess he thanks ya are ta gud ta walk back home like ya walked away. Don't know if Pa even wants ya to come home, but sumbudy has to take keer of him and I got all I can do. I guess wul see ya when ya git here. Ya probably ain't in ta big a hurry to leave that thar cushy job and cum home where nobody is gonna pet ya like them thar people do. Luv Esther."

"Anna, I think you have the solution. But, I don't know how we can get along without you. You've been a joy to us."

Anna left the room thinking, *Esther's not the solution – she's the problem - or at least part of it. She not only is a pain in my neck; she's a thorn in my side.* Anna walked through the kitchen to the back porch where she picked up a bucket and went to gather the eggs. After supper that night Anna and the Muellers discussed the situation.

"We don't have the right to keep you here when you're needed at home," Mr. Mueller said. "If you pack your things tonight I will drive you to your Uncle's house in the morning instead of you waiting for the next train. That will save a little time. This is the day Tom wanted to leave, isn't it?"

"Yes."

"Anna, you know we don't want you to go," said Mrs. Mueller. "We don't know why God has arranged things like this. Don't forget God said He would never leave us or forsake us, so that means He's going to go home with you and stay with you. Remember, too, that we'll pray for you and for your family every day."

Mrs. Mueller prepared several boxes of food items to send with her. When Anna protested she said, "Anna, without all the work you've done, with canning and tending the garden, we wouldn't have had food to give you."

The next morning Anna carried her things to the wagon and when they were ready to leave the girls hugged her several times and chorused, "We don't want you to go." As the wagon pulled out of the drive, Mrs. Mueller had tears in her eyes and little Sarah was sobbing.

On the way Mr. Mueller dropped Martha off at school, and then turned the horses west leaving behind the life that had grown dear to Anna. Would she ever see the Petersons again? And John? She hadn't even been able to tell him good-bye.

When they arrived at her uncle's house, Aunt Nettie welcomed her with a hug.

Uncle Chris said, "We'll see that she gets home safely. Thanks for bringing her."

Mr. Mueller slipped some money into her hand when he gave his farewell.

"How can I thank you for all you and Mrs. Mueller have done? I'll never forget you."

"I don't know how we would have made it this last year without you, Anna. You've become more than a hired girl to us. You're welcome to come back anytime."

When Mr. Mueller left, Uncle Chris helped her into his wagon and they began the journey back to her home. Anna said, "Uncle Chris. Do you know anything about Ma?"

"Terrible thing, her being taken to that mental hospital. Don't think I would have allowed it, but then your Pa's in no shape to care for her, so maybe she's better off. Last I heard the doctor at Fort Supply didn't want her to have visitors. Maybe Lucy's heard something more."

"I want to go see Ma as soon as I can."

~~~~~~~~

The trip on to Anna's home took over eight hours. As they bounced along, Anna thought about the changes in her life in the last few months. She thanked God for allowing her to know the Muellers and for the opportunity of learning about Him. Uncle Chris's voice brought her out of her deep meditations.

"I'm sorry you have to go back to that mess at your pa's house," he said. "I'm not sure what we will find, but I hear things aren't good."

Oh, Uncle Chris, I didn't want to go. I'm so thankful for the Muellers. I learned a lot, but best of all, they taught me about God."

By the time they turned the horses up the path into the Ebbessen's farm yard, the sun had set, leaving a star sprinkled sky and the glow of a full moon.

Anna felt exhausted from the long drive. "I feel like my bones have been bounced and rattled until they don't know where to settle back into place," she said. "Uncle Chris, your bones must be more shaken than mine, since you're older."

Uncle Chris laughed.

Anna stepped off the wagon and helped Uncle Chris unload her things.

"It looks like they sent you plenty of food to eat until you can grow some. I can spare a little money. I'm sure your pa won't have any."

"That's real kind of you, Uncle Chris, but Mr. Mueller gave me some extra money and I still have my last month's pay. I hadn't had time to send any to Tom. Now I'm glad I didn't."

"Anna, don't give your pa any money. Keep your money hidden and don't let your pa know where it is."

"Do you know how often Tom will come home, or how far away he is?"

"No, I don't."

"Maybe Esther or Lucy can tell me.

"I see Pa isn't home. Uncle Chris, it's almost dark. Please, stay the night. Eat something, and then I'll make you a bed."

"I'll rest the horses while I have some coffee and a bite to eat. But I can't stay the night. I must get back home by daylight."

A little while later Uncle Chris hitched up the horses and said, "Anna, take care of yourself, and let me know if things get too bad."

"Good-bye, Uncle Chris. Thanks for everything."

Uncle Chris turned the horses and drove out of the yard. Anna felt overwhelmed with sadness and loss. How would she cope with her pa, without her ma or Tom to support her? Feeling exhausted, she put the money in a small bag and penned it inside her clothing. She checked her sheets; they were covered with dirt. She stripped the bed and began looking for clean linens. Finally she stretched a light quilt over the corn shuck mattress, lay down, and pulled another quilt over her and fell fast asleep.

She didn't know how long she had slept when she was awakened by yelling and banging. She sat up in bed, disoriented, and then realized it was Pa. "Pa, what's going on?"

The hollering and cursing continued. "Tarnation, girl what you doin' here? Can't evn' get in my own house."

Anna jumped up and lit the lantern. "Are you hungry, Pa? I'll fix you something to eat."

"I ain't et much today. Might as well."

No welcome home from Pa. Well, I didn't really expect one.

"I brought some eggs home with me, and some ham. Would you like some of that?"

Pa grunted in reply.

Anna stirred up the coals in the stove and added small sticks of wood that would burn fast and hot. She sliced some ham into a skillet and set it over the fire. Then she broke three eggs into the skillet and in just a few minutes she had the food ready. Pa sat slumped over in his chair, head nodding. Anna could smell liquor on his breath. He stunk from need of a bath as well.

"Come on Pa, eat while it's hot."

He began eating, wolfing down the food as if he hadn't eaten in some time. After wiping out his plate with a piece of bread, he shuffled over to his bed and flopped down, shoes still on his feet, and in a short time was sound asleep. Anna found a quilt and spread

it over him and stood looking down at him.
"What a waste of a human being, Lord."

CHAPTER 19

The next morning a misty light, peeking through the narrow cracks of the soddy, awakened Anna. From his bed on the other side of the quilt she heard her pa snoring. She sat up, dragged her bone-weary body out of bed and looked around. Last night's lamplight hadn't revealed the squalor and filth. Dirty clothes, leftover food, ashes from the stove, and trash beyond description confronted her.

How could my sisters have allowed Pa and Tom to live like this?

She decided to go outside. Maybe some fresh air would make her feel better. She glanced around at the buildings. The barn, a poorly built structure, looked as if it might blow over with the next strong wind. The door's leather hinge looked frayed and ready to break. She peeked inside. It hadn't been mucked out in ages. How could even horses live in this squalor? The mane of Pa's horse was matted and full of Russian thistles and she wondered when he had last been groomed. Had her pa even fed and watered his horse after he brought him into the barn last night? She found a bit of moldy hay and a little grain and tossed it to him, and after he had gobbled it down she led him out to the horse tank for a drink.

Anna stepped around to the outhouse and found the condition there as bad as the barn.

It'll probably be me that digs a new hole and moves the privy. Don't blame Tom for moving out, but he could've done better than this!

She looked around for some farm animals. The chicken yard and hog pen were empty and if there were cattle, they were out of sight. *How could things have come to this?* As she stumbled back to the house, she prayed for strength.

"Lord, I feel like running back to the Muellers. How can I cope? Help me to remember that you'll be with me."

Now she must deal with her pa. She returned to the kitchen and stirred up the fire and set a skillet lined with bacon strips on the burner. The milk she brought with her had soured so she used it to make biscuits. The scent of coffee and sizzling bacon awakened her pa and he yelled, "What in tarnation's all that blasted racket?"

"Come on, Pa, wake up. I have a pan of water fixed so you can wash."

Pa grumbled, and stumbled to the door, the effects of the liquor still in his body. He went outside to relieve himself and swish around in the wash pan. When he returned Anna had the meal on the table, but he only pushed the food around on the plate, and sipped his coffee.

"What are your plans for today, Pa?"

"I don't make no plans, I just do what I want to."

"When you feel a little better, later today, would you plow me a garden spot?"

Pa grunted and stared at her. I'll probably have to do my own plowing. I guess I can if I must.

Anna stacked the dirty dishes into a pan and set them aside while she gathered the dirty clothes. She stripped the beds and turned the mattresses and shook them to soften up the corn shucks that filled them.

"I wonder where the wash tubs are? Better quit

talking to myself, anyone hearing me is going to think something is wrong with me, too." She found wash tubs and a bench beside the barn and lugged them over near the front door of the soddy. After she heated a bucket of water she poured it into the tub, tossed in some soap chips, and then threw the dirty clothes in to soak. Anna felt grateful Mrs. Mueller had included the homemade soap in the boxes of supplies she had sent with her.

"Thank You, Lord, for giving Mrs. Mueller the wisdom to know what I was going to need." She carried water from the windmill and poured it into the rinse tub.

When she returned to the soddy her pa was gone. She found several empty liquor bottles and butts from some homemade cigarettes.

I didn't see Pa smoke, so I imagine Tom has started using tobacco.

She grabbed the broom and swept it across the dirt floor in an attempt to tidy up. After sweeping, Anna sprinkled a little water on the floor to help settle the dust and then she went to look for Pa.

"Pa, where are you?" she called. No answer. She peeked into the barn and found him lying on the barn floor sound asleep. Without waking him, she returned to her inside work.

She cleaned the rubbish off the table and poured hot water into the dish-pan. After she washed the dishes she left them to air dry while she finished the laundry. Grabbing the washboard she headed outside and began scrubbing the clothes she had left to soak. A few minutes later, she heard the sound of Pa's horse walking across the yard and ran to catch him.

"Pa, do you want me to pack a lunch for you"

He shook his head.

"Will you be home for supper?"

"None o' your dad burn business!" he said and with a jab to his horse's ribs he galloped away.

So much for getting the plowing done; it would have to wait one more day. Anna spread the freshly washed clothes onto the drooping fence and sagging clothes line. After putting another tub of clothes to soak, she decided to put away the food she had brought from the Muellers'. The dugout cave Pa had fixed years ago would make a cool place, but after checking it she saw that part of it had fallen in and the rest of it was a mess. Clearing out a corner on the kitchen floor, she set the boxes down while she took inventory of the perishable foods. The days were still cool, but with May coming on they would heat up fast. She wished they had a milk house like the Muellers had to keep the food cool.

When all the items had been sorted Anna returned to her washing. One more tub of laundry and she would be finished. Sweat dripped off her face and her fingers felt numb after scrubbing the last tub of laundry and leaving it in the rinse water. She gathered the dry clothes and carried them inside and put them away.

Anna took off her apron and rolled her shoulders. That chair sure looked inviting, but if she sat down she would not be able to get up again, and she really needed to go see her sisters today. Did she have the strength to walk five more miles? Maybe someone would come along and she could hitch a ride. After combing her hair and putting on her sunbonnet, she began the journey, and after walking two of the five miles to Esther's house a neighbor came by and gave her a ride in his wagon.

Esther's house stood at the end of a narrow lane. Weeds, tall scraggly grass, and trash littered the front yard. It looked worse than it did before Anna left. A pack of dogs started howling as she entered the yard. No one could sneak up on Esther with that racket.

I hope the dogs remember me. They're vicious with strangers, she thought as she scurried across the yard and up the porch steps and knocked on the door. After a few minutes, Esther, rubbing her eyes and yawning as if she had been awakened from a nap, opened the door.

"Oh, it's you." Esther said.

So much for a welcome from Esther.

"Well, you might as well come on in," Esther shrugged and opened the door.

Anna stepped into the house and tried not to look around or let her expression show her disgust. Esther's house looked almost as bad as Pa's.

"How are you?" Anna asked.

"I'm tired. I just didn't feel like doing nothin' this morning, so laid down after Howard left." Esther's sullen face and whiney voice made Anna want to run away. "You wouldn't understand since you don't have no kids. You can help me clean up while you're here."

"What would you like me to do?"

"Start with the kitchen. I need ta walk up to the big house and ask Howard's mother something. If I don't, she'll be coming down here. The baby's asleep, so I'll just leave him with you."

Anna walked into the kitchen and gagged at the smell of rotten food and spoiled milk. She looked around and groaned. She closed her eyes, and then opened them again. The kitchen looked the same. Soiled dishes covered every available area; the fire was out and no hot water was in the teakettle. Kicking the empty wood box she made a quick trip outside to get kindling and then returned to the pump and filled the water bucket. After cleaning out the ashes in the stove, she filled it with wood and stirred up the fire and poured water into the tea kettle to heat. She piled dishes into the dish pan and cleaned off an area to have some space to work.

Anna tried to think what Esther had looked like a year ago. She had gained weight since the baby came. Still, she didn't remember her looking quite so disheveled. Her hair looked as if it hadn't been combed in some time, and her dress was soiled and wrinkled. Esther had always been a bit sloppy and self-centered, but never lazy as she seemed to be now. Shaking her head she put aside her critical thoughts.

Esther had still not returned when she had finished her tasks. The baby was still asleep so Anna decided to straighten up the front room. She sorted through the mess, stacked the newspapers in one pile and dirty laundry in another. When the baby started crying, Anna went to pick him up. He began routing around making sucking sounds.

"Poor thing, must be feeding time," Anna cooed. Why wasn't Esther home from her mother-in-laws house? She must know it was time to nurse the baby. Anna bundled up the child and went to find her.

When she knocked on the Elmore's front door

Esther opened it and with a curt, snappish voice said, "Oh, it's you again."

Mrs. Elmore came to the door and said, "Anna, it is good to see you. Come on in."

"Thank you. I just brought the baby to Esther. I need to get home before dark." She handed the baby to her sister and left. On the way across the yard, she stopped at the well, pumped up a fresh stream of water, caught it in her cupped her hand, took a long drink, and then splashed some on her face and neck. Maybe the cool water would sooth her anger at her sister's unkind, careless behavior.

"Lord, give me patience. Help me to remember your patience with me."

Anna walked most of the way home before a neighbor came along and offered her a ride in his wagon. When she got inside the soddy she sank into a chair and looked around. She pulled off her shoes and wiggled her toes.

She gathered the laundry she had left spread about the house and folded it. Then she decided there was time to wash the clothes she left soaking. Maybe they would dry before dark. Pa should be home soon. Anna set out a simple meal, and then sat down to wait for her pa. As she waited, her mind spun like a tornado stirring up trouble.

If we have leftovers from supper how will I keep them from spoiling? She bit her lip. *Why am I worrying about leftovers when all the food we have is what Mrs. Mueller sent with me and that won't last long.*

Anna shifted around in the chair. She needed to talk to Tom. Perhaps he could advise her on how to improve the farm so that it would support them. Maybe Lucy or her husband would help, but if they didn't, what would she do? No money, no food, no supplies. Problems bigger than she could solve tumbled around in her head. Then she remembered she knew the One who held the world in His hands.

"Father God, don't let me forget that you're with me, even in this desolate place."

Anna sniffed the gravy she had made from bacon drippings. M-m-m it smelled good. Her stomach rumbled. Where was that man? Finally, she ate supper alone and covered the rest of the food with a dish towel. After putting on her night gown and tying an apron over it, she lay down to wait for Pa.

Thud! The sound of something hitting the floor broke her sleep. She jumped up just as her pa stumbled in the door.

"Pa, supper's waiting."

"Don't want nothin' ta eat, gal. Leave me alone." He shuffled over to his bed and flopped down, shoes and clothes still on. Anna covered him with a quilt. He reeked with alcohol and the stench of an unwashed body.

"Tomorrow you're going to take a bath before you leave this place." He answered with a snore. What if he lost his temper and hit her as he had her ma? What would she do? In his drunken, sickly state, she was stronger than he, still if he got angry enough he might strike her. Even so, she would insist he bathe. She couldn't live in this house with his disgusting smell.

Anna pulled the box in which she stored her personal items from under her bed and took out her

Bible and the little book John had given her for Christmas and turned to Psalms One, the reading for that day. She read through the comments and Scripture. When she came to verse six, she stopped and reread it.

"The Lord watches over the way of the righteous." *Lord, I want to be like the righteous man. Still it's hard not to feel resentment toward Pa. And Esther acts like I'm her servant. Watch over my ways and help me overcome my temper.*

Carefully she put her Bible and the little book of readings back in the box, slid them under her bed, snuffed out the lantern and closed her eyes. But sleep had escaped her and she tossed about making a mental list of things to be done. *The chicken house needs repair ... need some baby chicks. ..a sow... a cow,.. maybe with a calf.... We need a buggy - I wonder where ours is.... Ma. How did you live like this? Oh, when can I see you?* At last she dozed off; all these ideas rattling around inside her head.

CHAPTER 20

The next morning she lugged a wash tub into the barn and filled it with warm water. When Pa came outside to use the 'necessary' she said, "Pa, your bath is ready."

"Aint taking no bath," he shouted at her as he stomped into the outhouse.

She waited until he came out and said, "Pa, you stink. I've hidden your shoes and you'll not get them back until you take a bath." He marched toward her, hands made into fists. As he approached she tossed him a towel and said, "Here's a towel to use to dry off. I'll be back with your shoes when you're finished."

"You might as well get used to it, because you're going to take a bath, even if I have to put you in the horse tank. I'm big enough to do it."

Mr. Ebbessen glared at her. His eyes blazed with fury, the way they did when he was angry with her ma, and then he turned his back and began mumbling obscenities.

"I'll go start breakfast and be back in ten minutes." As she walked to the house she giggled a bit and thought, *maybe I should have tied the horse in a sand-burr patch, but I don't want to provoke him anymore than I have to.*

When she returned to the barn Pa had finished bathing and had on his pants. She gave him his shoes and socks, watched him put them on and then walked with him back to the house and they began eating.

"Pa, what happened to Ma. Why can't we see her?"

He shrugged his shoulders and snatched up his

coffee.

"Pa, where's Tom? I need to talk to him."

He ignored her.

"Please, plow the garden and help me dig a new privy today."

He scowled and shoved in a few more bites. Without a word, he gulped down his coffee, pushed back his chair, and slammed out the kitchen door. A few minutes later she heard him ride away. She slumped in her chair. How had her ma tolerated the man? Anna cleared away breakfast and washed dishes, and then carried the dishwater out to where she planned to plant her garden and dumped it. She then hauled Pa's bath water to the same spot and poured it out.

After she returned to the soddy she sat down at the table and made a list of things to do. First she needed to repair the chicken house and pigpen. She thought she might have money enough for these things if she could find someone to do the work. Maybe she could exchange garden or house work for their labor. Her work should be worth as much as any man's. She decided to go see Lucy and see if she had any suggestions. Almost as soon as she walked out to the road she saw a neighbor drive by and rode most of the way to Lucy's house.

Lucy lived across the road from Esther, but in contrast to the mess at Esther's, Lucy's yard was trimmed and neat. At the door Lucy welcomed Anna.

"I'm glad you're home. It must have been hard to leave the Muellers', but someone has to stay with Pa. How is he, by the way?"

Lucy brushed back wisps of dark curls that had

escaped her pins and smoothed her apron down over her clean, cotton house dress. She was almost as tall as Anna but had delicate bones and poise that Anna wished she had.

"Come in. Let's sit a spell, and then I need to get back to fixing dinner," Lucy led the way to her uncluttered, simply furnished parlor.

After they sat down Anna said, "When he left home, he was surely fired up at me. He's been drunk the last two nights and hadn't sobered up when he left this morning. Where does he go, Lucy?"

"He goes to the man's house down the road from you. I think his name is Taylor. I don't know for sure, but Esther thinks he's a Moonshiner, and Pa helps him for all the booze he can drink. Why is Pa mad at you?"

"This morning I fixed him a tub of water out in the barn and said he had to bathe before he left. I told him he wouldn't get his shoes until he did because I had hidden them."

"Anna, I can't believe you did that." The sisters laughed at Anna's prank.

Lucy said, "We haven't seen Pa for some time. He leaves the house early and gets home late. Tom left things in a real mess, but I couldn't take my babies over there to clean up and didn't want to leave them with Esther." Lucy stood up and walked toward the kitchen. "It's almost noon. Are you hungry?"

"Thanks Lucy, but I didn't know how long it would take for me to get here if I had to walk all the way, so I brought my lunch with me."

"Mike will be in from the field soon. We'll eat when he gets here. Danny's with him and Marie's having her morning nap. Come on into the kitchen while I get the meal on the table."

Anna found a chair and looked around the orderly kitchen, free of clutter. The starched, yellow gingham curtains fluttered in the open windows. Lucy's house was quite a contrast to the dismal mess at Esther's.

"Sit down while I finish," Lucy said.

"Do you know how Ma is? I want to go see her."

"Me too, but the last time we heard she still wasn't allowed visitors."

"Lucy, we're family. We should be able to see her."

"I know Anna, but we can't go against the doctor's orders."

Anna turned away and pressed her lips into a line, fighting to silence her angry thoughts.

"Anna, do you need money? We will help as much as we can."

"I have a little money, but it won't last anytime. Do you know how I can find work?"

"Let's talk to Mike. Here he comes now."

Anna had great respect for Mike. His father, a German immigrant, had taught him the love of work and tough discipline. From his mother, a half-Ponca-Indian, he had learned to live in rhythm with the earth and value the land. Everything he planted grew and flourished. Mike's black eyes, high cheek bones, and black hair came from his ma. His husky, muscular build came from his pa. He gave Anna a welcoming smile.

"Good to see you. Did you and Lucy catch up on the happenings around here?"

Little Danny came over and leaned his elbows on Anna's knees. "You don't know me, do you?" he said.

Anna looked at him, "Well, you look like someone I've seen before. Is your name Elmer? Jimmy? Moses?"

Danny shook his head at each name.

"My name's Danny."

"Oh, I remember now. How are you Danny? You look like your good-looking Dad. Did you know that?"

Danny grinned. He was neatly dressed, but his face was streaked with dirt.

"You've been making mud pies? You have some right here and here." Anna touched his handsome little face.

"Dinner is ready," Lucy called.

"I want to sit by Aunt Anna," Danny said.

"Fried chicken. My favorite." Mike gave his wife a pat on the arm.

Anna wondered what it would be like to have a husband like Mike. She felt happy for her sister.

After dinner Lucy said, "Mike, Anna needs some help and advice about some problems."

Mike laughed and asked, "Surely there aren't any problems on that place?"

"Not any little ones," Anna answered. "I made a list of the things I think we need. I have a little money, but not near enough to buy everything. I thought I might be able to trade some work for the things I can't do myself. I'll need a horse or mule, to ride to work. Do you have any idea what one would cost?"

"Let me ask around, Anna, and see what I can come up with. Some of the neighbors may have an animal they would trade. Our close neighbor's wife,

Mrs. Long, is going to have a baby soon. She's been having trouble and has to stay in bed a lot. Her husband might need your help and make some kind of trade. They're good people. Would you like to go see them now?"

"Okay, but let's talk before we go. I'm a hard worker and a fast one. I feel that my time's worth the same as a man's. I can't do everything a man can, but I can do many things a man doesn't want to do."

"I don't know, if you can get a man to admit that or not. Whatever you agree to, get it in writing. I'll go hitch the horses to the wagon. I'll be ready in about ten minutes. Is a little somebody too sleepy to go?" He looked at Danny.

"No, Pa. I'll help with the horses."

~~~~~~~~~

Mr. Long met them at the door of a white frame house. He was short, hardly came up to Anna's chin, and wore overalls that looked a size too big. His head was bald with a fringe of black hair that stretched between his ears. His face showed signs of worry and the lines crisscrossing his forehead now knitted with strain.

"Come in, folks." Mr. Long walked them into the parlor where his wife stood leaning against the couch.

Mrs. Long, shorter even than her husband, appeared to be in the last days of her pregnancy. Her large belly pushed against her simple cotton frock and from below its hem Anna could see ankles swollen twice the size of normal.

Mike said, "Mr. and Mrs. Long, I would like for you to meet my sister-in-law, Anna. She wondered if you needed a hired girl for a while."

"We really need the help. Right now our children are with Mary's folks in Freedom, but I don't know how long her mother can keep them," Mr. Long said. "Mike, let's go out in the kitchen while Anna and Mary get acquainted." Mike and Danny followed him into the kitchen.

Mrs. Long stood awkwardly leaning against a chair. She said, "Please, forgive this mess." she waved her hand over the dirty laundry piled on the couch. "I've not been able to keep up with things the last two weeks."

"Mrs. Long, would you like help into bed?" Anna asked.

"Call me Mary. I am so tired and feel so bad I've had to let things go."

"Your feet and ankles look quite swollen. May I check your legs?" Anna lifted Mrs. Long's hems a bit and saw that her legs from the knees down were so swollen Mary would have trouble getting them up on a bed. Anna helped the woman onto the bed.

Mary continued, "This is my third baby. I never had problems in the past. The baby's due in two weeks, but I wouldn't care if it came a little early."

"While you rest, I'll go see what the men have decided."

Anna found the men sitting at the kitchen table drinking coffee. Danny had found a toy car and was pushing it back and forth across the floor. Mike looked up as Anna entered and said, "Mr. Long has a sow that he wants to get rid of. It's almost ready to farrow. The sow's worth fifteen dollars but if you trade back a young one he'll let you have it for ten dollars."

"That sounds like a fair deal, but right now I

don't have a decent place to keep a sow."

"If you can pay for supplies to repair your pigpen, Mr. Long will do the work. If you work for them, he'll trade you even up on the hours you both work. How much can you work, Anna?"

"I can leave home when I get Pa fed. I would need to leave here early enough to get home before dark. It's quite a piece to walk each day and I don't have an animal to ride."

"I think we can help you out on that," Mr. Long said. "We'll lend you a horse to ride back and forth."

"When the baby comes, maybe I can stay every other night, if I can get Pa to eat on his own."

"When can you start?" Mr. Long asked.

"In the morning. Or, I could stay now, if you like. Is the horse so I can ride it home tonight?"

"Oh, Anna, please stay. I'm about to my wit's end. So many things need to be done." Mr. Long pulled out his large handkerchief and blew his nose.

Anna walked out to the wagon with Mike.

"I don't know how to thank you."

"Don't worry about it. I feel like you got the short end of the stick. You're going to have your hands full. If you stake out the garden spot, I'll plow it for you."

"I almost forgot to ask about Tom. Where is he, and how far away?"

"He's working for some people named Morrison who live about twenty miles east and a little north from you. He's so head over heels in love with their daughter, I don't know if he's worth his salt. Doubt he knows you're home."

"In case he comes home, I'll leave a note to tell him where I am."

"Anna, I imagine when he walks into the house, he'll know you have been there." Mike laughed and hopped onto the wagon.

"Mike, I don't want to make a hardship on you or Lucy, but sometimes I may need some things from town. If I make a list, could you get them for me? Uncle Chris told me not to give Pa any money to buy things I needed."

"We'll help all we can. My little helper and I must get home now. See you later."

CHAPTER 21

When Anna returned to the house, Mr. Long was waiting to speak to her.

"I'm not a rich man, but I want what is best for Mary. She's not felt good for several weeks. Do you want to write out some kind of contract like Mike suggested?" He pulled some paper out of a small secretary in the corner.

"Let's write a simple one in case I have to do it anyplace else. I trust you and I think you trust me, but some time I might have to remind someone else that I asked you for a contract." Anna paused.

"I do have some personal concerns. If I work here every day, I won't have time to bake bread for home. Could I make extra and take it home with me? Also, if it's all right, when I do the laundry here, I will add my personal things. I'll work an extra hour to make up for it. Is that all right?"

"That's fine, and you don't have to work any extra time. What shall we write?" Mr. Long dipped his pen in the inkwell.

"How about: 'We will exchange work, hour for hour. I'll pay for all supplies you need.' I expect you to be as careful of my money as I am, but you don't need to write that down. 'I'll work out animals, or anything else I get from you at a dollar a day.' Does that sound like a fair price, or is it too much?"

"That sounds fair." Mr. Long wrote out a contract and they both signed it.

Anna said, "I must get to work or this day will be gone. Do you have a cellar where food is stored? Are there any foods you don't like?"

"I'll show you where the cellar is, and we like most anything. Mary hasn't been eating much lately. I'm not much of a cook."

Anna made an inventory of the available food and returned to the house. She decided she had better plan supper after Mary awakened, so she could ask her for suggestions. She didn't want to be too forward on her first day.

After she mopped the kitchen floor she decided to look around outside. Several cows wandered around the corral chewing their cud and swatting flies with their tails. Mr. Long went into the large, weather-faded barn carrying a milk bucket. Three cows waited in their stalls.

"Do you want me to help with milking?" Anna asked.

"I'll take care of it, Anna. We have two more milk cows. One has just calved and the other's due any day now."

Mr. Long filled the milk bucket and took it over to feed a calf. He put its head into the milk but the calf bawled, bucked, and snorted, spreading milk everywhere. Mr. Long continued poking the calf's' head into the milk and after a time it began wolfing it down, making loud sucking sounds. After he finished, Mr. Long said, "I'm not sure if Mary got the separator washed this morning. I forgot to show you where the milk house is. I'll show you now."

Anna had to stifle a giggle as she watched Mr. Long's oversized overalls jiggled as he walked across the yard. The milk house had a stone floor with walls that were made of wood. A trough of cold water ran through the building to keep the food and cream cold.

Anna grabbed the dirty separator and carried it into the house and after the water was hot she began to scrub it down. By then Mary was awake.

"Anna, would you help me to the outhouse?"

As they walked Anna noted the swelling in Mary's ankles looked a little less but walking still seemed difficult for her.

"Mary, would you like for me to help you take a bath? It might make you feel better."

"Please do. Just a sponge bath. I don't think I could huddle into that tub."

Anna found clean sheets and remade the bed. After helping Mary wash her back and legs, she helped her into a clean gown.

"Do you feel like sitting in the kitchen so that I may ask you about the food situation?" Anna asked.

"I don't have much of an appetite. If you have time, would you make some fried potatoes and heat up some canned pork for my husband? I think the bread's all gone. Just make biscuits. Make a few extra for Calvin's breakfast. Poor man, he's really lost weight since I haven't been able to cook much. I feel like this baby may come early. I sure hope so"

"What do I need to do to help you prepare?" Anna asked.

"I think everything's ready. You'll find them wrapped in a sheet in the bottom drawer of the chest. The things I need for the birthing are in the next drawer."

Anna helped Mary back to bed and then looked at the clock. She needed to get the separator put back together. Then she would gather the eggs, and start supper. As she was walking across the yard Mr. Long asked, "Are you used to riding a horse?"

"It's been awhile, but I think I'll be all right. May I leave the horse tied outside tonight? If Pa finds a strange horse in the barn, he might get upset. What's your horse called?"

"Sandy. You probably need to allow at least an hour to get home, maybe a little longer."

"After I gather the eggs, I'll start supper."

After supper she helped Mary outside again, then back to bed. She said, "Do you like to read? Maybe I can find you a book."

"I love to read, but I don't feel like it right now."

Anna set the sponge for tomorrow's bread baking and prepared to leave. Mr. Long saddled up Sandy for her to ride home. As Anna was leaving, she asked, "How long has it been since Mary has seen the doctor?"

"It's been at least a month."

"That swelling in her legs doesn't seem normal. At least I don't think so. I'll see you in the morning when I can get here. Good night."

Anna patted the horse's silky mane.

"I've never ridden a horse quite this grand. Sandy's a good name for you. Not quite a roan and not quite palomino. I need a good friend and I think you do, too." The mare whinnied and tossed her head. "Let's go girl. It's a long ride."

As she rode, Anna could hear the howl of coyotes. Tumbleweeds drifted about, growing larger as they rolled along. She thought about her day: How blessed she was to have found a job so quickly. The Longs seemed pleasant; still she really missed the

Muellers. And John. She missed him most of all. She wished she could hear his deep chuckle and listen to one of his amusing stories.

I really like John. Well, maybe just a little bit more than like.

When she got home, she watered the mare, and tied her to a fence post. She decided to stake out her garden while there was still light. Meanwhile, she put water on to heat for a bath.

Oh how I miss the Mueller's bath tub, she thought as she poured the water into one of the wash tubs sitting on the bench out in the yard. She rushed through her bath, hoping to finish before Pa arrived. After she bathed, she slipped on one of her old flour sack dresses, put her shoes on, and hurried to the house.

Planning to stay awake until Pa came home so that she could explain the strange horse in the yard, Anna took the little book John had given her out of the box under her bed. She read that day's selection titled *Trust and Guidance.*

"You can depend on God for all your needs. Jesus said he would send His Spirit to guide and comfort you no matter what your situation. Do you trust in Him or yourself?" She opened to the Scripture reference. "Trust in the Lord with all thine heart; and lean not unto thine own understanding. In all thy ways acknowledge Him and He shall direct thy path." Proverbs 3:4-5.

Did she really trust God, or was her confidence founded on her own ability? She put the book and Bible away and bowed her head and prayed, "Father God, help me to trust you with all my problems and be content, and not whine and feel sorry for myself. Watch over Ma and make a way for me to see her."

When she heard the sound of a horse's hoofs coming into the farmyard, she jumped up and ran outside. Pa was climbing off his horse and staring at Sandy.

"Pa, I got a job at the Long's today," Anna said, "They loaned me this horse."

Mr. Ebbessen just grunted and ambled into the house. He pulled up a chair and flopped down, still not speaking. His breath smelled strong of liquor.

"Pa, if I don't come home some night, it will be because Mrs. Long needs me. I'll try not to stay unless I can make some arrangement for you. I'll make you some eggs and toast for supper."

She fried the eggs, and then took the lid off a burner of the stove top and held the bread over the flame with a long stick until it turned a golden brown. She wished she had some butter to put on it but until they had a milk cow that would not be possible. How could she afford a milk cow?

"Pa what happened to our milk cow? Could you bring some milk home from where you work? Then I could churn some butter." Her pa just grunted. "I guess that's a no." Anna grumbled, hoping her pa didn't hear her.

She put the eggs and toast on a plate and set it in front of her pa. He took a few bites, made a face, and pushed the food away. What should she do? She couldn't force him to eat.

Mr. Ebbessen stumbled into his bed and lay down. She banked the fire for the night and went to bed.

Anna tried to push away her anger. She wanted to dump the leftover food on her pa's head and yell at him. Then maybe she could get rid of the knots in her stomach.

"Lord," she prayed, "Help me to love him as you love me." She drifted off to sleep listening to Pa's drunken snores.

~~~~~~~~

Before her pa stirred the next morning Anna put on her clothes, and went to muck out the barn enough for Sandy to stay in it. As she scooped up the nasty smelling manure she tried to count her blessings and not fret over problems.

I have a job, Mike's going to help with the plowing, and I have a horse to ride. I said I could work like a man, so I better quit complaining about cleaning up this mess.

She shoveled up the last of the waste and hauled it out to the dump behind the corral. After she finished she went back into the soddie to get a clean dress and then pumped water to fill the wash basin and carried it, along with a towel and her clean dress, out behind the barn. She stripped down to her petticoat, washed off, and put on her dress. Removing the dish towel she had tied over her head, she unpinned her hair, brushed it and tied it into a twist at the back of her neck. She returned to the house and prepared breakfast.

Pa was slow getting around that morning and Anna had to work at being patient with him. Finally, he washed up a bit and dropped into a chair. While he ate, Anna tried to explain to him where she would be during the day.

"Pa, I'm working at the Longs. Mr. Long will do some work for me without charging. I want to get some farm animals and plant a garden."

Her pa just shrugged his shoulders and muttered, disinterested in the whole matter. When she left, Pa was still messing around in the barn. Would he decide to plow the garden for her? That would be a wonderful surprise, but too much to count on.

CHAPTER 22

The next morning when Anna arrived at the Longs she found Mrs. Long making a list of things for Mr. Long to bring back from town. Anna said, "While you are in town would you buy some things for me?"

"Certainly, what do you need?" Mr. Long said.

"I want to get supplies to repair the chicken house and also the pigpen. I may have to put off buying baby chicks until I can stay at home to take care of them, but if I don't spend my money to buy the materials, it will go for something else. Could you buy what I will need?"

"I'll go by your place and see what you need for the repairs and maybe I can get them in Freedom."

"How much money do you need? Is ten dollars enough?"

Anna went into the milk house and unpinned her little bag of money from inside her dress and brought it to Mr. Long.

Mr. Long took the money and said, "I'll not be home until afternoon, maybe late. Please stay with Mary until I get back."

"I'll stay, don't worry. I can ride home in the dark if I must." In truth she was terrified to ride at night because she knew that mountain lions sometimes roamed about the area after dark, but she would just have to trust God to protect her.

After he left, the ladies discussed the work schedule.

"I don't know how long my mother can keep the children," Mary said. "Why don't you clean their room? It will be easier to do while they are gone. If you have time, clean the front room, in case some of the neighbors come to see the new baby. When it comes that is, but I think it will be soon."

After putting the bread to rise, Anna cleaned the other rooms. By 11 o'clock she had finished and went to the milk house to check on the food cooling in the water trough. She fixed some bread and fruit for dinner. The doctor dropped by just as they finished eating.

"Looks like your birthing's close, Mary. Don't want to scare you but I don't like what I see. Try to give Calvin time to get to town to fetch me if you can. I need to be here." He looked at Anna, and asked, "Aren't you Anna Ebbessen?"

"I am."

"Are you going to be with Mary after the baby comes?"

"That is my plan. Right now I'm only working days. I'm really home to take care of Pa. If he behaves himself, then I can stay. I don't know what to do about him."

"That old rascal. Do you know anything about your ma?"

Tears ran from Anna's eyes. "No and they won't let us visit her. What is your opinion? Wouldn't it be better for her see her family?'

"Mental problems aren't my area, but I know that's the usual policy at those institutions. I'm just a country doctor, but I think seeing family would hurry the cure. Still, in your ma's case it seems that it was family problems that caused her condition."

When Anna returned to the house, Mary had dozed off. She went out to check the garden. The dusty soil whipped around Anna's shoes and the plants wilted from lack of moisture. She wondered how long it had been since a soaking rain had fallen. It was April, time for spring showers and if they didn't start soon the little plants would die. She returned to the kitchen and carried the bucket of water she had saved from washing the dishes, and then tossed it on a couple rows of potatoes. She kicked at a clump of Johnson grass. Weeds threatened to crowd out the seedlings.

Weeds hardly need rain to grow. Doesn't seem right. The pesky invaders must be destroyed before they sucked up whatever moisture there was. She located the hoe, and began chopping away at the trespassers.

After she had finished, she checked the chicken house and decided to clean it. As she thought of her experience with Carl, she began to laugh. "My favorite job," she muttered. In the tool shed she found the rake, pitchfork and wheel barrow and returned to the chicken house. After stripping down to her petticoat and hanging her dress close by so she could grab it if anyone came, she tackled the work. When she finished she washed herself and her petticoat. Mr. Long pulled his wagon into the yard just as she put on her dress.

"How is Mary? Did Doctor Rodgers come?"

"Yes, and he checked her over and said for her to stay in bed when possible. He thinks she could give birth anytime."

Anna grabbed an arm load of packages and carried them to the house. When she entered, she heard Mr. Long ask Mary, "Don't you think we should get the cradle down out of the attic?"

"Yes, it won't be long, I'm thinking."

Anna spent a little time washing and drying the cradle and finding the right pillow for it. By the time she finished, it was late and she knew she must still get supper on the table.

While the bread was baking she made Mary some chicken and rice soup. The rest of the chicken and broth simmered on the back of the stove. She stirred up the fire, pulled the kettle to the front, and hurriedly made some drop dumplings. She opened a jar of green beans and put them on to heat. With the fresh bread and bread pudding, she thought this would be enough supper. Anna went to check on Mrs. Long.

"Do you need anything?" she asked.

"Yes, please help me go to the outhouse."

As they walked back to the house Mary said, "Mr. Long stopped by to see the children and they are anxious for the baby to come. I'm sure my parents are spoiling them rotten." Mary rubbed the back of her neck. "I really miss them."

As Anna prepared to leave she asked Mr. Long about the chicks.

He said, "How many do you plan to buy? We usually bought about one hundred."

"About fifty. Do you have a place for me to keep them here for a while?"

"We'll arrange something."

"May I keep them here until I leave? Then I would take one-third of those that survive."

"Do you think you can take on that much more work with a new baby and all?"

"I think so. How soon can we get the chicks?"

"Anna, I think you are a glutton for punishment.

I'll talk it over with Mary."

"If it's all right, I'll work at least three weeks after the baby comes, then if Mary and the baby are all right, I'll work two or three days a week until you don't need me. I must go now, I want to stop at Lucy's and ask about Ma."

Lucy met Anna at the door.

"Come in, Anna."

"I must hurry home before dark. But I wondered if you have heard anything about Ma. Also, do you know if Tom comes home on weekends?"

"We haven't heard from the doctor since he told Pa and Tom not to come see ma for a while. He hasn't answered our letters. I'll write again and find out if there's been any change.

"Thank you, Lucy. Since we can't see her, I'm quite anxious to know how she's doing"

"I'll let you know when I hear from them. Take care."

~~~~~~~~~

One morning, a week after Anna began working for the Longs, she rode into the yard and saw a horse saddled up. She rushed into the house and found Mr. Long, his face creased with worry, pacing about the kitchen.

"Oh, thank the Lord. 'fraid I'd have to leave before you made it." Mr. Long grabbed his hat off the kitchen table. "Pains coming real fast... I'll be back soon as I can... Coffee on the stove." He ran out the back door and jumped on the waiting horse.

Anna dashed into Mrs. Long's bedroom and found her panting and groaning. She didn't know what to do so she ran back to the kitchen and put water on to heat. Hadn't she seen the doctor do that? She got a pan of cool water and clean rag and raced back to the bedroom. Mrs. Long was on her side gritting her teeth and moaning.

When her pains eased, she said, "Anna, my water could break at any time. Get the birthing things out of that drawer."

Anna removed the birthing pack and swiftly slipped the rubber sheet and other sheets under Mrs. Long. When they were in place Mrs. Long rolled over and began crying, "Oh, God, don't let me lose this baby."

Anna brought the pan of hot water into the room. She paced the floor and twisted her hands together. Anna, who seemed to always know what to do, was in a panic at seeing the woman's pain and fear. Then she heard a gentle whisper, "Lo I am with thee always…"

Anna sat down and said, "Dear Father God, forgive me." A calm peace replaced her panic. She turned to Mrs. Long and said, "May I pray with you? I'm at a loss of how to help, but I do know One who does."

Mrs. Long nodded. When her pain had lessened a bit, Anna took hold of her hand and prayed, "Lord, you know our needs. You know how helpless I feel. Help Mrs. Long with this pain. Please, let the doctor get here *soon*. Give her a healthy baby."

Mrs. Long began to moan and Anna paused until she relaxed again. "Give me wisdom to know what to do. In Jesus name, amen."

After the prayer Mrs. Long settled down a bit and said, "Help me to my feet, I think if I walked around it might help. It seems like this baby is pushing a hole in my back."

Anna prayed as Mrs. Long walked back and forth, pausing often and moaning in agony. The morning wore on and still the doctor had not arrived. When Mrs. Long's anguish increased and the pains came closer she lay down. Anna wiped cool water across her face.

"Thank you Anna. I think this baby is going to get here before the doctor arrives."

To get their thoughts off the desperate situation Anna began to talk about her time with the Muellers.

"I had never heard God's name spoken in a reverent manner. I didn't know I was a sinner and needed to be saved by believing in Jesus, who died for my sins."

Mrs. Long groaned, took a deep breath and said, "Oh, Anna, I'm so glad you are a Christian. I haven't felt like talking about this with you. Oh, dear me, this is a hard one." She let out a scream, "The doctor's not going to make it. Oh! ... Oh! I think the baby's here! Take a look."

Anna, wide-eyed and dazed, pulled back the cover. She could see a tiny head pushing out. She gently touched and guided it as the baby moved forward.

"It's a boy. A boy! What do I do about this cord?" Anna was shaking until she thought she would drop the little bundle. Mrs. Long's face beamed with the joy at hearing the news. The baby let out a cry and gulped in the air. Her pain forgotten, Mrs. Long said, "Anna, wrap the baby and give him to me. There's a piece of string and some scissors on the dresser. Pour that boiled water over it then wrap the string around the cord in two places and cut it in between. Must be done soon! Can you do that?"

Anna's eyes grew large with fear.

"Bring the things over here and I'll help you."

Anna picked up the string like she thought it was a snake.

"This has to be done, Anna, and there isn't anyone but you here to do it. I'll help you."

Finally, Anna carried the string and scissors over to the bed.

"I'm okay now. Where should I start?

"Wrap it about eight inches down. That's right. Now cut the string and tie a knot in it." Anna did as she was told.

"Now move up about four inches, and make the second tie. Okay, cut the cord in between where you tied it. Leave it a little longer on the baby's side. That wasn't hard, was it? The after birth should deliver soon."

"After birth! You don't have to eat it like some animals do, do you?"

"Anna! Of course not!"

After everything had been taken care of, and the baby had been sponged off and nursed, they both fell asleep. Anna sat down. Her heart pounded but her spirit felt light.

"I did it. No, we did it. Thank you, Father God. Thank you." She felt exhausted and soon her head began to nod. A door banged and Anna nearly fell off her chair.

"We're here," Mr. Long called as they bounded into the bedroom. Mr. Long looked at his wife and new born and cried, "Well, praise the Lord." He then kissed his wife.

"We have a boy, want to hold him?" Mrs. Long said.

The doctor said, "It looks like you girls did a great job. Now let's see if we can get you on the road to recovery."

He turned to Mary and said, "Drink plenty of liquid, especially milk, so you can nurse the baby. Take it easy and stay in bed until all the swelling is gone from your legs. It's hard to tell these new mothers to stay in bed, but since you haven't been well, you need to cooperate." He gave Mrs. Long a little pat and turned to her husband.

"If you have any problems, send Calvin to get me."

Little Scottie was a lusty, demanding baby and Mrs. Long, still frail, had all she could do to keep him fed and his dirty diapers changed. The children returned home from their grandparents and fought for their mother's attention, jealous of the new baby and each other. Until Mrs. Long could be up and about, Anna was responsible for all the inside duties, as well as looking after the children and taking care of the chickens. She felt she had more to do than time to do it and often fell into bed at night too tired to take off her dress. Had she been this weary working harvest season at the Muellers? There she also had Mr. and Mrs. Peterson's help.

~~~~~~~~

At last spring rains came with a flourish; thunder, and lightning broke the quiet of the prairie and changed the dry, crusty red earth and dead buffalo grass into a green carpet, splashed with the colors of wild flowers, purple wine-cup poppies, orange-red Indian paintbrush, and the yellow-gold of sunchokes and primrose.

The birds returned from their winter flight and their chirps and warbles filled the air. Farm animals gave birth to their young. The old sow, for which Anna had agreed to trade, now had eight piglets. The baby chicks Mr. Long brought back from Alva needed special care as April nights in Oklahoma were still cool; so extra heat was provided by suspending a kerosene lantern from a rafter in the barn. Emily and little Jake loved to pick up the baby chicks and didn't realize their hugs could kill the fragile little creatures. The children required careful watching and Anna often wished for a dog like Ben to guard over them. She even suggested this to Mr. Long but nothing came of it.

Mr. Long usually took care of the outside work, but one morning he came into the kitchen where Anna was scrubbing the floor and said, "I know you've got your hands full with the house and all, but I must make a trip into Alva for some seed and I'm going to need your help with milking and these new calves while I'm gone. Two cows have recently given birth; one calf won't drink from a bucket and has to be fed several times a day with a teat-bag. Have you ever weaned and bottle fed a calf?" Mr. Long asked.

"I was young when we had milk cows. Ma and my older brothers took care of all that. For some time we haven't had a cow."

"Well, if you're planning to get one, you better learn how to wean calves. Sometimes it's not pleasant."

Anna dried her hands, set her mopping supplies outside, and followed Mr. Long out to the barn. The bawls and pitiful honking wails of the calves bounced off the barn walls, announcing their distress at being separated from their mothers. Their wretched moans broke Anna's heart but she knew Mr. Long was doing what had to be done so that the milk of the mother cows could be used for the needs of his family.

When they entered the barn, the young calves came prancing, dancing, lopsided and wobbling toward them.

Mr. Long said, "Stay on this side of their pen. They're stronger than they look and could knock you down with their need for milk." He put some milk in his hand and offered it to the babies. The little calves began to slobber and suck the warm liquid. While they were licking his hand, he dipped it down into the bucket and the calves ducked their heads into the pail and continued lapping up the milk.

"Keep this up for a few days and then they'll learn to drink from a bucket. This runt must be fed from the teat-bag. He was born a few days ago and still refuses to drink from the pail."

While Anna continued feeding the other calves, Mr. Long poured milk into the teat-bag and the little runt, ribs protruding and bowed legs bouncing, began sucking and pulling at the bag, slobbering and snorting loudly. For the next few days this duty was added to Anna's responsibilities. She fell in love with the frisky, bouncing, little fellows and then Mr. Long returned and took over the job.

After a few weeks, Mary was on her feet and able to take over many of the duties, allowing Anna to return to her home at night. She knew that her time working for the Longs would soon end and she began to fret about where she would find work when that time came. The food the Muellers had sent home with her had just about run out and the Longs now insisted that she take food home each evening for her pa's supper. Without this job, how would she provide for herself, her pa, and the farm animals she would be taking home with her when she left? How had her mother managed all those years after Pa began drinking?

Pa's only greeting after she stayed three weeks, night and day, at the Longs was a complaint.

"'Bout time you got yourself home. Been up to no good, I reckon."

He behaved crabby and morose, and refused to have any kind of a conversation, and only mumbled answers to Anna's questions. Bath mornings became an all out war between the two, but one that Anna determined she would win. Who would have thought that a daughter would have to make her pa bathe?

CHAPTER 23

Mr. Long repaired the chicken house and pig pen, and Anna worked enough days to pay for the pig and all the work Mr. Long did for her. Baby Scottie was now four and a-half weeks old. The swelling had gone from Mrs. Long's legs and she was up part of the day helping with the simple tasks.

"Anna, we're now going to need you only two days a week," Mr. Long said. "Mary will need some help with the washing and ironing and some of the heavy cleaning for a while. You'll be free to work for someone else the other days."

"Thank you, Mr. Long. I don't have another family to work for at this time and I really do need to work."

"I'll keep my ears open for anyone in the neighborhood that needs help. When do you want me to bring your sow and chickens over?"

"I'll let you know." She saddled up Sandy and urged her out onto the road toward home. As the horse trotted along Anna began to fret about her future. How would she feed these animals? She wasn't even sure how she would feed herself and Pa? She was thankful for the garden spot Mike plowed and she had already planted a few rows of vegetables, but until they were producing she had to think of a way to keep food on the table.

Would she have to ask Lucy and Mike to help her out? They certainly had done more than their share already. What about Esther and Howard? No, she could not ask them for help. She really didn't know if they were able, but even so she would not want to face Esther's scorn at such a request. No, she would just have to find a way on her own.

Pa did not come home until after dark that night. He ate only a few bites, drank a cup of coffee, and went to bed. After she cleaned up the kitchen, she went to her bed, dug under it, pulled out her box, and removed her Bible and *Book of Reading*. The scripture for that night was Matthew 6:25-34. She read the verses and then read from her *Book of Readings*.

"We are not to be concerned or anxious about our yesterdays nor our tomorrows. Yesterday is gone. It was ours. Now it is God's. As well, tomorrow is beyond our present control. The sun will rise; the moon will appear in its time. The One who holds our yesterdays also holds our tomorrows. The One, who cares for the sparrows, also cares for us. The fields are clothed with His glory. Do you think He cares less for His human creation?" Anna closed the book and her Bible and put them away.

"Forgive me dear Father God. I will rest in you and with your help I will cease to fret about my tomorrows."

~~~~~~~~

Two weeks later she rode Sandy to the Longs for the last time. She gathered her clean laundry and borrowed some starter to make bread at home. Mary walked her to the door.

"You came to us as an answer to our prayers. I don't know how to thank you. I feel I have found a real friend in you."

Mr. Long met her at the barn.

"Anna, I don't know what we would have done without you. You're one of the best workers I've ever seen. I know you have a hard time ahead of you at home. Let me know anytime I can help."

She handed Mr. Long the reins of Sandy's bridle.

"Thank you for loaning Sandy to me. She's been a real friend." Anna stroked the soft mane and patted the gentle horse on the neck.

"Go ahead and keep the mare for a while. You'll need a way to get around when you do find another job. We can spare her a little longer," Mr. Long said.

Tears pooled in Anna's eyes until she could hardly see.

"I need one more favor. Could you help me get the chicks and pigs home? I would work one more day for you, if you would help me. Also, can you tell me where to buy some grain?" Her money for provisions was almost gone but somehow, when the time came, God would provide for her needs.

"Mike might be able to help you with the feed. Would you like me to bring your animals over this afternoon?"

"Yes, please."

"Why don't you talk to Mike and see if he can help me. If he can't, come back this evening and you can help me."

When Anna rode into Lucy's farm yard she was sitting on the porch snapping beans.

"Anna it's been a while since we've seen you." Lucy set the beans aside and welcomed Anna into the house. "It's already getting warm. Would you like a glass of cool water?"

"Yes, thanks. I stayed at the Longs for four weeks after the birth of their baby," Anna was grateful for the cool water.

"You have a reputation for being a hard worker. You know how news gets around out here. I think it blows on the wind."

"Have you heard from the doctor yet?"

"No, mail's real slow or the doctor's too busy to write."

Anna dropped her head, trying to hide her disappointment.

"I need to see Mike. Is he home?"

"He's at a neighbor's. He'll be back for dinner. You know a man would never miss his meals." Lucy's mouth twitched with mirth. "Will you eat with us?"

"Thanks Lucy. I need to talk to him about helping Mr. Long bring my animals home."

"How will you feed them?" Lucy asked.

"I have a little money now but it won't last long. If Pa's bringing any money home, he hasn't told me. He hasn't asked me for any money; in fact, he doesn't talk to me at all. I have Mr. Long to thank for repairing the chicken house and pig pen, and fixing the barn door so it will close. And I have the sow paid for. She has eight babies."

"It's a while before dinner. Want to go over to see Esther? Tell her I said you must be back in an hour."

The dogs howled as Anna entered Esther's farm yard. The scanty patches of grass were knee high, and trash and old tools were scattered about. Esther met her at the door.

"Well, I thought you were ta good to come see me."

"Esther, I've worked as many hours a day as I could cram in and still get home in time to feed Pa."

"I heard that Mr. Long was doin' some work for

you. I don't know why you're tryin' to fix up that place."

"I have to do something so that we'll have some food and a little money. I bought some chicks that will soon be grown and produce eggs. Pa doesn't seem to be making any."

"If he's makin' any, he's drinkin' it up. Howard wanted ta get us some chicks, but I told him I don't have no strength ta raise them."

"Are you sick, Esther?"

"Well, sometimes I don't feel ta good." Esther puckered her thin lips.

"Where are the children?" Anna asked.

"I took the baby up ta Mrs. Elmore's and Jimmy's out in the field with his pa. You can help me with dishes."

Anna agreed and the sisters walked into the kitchen. The scene hadn't changed much from the one Anna saw when she was there the last time. Anna said, "I'll wash and you can rinse and dry." She went after water, and brought in some kindling for the fire. By the time the water was hot, she had made a place to work.

Esther watched her work, then said, "I'm so tired, I'll jus' sit here."

When it came time to leave, the job wasn't finished but Anna dried her hands and said, "I must go now. Good bye Esther."

"You still have time. Won't make no difference ta Lucy if you stayed and finished," Esther glared at Anna and her mouth turned down in a frown.

Anna left. Esther didn't even get up to walk her to the door. As she rode Sandy down the road she prayed, "Lord, help me not to carry tales from one sister to the other. Help me be tolerant of Esther."

When she got to Lucy's house Mike and Danny were washing up for dinner. Anna greeted them and while they ate she told Mike about her plans to bring home the animals from the Longs.

"Danny and I will help him bring the animals over to Pa's. What are you going to do for feed?"

"I'm not sure. My money's almost gone and I don't have another job yet." Anna tried to keep the worry out of her voice.

"I'll give you a bag of corn for the pigs. That should tide you over for a while. We'll help all we can."

"Thanks Mike. You and Lucy have done more than your share. I wish I could buy some hens, enough to keep us in eggs until my chicks are grown. I hope to find a job soon."

"Mike, do you think I could make more money having a field plowed and planted in broom corn like we used to, or work for cash?"

"Be easier to work for cash. I don't think you could take care of the broom corn by yourself. Your pa probably wouldn't help you."

"No, I can't count on him. I'll go on home now and get things ready. I really appreciate what you're doing and have done for me."

CHAPTER 24

It wasn't long before the wagon with her animals came rolling down the lane. Mr. Long pulled the wagon around to the newly repaired pig pen, opened the gate and removed a long board and leaned it against the back of the wagon. The sow had a rope tied around her neck. Mr. Long grabbed the rope and tried to lead the pig down the board but the stubborn animal squealed and refused to budge.

Mike got behind the sow and tried to push, but she sat on her rump and shrieked louder. The sight was quite comical and they laughed so hard they could hardly manage the pig. Finally, after much wailing and grunting, pushing and pulling the sow went into the pig pen and Mike fastened the gate. After circling the pen to make sure all her piglets were safe, the old sow settled down. It was then time to unload the baby chicks, and after wrestling the sow into the pig pen, getting the chicks into the chicken house was a simple matter.

Anna heard clucking and crowing sounds from a box wired to the side of the wagon. She said, "Mr. Long what are these hens and rooster doing here?"

"The hens are from Mary and me. You went the extra mile for us. Thanks to you we have a healthy baby and Mary is still with us. The rooster is from Mike and Lucy."

"Thank you both. Mike, I really didn't do anything for you."

"Think of the trouble you saved us by coming home and taking care of your Pa. I'll keep you in feed until I can get to town and buy you some. There's a bucket of milk under the wagon seat. Hang it in the water tank to keep it cool and it should be okay for a few days. Lucy sent it."

Anna waved as the two men hopped on the wagon and drove out to the road. No time for daydreaming, the animals needed to be fed and supper prepared. She put hay out for Sandy and Pa's horse and then checked the pigs and the baby chicks and put out feed for them. She carried a tub to the chicken house, turned it upside down and propped one side up with a rock so the babies could get under the tub if they got cold, and then she locked the hens and rooster in the chicken house. That should keep them safe from the coyotes that roamed about in the night.

By the time she started supper, it was dusk, and she had to light the lanterns to cook. When the meal was ready Pa still hadn't arrived, but she decided to eat anyway. An hour later she heard a horse coming up the lane and carried the lantern out to help Pa care for his horse. He slumped over, hardly able to stay in the saddle. Anna felt disgust. Why would he let himself get in this condition? She wanted to shake some sense into him, but instead she helped him down and into the house.

When Pa was seated at the table, she said, "I'll put your horse away. Go ahead and eat." When she returned his plate hadn't been touched and he had his head on the table asleep.

"Pa wake up and eat something."

"Leave me alone, Gal," he grunted. Finally, he drank a little milk, and Anna helped him to bed.

That night Anna could hear the coyotes howling as they circled nearer to the farm yard. She hated the sound of their cries and knew they prowled about hoping to find a way into the henhouse. She prayed that the door was secure.

The next morning Anna made morning rounds and found the piglets sucking contently at their mother. Anna set out feed for the sow and went to fill the water trough. The breeze blew briskly from the southwest. She set the windmill so that its blades would catch the wind and as the blades began to turn water trickled into the horse tank. She opened the chicken house and let the hens and rooster out. All seemed well and she felt thankful that they had survived the first night in their new home.

She wondered if the low fence Mr. Long had stretched out around the garden was high enough to keep the chickens out. She fed the little chicks and filled some shallow pans with water, making sure the water was not deep enough to drown them if they fell in. She decided not to put pans of water out for the hens; surely they could find the puddles around the horse tank.

As she scattered cracked corn for the chickens she said, "Well, I learned one thing today already: The more things you have, the more time you have to spend taking care of them." When she got back to the soddy, her pa still slept. She shook him gently, and then a little harder until he awoke.

"Come on, Pa, get up. I fixed you a pan of water so you can wash."

He staggered and fell against her as she helped him put on his shoes and walk outside to clean up. Was he sick or just suffering from a hangover? No way to tell; nevertheless, she would have to take a chance on him being all right by himself today. She planned to search the fields for edible plants and fuel for the cook-stove. Tomorrow she would follow Pa and find out where he went. Today she needed to forage for food so that they would not go hungry until she could find work again. All of her cash money must be saved to buy supplies for the animals.

Pa half-heartedly splashed water on his face but refused to wash any place else. When he finished he returned to the house and sat down at the table where Anna served him biscuits she had brought from the Longs. He ate a little, and then drank some coffee. Coffee seemed to be all Pa wanted and that would soon run out. Tomorrow she would have to start reusing the coffee grounds.

"Pa, I'm worried about you. If you won't eat, please drink a glass of milk." She set the milk in front of him and then went to his bed and laid out some clean clothes. She brought in the wash pan and a cloth.

"Pa, sponge off and get out of those clothes so I can wash them. I'm going out to water the horses." Outside, she led Sandy and Pa's horse to the horse tank, gave them both a little corn, more water, then tied them to a post.

By the time she returned to the soddy, Pa had on his clean clothes. After helping him with his socks, she asked him if he wouldn't like to lie back down for awhile. He fell back on the bed.

"Stay home today, Pa. I'll cover up the rest of the biscuits and you can eat them for lunch. I'll be home as soon as I can."

Anna didn't like leaving Pa, but she didn't know

what else to do. She saddled Sandy, got a large burlap bag, shoved her tools and lunch into the sack, tied it onto the saddle, stepped up onto the mare and rode out of the farm yard and across the open field. In the spring Ma had often sent them out to look for edible plants, but that had been a long time ago. She hoped she could remember how to identify them.

As she rode along she saw some sand plum bushes growing along the fence line. The stunted trees were covered with fragrant, white blossoms, which in a few months would become plump little balls of fruit. These plums made delicious jelly. Her mouth watered thinking of its sweet taste.

She studied the sky and saw a few scattered dark clouds, but it didn't look like it would rain today. Spring rains had been scanty this year, and even if she were caught out in it she would be thankful for the moisture.

She could now see the tree belt and knew that the creek was nearby. Could she catch some frogs today? Pa loved frog legs. Maybe they would give him more of an appetite and she could get him to eat. Fishing for frogs would be last on her list; first she wanted to find some pokeweed. They had always gathered pokeweeds in the spring when the plant was safe to eat. Its leaves made a delicious salad and the tender stalks were good for cooking with bacon grease. She began to search for the tall emerald green plants. When she located them, she hopped off Sandy, tied her to a tree, untied the sack and pulled out her knife.

Anna prodded around in the plants until she found stalks about the size of her little finger. She sliced off these stalks, with their leaves, and piled them on the ground. Sandy whinnied and pawed the ground. Anna looked up.

"What's wrong girl?" She noticed that a dark wall cloud had formed in the Southwest. Could Sandy feel or hear a storm coming?

"Looks like we might get some rain. We'll be going as soon as I finish. A little rain won't hurt us." She patted the mare and returned to her task.

A sudden gale of wind scattered her pile of plants. Anna grabbed them and stuffed them into her sack just as large drops of rain fell. She looked up and saw that dark, turbulent clouds had gathered above.

Time to head home.

The sound of Sandy's hoofs pawing and pounding the earth startled Anna. She turned and watched as the horse began throwing up her head, flaring her nostrils, and frantically pulling at the rope attached to the tree. What was happening?

The air went still; didn't feel right. The mare reared, whinnied, and bolted, breaking loose the rope that held her. The air began to stir.

Anna watched as a tail formed in the wall cloud. It seemed to be moving in her direction.

Oh, dear God, could this be a tornado?

Sandy began to gallop and whicker wildly. Anna watched as the black swirl moved toward her. Rain poured down. The horse disappeared from her view just as Anna heard a sound, like a freight train, drawing nearer.

She stood frozen in fear as the monster sped in upon her. What should she do? There was no safe place to run, nor time to do it. Out in the open her only hope would be to find a gully, but she didn't remember seeing one nearby. Just as she saw a pea colored light she fell on her stomach and rolled to the lowest place she could find. She closed her eyes in terror as she saw the greenish, whirling funnel come close.

As the spinning mass churned in Anna's direction it sounded like dynamite exploding. A blast of wind, like she had never before experienced, hit her and she felt as if her breath had been sucked from her. The wind tore at the ground where she sprawled, its fingers grasping, sweeping everything up into the circling monster. Tree limbs and other debris smashed against her prostrate form.

The raging giant continued to pull and suck everything that stood in its path. Anna clutched at the grass under her and prayed that somehow she would live through this horror. She felt as if she were being yanked into its funnel, lifted off the ground. She screamed and screamed and then everything went black.

CHAPTER 25

When Anna awoke, rain fell in sheets and her body felt as if a mule had stomped on her. Why was she lying on the ground? She rubbed her head and tried to remember what had happened. As she stood up and surveyed the chaos, the memory of the terror returned.

"Dear Father God, thank you for sparing my life. Please, help me find my way home."

Sandy! Where was the horse?

"Sandy, come here girl," she called and called but the sound of the rain gobbled up her voice. She had no idea how far she was from home. Would she even have a home left? What about her animals? She felt desperate to get back and check on them.

Where was she? Nothing looked familiar. Had the tornado sucked her into its funnel, and carried her away and then dropped her? She had seen that happen with things. Surely she would remember an experience such as that. Where was she? She had ridden south toward the creek when she left home; therefore, to return she must walk north. She started walking in the direction she guessed was north, but couldn't be sure because the rain and clouds hid the position of the sun. Trudging through the rubble of debris left in the wake of the tornado, and fighting the gusting wind and pouring rain, she began her hike homeward.

After walking what seemed a great distance she heard a cry, something like a baby's. She stopped and listened, then followed the direction of the sound. When she came to a pile of boards and branches, she crouched over and dug around under the heap until she felt the soft fur of an animal caught under the wreckage and gently freed the creature. It was a puppy, its fur soaked. The puppy sniffed at Anna and licked her hand.

"Poor little thing. Where's your ma?" Anna snuggled the puppy to her breast and covered it with her hand, hoping to warm it a bit. "You're going home with me," she crooned. "That is if I can find home."

Anna stood up, tucked the puppy into her apron bib, and continued her journey. After walking what seemed like hours, the rain stopped and the clouds lifted. She studied the sky and saw that the sun was now midway in the west. It looked to be around three o'clock. She had been walking toward the sun and not north as she thought. Nothing looked familiar. She put her hands to her eyes and peered across the field trying to see if there were any buildings nearby. If she found a house, maybe she could find someone to take her home.

Home? Had the tornado struck there as well?

All her bones ached and her feet hurt, but still she must hurry. She stepped up her pace, and soon saw the outline of buildings in the distance. Running, she headed toward them. The area looked familiar, and she thought she might be somewhere near her sister Lucy's, about five miles from where she lived. All around her she saw broken branches and scattered wreckage, but the buildings looked untouched. She approached the farm house.

At her knock a man opened the door. His eyebrows shot up and his eyes widened in shock at seeing a young girl, hair tangled and falling down her back, in very wet muddy clothes standing on his porch.

"Young lady, what happened to you?" he said.

"Please, I'm trying to find my way home. I was caught in the storm."

"Come on in. You look frozen. Would you like a cup of coffee?"

"Thank you. I'm really quite a mess. Maybe I should stay out on the porch so that I won't get your house wet."

A voice called, "Fred, who's at the door?"

"Bell put on the kettle. We have a visitor." He looked at Anna. "What's your name young lady?"

"Anna Ebbessen"

"Come in, dear. Let's warm you up."

The woman took Anna's hand and brought her into the house.

About that time the little puppy, tucked into Anna's apron bib, poked its head out and gave a little whine.

"Oh, my! I forgot about you little fellow. I hope you don't mind if I bring this puppy in. He's as cold and wet as I am."

"Not at all," said the woman.

Anna followed the woman into the kitchen. A bucket of water, with a dipper hanging on the side, sat on a small table near the sink. The woman poked at the coals in the cook stove.

"Come on over here and warm up," she said. "Fred, get a towel for Anna." The woman poured steaming coffee in a cup and handed it to Anna. She then poured a little milk into a small bowl and gave it to the puppy.

Anna took the coffee and said, "Thank you for your hospitality. I really need to get home to see about my pa and the animals." She took a sip of the coffee, swallowing the warm liquid slowly. "I think my sister and her husband, Lucy and Mike Greiner live near here. Could you take me to their house?"

"Yes, they live down the road about two miles," Fred said. "I'll go get the wagon ready."

"I don't know what happened to my horse," Anna said. "Would you keep a look out for her? She's sandy red and may still have her saddle on. I'm really worried about her."

"Certainly, we'll do what we can to help you locate her," Fred said as he grabbed his jacket and headed out the door.

"Thank you. I must be on my way now." Anna finished her coffee and set the cup on the table. She picked up the puppy, tucked it into her apron bib again, and went out to the wagon.

When they pulled into the Greiner's farm yard, Anna saw no damage to the buildings, but broken branches from the cedar trees were scattered about and a blackjack tree near the barn had been ripped from the ground.

Anna thanked the man for the ride and said, "Would you like to come in?"

"I need to be getting back. About time to do chores," he said. "I'll keep my eye out for your mare and if I find her I'll let Mike know."

Mike heard the wagon pull into the drive and stood on the porch. When he saw Anna and his neighbor he came out to meet them.

"Good evening Mr. Rueffer." He turned to help

Anna down from the wagon seat. "Anna, what happened to you?"

"Mike, I've never been so happy to see anyone in my life. I'll tell you all about it later."

"Won't you come in Mr. Rueffer?" Mike asked.

"Thanks, but I must be getting back," the man said as he flipped the reins and drove his horses out onto the road.

Anna and Mike walked into the house. When Anna saw her sister, she threw her arms around her and began to cry. All the fear and worry she had felt for the last few hours spilled out in a gush of tears. Lucy, not used to such emotion from her sister, said, "Anna, come sit down. What happened to you?"

"Lucy, I've just been in a tornado. I need to get home and don't have time to tell you about it now. I must see if Pa's all right and if the twister hit our place. Mike would you take me home? I'm really worried about what might have happened there."

"I'll get the wagon ready."

"We saw the black clouds, and the rain and wind was terrible," Lucy said.

"Lucy, I found this puppy out in the storm. I want to take him home with me but don't know if I have any milk left to feed him. Could you send some with me?" Anna petted the little ball of fur. "I know Pa will have a fit if I bring him in the house, but right now he's too small to be left out in the barn without his ma."

"Anna, you look like you could use some warm milk as well as the puppy." Lucy poured milk in a bucket and put the lid on. By the time she finished Mike had the wagon ready.

"Thanks, Lucy. What would I do without you and Mike?" Anna picked up the pail and went out to the wagon.

As they drove into the farm yard Anna saw some stray debris, but it didn't look like the tornado had touched down. Anna said, "Thank God it looks like we've been spared. I pray the animals are okay." She jumped to the ground almost before Mike had pulled the wagon to a stop and ran to check on her animals.

"I'll look around with you and help you get all the chickens in the hen house. Then I've got to hurry back." Mike tied the wagon to the hitching post and lifted the bucket of milk out and carried it to the water tank and set it down.

Anna looked in the barn, hoping to see the mare. She said, "Looks like Pa's home. His horse is here, but I don't see Sandy. Mike what am I going to do? What if she's dead?" Anna nibbled at her lower lip.

"I'll check with my neighbors tomorrow. Don't worry, we'll find her."

Anna fed the sow while Mike checked on the chickens.

"Looks like they had sense enough to get inside the hen house when the storm hit," Mike said. "I think all the chicks are here, but tomorrow when it's lighter you can make sure," They need water, Anna. Could you take care of that?" Mike handed Anna a basket. "I found a few eggs. You may need these for supper."

"Thank you Mike," Anna said.

After Mike left, Anna poured fresh water for the sow and the baby chicks and then stopped to whisper a prayer.   "Dear Father God, thank you for sparing my home and these animals. Protect Sandy, wherever she is, and please help me find her."

Now I must see about Pa.

She locked the hen house, and picked up the milk pail. Would Pa yell at her for not being home and getting his supper? What was he going to say about her puppy? The little feller hadn't made a sound, nor moved in quite a while. She hoped he was all right.

Anna opened the door quietly in case Pa was sleeping. She found him in the kitchen slumped over the table. He had eaten the biscuits she left that morning and the coffee was also gone. She set the milk pail on the floor and the basket of eggs on the table.

"Pa, I'm home," Anna said as she touched his shoulder.

"Where ya been Gal? I want my supper," Pa said.

"I have some milk that Lucy sent." She poured him a glass then said, "I need to get into some dry clothes and then I'll fix you something."

He ignored her disheveled state. He only thought of himself. Anna tried to curb her anger, but she felt exhausted and without patience. Best to walk away and take care of her puppy before she said something she would regret.

She snatched up a small bowl and filled it with milk and found a rag to make him a bed and ducked behind the quilt into her room. After setting the bowl on the floor, she placed the puppy on the cloth. He whined a bit when she put him down, lapped up a little milk, and after circling the rag a few times, he sprawled out.

How could she keep the creature away from her pa until she figured out what to do with him? Her hair felt tangled and full of grit and she wanted a bath badly, but Pa might start fussing if she didn't get him something to eat. Pulling off her dirty apron and filthy dress, she slipped into clean garments and went back to the kitchen.

Anna served her pa, but she felt too tired to eat. After he finished, she helped him to his bed and then she stumbled into her room. How could she put on her night clothes without first bathing, and she had no strength left, not even to sponge off the grime. With a sigh she fell into bed, pulled up the light spread, and let her mind drift into a fitful slumber, filled with visions of flying objects.

CHAPTER 26

A few days after her experience in the tornado Anna surveyed the pile of buffalo and cow chips she had collected and stacked under the walnut tree. Her heart sang with thanksgiving that God had helped her find fuel and edible plants in the fields. Silly to feel so much joy over a pile of dried bovine manure, but for her it was as valuable as a stack of shiny, ebony coal. The chips would do nicely for kindling; and hopefully, before they were gone, she would find work.

Every day, for the last week she had scavenged the countryside surrounding the soddy. Pa had never raised cattle, not enough money to invest in a herd; still there were plenty of old patties left in their fields. From earliest times buffalo had roamed the area and after that, until the opening of the Cherokee Strip in the run of 1893, cowboys had driven their wild herds across the area from Texas to the stockyard in Dodge City. No, it didn't take much effort to find dried chips for firewood. It had been back breaking work, but when Anna considered the results she felt pleased.

Thanks to Mike, and his knowledge of herbs, she had found an abundant supply of non- poisonous plants as well as sunchokes to make flour or substitute for potatoes until hers were ready to dig. Yesterday she caught frogs from the creek and after cutting off the legs and sprinkling them with salt, she fried them in bacon grease until they were bubbly, tender just the way Pa liked them. She wished she had had a little cornmeal to dip them in but even so Pa had eaten them with relish and asked for more.

"Lord, forgive me for doubting that you would

supply our need."

It's time I quit woolgathering and tend my garden Anna thought when she felt her puppy's wet nose pushing against her ankle.

"Good morning, Survivor. I know it's time to get busy," she said. The lost puppy she found after the tornado, followed her as she circled the barn, found a hoe, and marched to her garden.

After last week's rain small plants had pushed through the soil, but at the same time the weeds had multiplied. Anna attacked these with passion. These pests would not rob her family of their food supply. Laughing, she remembered the wild plants she had gathered from the fields to use for food. Most people would count them as weeds, also.

Anna was jarred from her thoughts by the rattle of wagon wheels. She whirled around and saw a stranger pulling to a stop in front of the barn. He jumped from the wagon and tied his horses to the hitching post. She didn't know the man. Maybe he brought news of Sandy. The mare had not returned and no one had reported seeing her. Anna laid her hoe aside, wiped her hands down her apron, and walked over to greet the man.

"Good-morning. What can I do for you?"

"I'm looking for Anna Ebbessen. Doctor Rogers said I would find her here."

"I'm Anna Ebbessen."

"My name's Ralph Brown. The doctor said you might be looking for work." Mr. Brown combed his fingers through his thin white hair and tucked his hands in the pockets of his overalls. Smiling blue eyes matched his work shirt.

"Yes, I am," Anna said.

"I need someone to help out for a while," Mr. Brown said. "Could you work two or three days a week?"

Anna could hardly keep from dancing up and down with delight. She said, "Where do you live?"

"I talked to Calvin and Mary Long before I came over here. They gave you high praise. I live about five miles north of their place and back east three miles."

"That would be about twelve miles from here," Anna said. She rubbed her hand over her forehead. What should she do? That was too far to walk.

"Mr. Brown at this time I don't have a way to get there." Tears burned in eyes.

I must find Sandy. I must tell the Longs that Sandy's missing. Somehow, I will have to pay them for her loss, but if I don't work how can I pay them? It was too much. Anna blinked and squeezed back her tears. How could she let a stranger see her distress?

Mr. Brown licked his lips and scratched his chin.

"I was counting on your help. You see, my wife can't be left alone and I have to go to town for supplies tomorrow. Can't wait any longer." Mr. Brown let out a deep sigh.

"I just may have the answer. We have an old mule my wife used to ride. No count for plowing, but a gentle soul, and I could make you a deal on buying him. Probably not worth more than five dollars. People don't want a mule that won't work the fields. I could let you take him and pay out what you owe in exchange for your work."

That would not solve Anna's need for cash, but it

shouldn't take more than two weeks to pay out the animal and what other options did she have? She said, "Thank you, Mr. Brown. Would you like for me to go with you today? That way I can meet your wife and you can show me what you need done."

"When can you be ready?" said Mr. Brown.

"Let me make sure my animals have enough water and feed, and then we can leave." Anna wished she could invite Mr. Brown into her home but she was ashamed to let him see how they lived. After she took care of the animals, and made a safe place for Survivor in the barn, she climbed onto the wagon seat beside Mr. Brown. As they rode along Mr. Brown talked about his family.

"My wife isn't very strong any more. Sometimes, her mind wanders. Been married fifty years. A man couldn't ask for a better wife. My Jenny's worked right alongside of me in the fields when I needed her, and we raised four children." Mr. Brown pulled the reins to slow the horse as they crossed a narrow bridge.

"They've all moved away now, and have families of their own. I don't want them to know the condition Jenny's in. They couldn't come home and help out anyway."

Anna had trouble listening to Mr. Brown as he continued talking about his children and grandchildren. Her thoughts strayed to Sandy. She must talk to the Longs soon. Tomorrow when she returned from working at the Browns', she would stop by their farm. They were good people. Maybe she could work in exchange for the cost of the horse.

Poor Sandy, where are you? Are you dead..... ?

"Anna, did you hear me?" Mr. Brown asked.

"I'm sorry. I'm afraid I was day dreaming."

"We are almost to my place," Mr. Brown repeated as he pulled the wagon into the lane leading to a neat white washed cabin. The yard was free of trash and the outbuildings well built.

When they entered the house Mr. Brown said, "Thank you, Liza, for sitting with Jenny."

"She was a little nervous while you were gone but she didn't try running off or anything. I'll be going now," she said as she put on her bonnet and walked out the door.

"Liza's a neighbor girl," Mr. Brown told Anna. "She was home from school today and could help out, but I don't like to leave her long with Jenny. She's too young to know what to do if a problem comes up,"

They found Mrs. Brown pacing about the house and calling, "Ralph. Ralph." Mr. Brown took his wife's hand and led her into the parlor.

"Jenny, this is Anna Ebbessen," he said. "She's going to be helping us out for a while."

Mrs. Brown wore a simple house dress, with a clean apron over it. She was short, and so thin Anna thought she might blow away if a gust of Oklahoma wind hit her. Deep half-moon shaped smile lines framed her mouth, but today she wasn't smiling. Confusion and maybe fear showed in her hazel eyes.

No greeting or response came. Mr. Brown led his wife to a rocking chair in the corner of the room and the woman began rocking back and forth, making crooning sounds as she moved.

"This is one of her bad days. My leaving her alone, as I did this morning, pushes her into herself." Mr. Brown ran his fingers through his hair, frowned, and said, "I'll show you around and we can go over what needs to be done."

After walking Anna through the house and discussing the work he said, "You probably know more about all this than I do. Most important to me is that you keep careful watch on Jenny, and of course, getting meals for us. You can see she isn't able to cook much and has lost a lot of weight."

Mr. Brown made sure his wife was safe, and then led Anna out to the barn.

"At one time we had a large herd of cattle and several milk cows. I've sold off most of the herd and only have two milk cows left. Would you be interested in buying one of them?"

How could she feed another animal? Besides she needed to work for cash and still had to pay off the mule.

Lord, what should I do? She said, "Thank you, Mr. Brown. We certainly need a milk cow, but I have no money to pay you and my pa isn't any help."

Mr. Brown said, "Let's see how things work out here. We can talk about this again later."

They went back into the house. "Anna, why don't you fix us something for dinner and then come back tomorrow. I'll need to leave as soon as chores are done."

"I'll be here Mr. Brown," Anna said.

After they had finished eating Mr. Brown took Anna back out to the barn and introduced her to the mule. Anna had to hold her breath to keep from laughing at the funny creature, with its bowlegs and ears that flopped over like broken rabbit ears.

"Mr. Brown said, "Not much to look at, but he's

gentle and obeys as long as you don't hook him to a plow." He stroked the mule, patted its rump, and saddled it up. "I'll throw in the saddle and bridle with the deal. We don't have no use for them without the mule," he said. "We call him Bowlegs. Guess you can see why."

"Thank you, again. I'll be back early tomorrow," Anna said. She got on the mule, rubbed its neck and said, "Let's go girl. Guess I can call you 'girl' since mules have no gender," she laughed.

~~~~~~~~~

The next morning Mr. Brown met Anna at the door.

"Good morning, Anna. Come in." They walked into the parlor where his wife sat rocking peacefully.

"Looks like today may be one of her good days. Be sure to keep a watch that she doesn't go outside by herself. My greatest fear is that she'll wander off down the road and get lost." Mr. Brown ran his fingers through his hair.

"I'll hook up the wagon and be on my way. Do whatever housework and cooking you can, but most important keep an eye on Jenny. She's the dearest thing I have."

Mrs. Brown stared at him with unknowing eyes and continued rocking. He touched her cheek and sighed deeply; then he went outside.

"Mrs. Brown," Anna said, "I'm going to be with you today. If you need anything, please tell me." The woman made no response. Anna left the woman rocking and making little cooing sounds and went to clean the bedroom.

The day passed pleasantly as she tended Mrs.

Brown's needs, talking to her gently and, occasionally, walking her to the outhouse. Several times the woman had ambled through the house calling, "Ralph? Ralph?"

By late afternoon she seemed quite upset. Trying to distract her, Anna took her outside and they strolled about admiring the flowers. After a time Anna settled her back into her chair and went to prepare supper. She took the bread out of the oven and set it on the table. Her mouth watered. Why not cut a slice while it was warm? She spread butter on top and took a bite. Gladness bubbled up from her soul. God truly had kept His promise to provide; she now had work and her animals were doing well. The words of the song Mr. Mueller sang so long ago began to run through her mind.

In Shady green pastures so rich and so sweet,
God leads his dear children along. ...

Suddenly, Anna became aware that the rocking sound of Mrs. Brown's chair had stopped. She set the bread aside and rushed into the parlor. The chair was empty. Filled with concern, she scurried through the house calling, "Mrs. Brown, Mrs. Brown." When she realized that the woman was not in the house, she ran outside. First, she checked the privy.

"Mrs. Brown," Anna called. No answer. She opened the door; it was empty.

"Dear Father God, please help me find her. Soon!" She peered into the barn, but Mrs. Brown wasn't there.

Anna ran out to the road, praying, "Oh, please dear Father don't let anything happen to her." She looked back and forth across and up and down the road as far as she could see.

"Mrs. Brown? Mrs. Brown?" Anna shouted her heart pounding. Nothing. The woman could not have gone far. Anna returned to the farmyard, tears streaming down her face and shoulders shaking. If something had happened to the dear lady, how could she tell her husband? Anna wanted to die. She was a failure at everything. She had lost Sandy. Her mother was now in a hospital for the insane. Her father hated her. And now she had lost Mrs. Brown!

Movement in the garden caught her eye. She began running, praying as she ran. As she approached the green bean vines she saw Mrs. Brown, crouched over, fingers snatching at the plants. A jumble of beans and leaves filled her basket, but what did it matter?

Not wanting to scare the woman Anna slipped through the vines and said quietly, "Thank you for helping me pick beans. Now let's take them to the kitchen for supper." Anna took the woman's hand and together they walked back to the house.

Anna had Mrs. Brown settled in her rocker when she heard horses' hooves. Should she tell Mr. Brown what had happened? If she did, would he fire her?

Mr. Brown came into the room and said, "Anna, it looks like things went well today."

Anna knew she had to tell him about his wife and feared that when she did she would lose her job; still she had to be truthful.

"Mr. Brown, we did have one scare," she said and then told him what had happened. "I think it would be a good idea if you could put a lock on the door so that Mrs. Brown would not be able to leave again."

"Thank you for being honest with me. I like your idea. The same thing could have happened with me here. I'll put a lock on the door right away."

"Anna, today was kind of a test. I haven't left Jenny alone since her mind has gotten all mixed up. The Longs told me you were a calm person and wouldn't excite her, and you haven't. I appreciate that."

"Thank you. I'll do my best."

'I thought it would be easier on all of us if you went ahead and took the milk cow home with you as soon as you can. We don't need the milk and we'll trust you to pay us, either in work or money."

"Mr. Brown, what if my Pa gets worse and I can't work? He wasn't well this morning, but I had told you I would be here, so I left him. If I don't come, you will know I couldn't leave him."

"Don't worry Anna. If you can't work one day, you can make it up another. We'll see you Friday, if you can make it."

CHAPTER 27

The next day Pa saddled his horse and as he rode away Anna watched him out of sight. She planned to follow him later. She had been thinking about Ma. No one spoke of her. Were they trying to protect her from bad news? No matter that the doctor had said they could not visit. Somehow she would find a way to go see her and see for herself how Ma was doing.

She found a paper and fountain pen to write Mrs. Mueller and ask her to send some Bible verses she could read to her ma when she went. She wrote, "I miss all of you very much. I miss Davy and the girls. And the Petersons, and John. Are they all right?

"I haven't yet seen my ma and don't know her condition, but even if she doesn't talk someone could read to her. Would you send me some verses that tell of God's love and salvation? I'll write them out and send them to the hospital and ask if some of the staff would read them to her.

"The farm was empty when I got here. No animals, no garden, but things are better now as I worked for some animals and I have planted a garden. My sister, Lucy, and her husband, Mike, have been very helpful.

"Pa's drinking's getting worse. Today, I'm going to see if I can find where he goes and what he does. I am thankful for what you taught me about God and His love. Thank you. Thank you. Love to all, Anna."

After doing her morning duties, Anna saddled Bowlegs and rode to the Taylor's farm. The dilapidated house looked as if a blast of wind could blow it over.

Flattened tin cans covered holes in boards that had never seen a drop of paint. Broken bottles and other junk surrounded the shack. A stout woman with frizzy, bleached hair answered Anna's knock.

"I'm looking for my Pa, Mr. Ebbessen. Is he here?" Anna asked.

"Don't keep track of who's here and who ain't. If he's here, he's down behind the barn." She slammed the door.

Anna tied Bowlegs to a tree and picked her way through the weeds and trash to the barn. Mr. Taylor, her pa, and another man stood around a large pot filled with liquid. The stranger turned and eyed Anna up and down, stopping to stare at her chest. Tobacco juice dripped from the corner of his mouth. With a leer he said, "Well, well. Look who's here."

His bold stare and sneering voice made Anna uncomfortable. He ambled toward her, brushed against her arm, without even an 'excuse me' and continued to gawk as he took his horse by the reins, hefted himself into the saddle, and rode away.

The man's rude behavior shocked Anna. She had never met anyone so bold and offensive. Surely it was an accident that he bumped into her. She turned back to her pa standing beside the large iron pot.

The putrid smelling liquid must be the Moonshine, Anna thought. Her Pa looked at her with bleary eyes.

"What ya doin here, Gal? Got no business checking up on me."

"I just came to see where you spend all your time. I could use some help at home."

"Can't tell your Pa what to do." He glared at her and punched at the air as if he wanted to strike her.

Mr. Taylor laughed. Anna turned; head high and spine straight, and marched back to her mule.

I guess I found out what I wanted to know. But, what good has come of it? He'll never change.

Anna's head fell, her bravado gone; she mounted Bowlegs to return home. As she started to leave a voice called, "Aint you the girl that hires out to work for people?" The disheveled blond woman she had seen earlier stood in the door of the house.

"Yes," Anna said.

"People a mile south of here may be interested. The woman's ailing and they have a bunch of kids. Woman's a friend o' mine. They're looking for help."

"What's their name?"

"Foster. I'll see him later."

Anna stopped to think.

"I could work for them on Monday," she said. "My charge is a dollar a day. Can you tell them?"

"Maybe they can slop along until Monday. Yeah, I'll tell them."

On the way home, Anna thought about Mrs. Taylor's comment, "I'll see him later." *Was Mrs. Foster the wife* of *that rude man she had seen with her pa?*

Monday morning when Anna arrived at the Fosters' home the vulgar man she had encountered at the Taylors' answered the door. Her first impulse was to leave, but she desperately needed the work.

Mr. Foster leered at her, then said, "Well, young lady we meet again." His lips curled into a smile that didn't reach his sadistic, black eyes.

"Go on back." He pointed at a small door behind him. "You'll find my wife in there. She'll tell you what to do."

On a sagging iron bed, in the small airless room, Anna saw a woman so emaciated and pale she was hardly visible under the lumpy quilt. The woman, eyes filled with pain and despair, looked up as Anna approached, but she remained silent.

Overcome by compassion for the miserable soul, Anna decided she would stay and do what she could to help the wretched woman.

"Have you had anything to eat?" Anna asked.

The woman shook her head.

"Would you like for me to make you a cup of tea?"

"Yes, please."

Anna went to the kitchen. Unwashed dishes, rotting food, trash and dirty rags littered the place. What a mess! She remembered Mrs. Taylor saying something like, "Maybe they can slop along until Monday." That pretty well described the kitchen. After digging around in the cupboard, Anna found some tea and made Mrs. Foster a cup.

Anna lifted the woman and placed a pillow at her back, but Mrs. Foster was too weak to hold the cup without her help.

"Mrs. Foster, where are your children?"

"Maybe .. garden .. or fields. Herrick keeps 'm working outside." she answered, her voice so faint Anna could hardly hear it.

Mrs. Foster said, "Tired ... need to sleep."

Anna lowered the woman back down on the bed and went to clean up the mess in the kitchen. After two hours she had cleared away the trash and dirty dishes and organized the cupboards. She paused, wondering what to do next, when Mr. Foster entered the kitchen. He walked up close to Anna and grinned, showing crooked, tobacco stained teeth. Anna tried to move away, but he grabbed her by the shoulder and began rubbing it in a familiar way.

Anna jerked away and doubled her hands into fists. She wanted to sock the man in the jaw. Instead she gritted her teeth and said, "The first time you touched me, I considered it an accident. Now, I know it wasn't. If you even look like you want to get close to me again, you will find yourself on the floor." She narrowed her eyes and stared into the man's shocked face.

"And while you're down, I might kick you in the ribs and step on your fingers. Do you understand me? If I didn't know your wife needed me, I'd walk out the door right now. You could wallow in this filth for all I care.

"Do you want me to fix a meal for you and your children, or wash the dirty laundry?"

He gave a toothy grin and said, "Fix me and you something. The brats have some bread and cheese. That's all they need."

"If bread and cheese is good enough for your children, it's good enough for you. Now get out of here and let me get on with my work."

Mr. Foster left, slamming the door behind him. Anna grumbled, "I now know what the term 'scum of the earth' means."

The banging door had awakened Mrs. Foster. Anna bathed her and changed the filthy sheets on her bed. She then gathered up the dirty clothes, along with the soiled linens, and dumped them in a pile. In the next room, quilts were spread out on the floor for the children's beds. She gathered the dirty garments scattered around and took them, along with the other laundry, outside. She found the wash tubs, filled one tub with the washing and then added soap and water.

It will take a week's soaking to get these clothes clean.

As Anna worked, her conscience began pricking her about the way she had talked to Mr. Foster. She had behaved like the old Anna, the one that didn't know the saving grace of Jesus. Still, the man was out of line and deserved a beating, which she felt perfectly capable of giving. She would not stand for his vulgar advances. What should she have done? What would she do if it continued?

"Speak the truth with love," a tender voice whispered.

Love! Love him! That... that...

"Be careful, Anna. Remember I love him too."

All right, Lord. What do You want me to do?

"Apologize."

She did not want to apologize. She would not! He should apologize to *her*.

Anna rubbed the clothes with a fury she wanted to release on the horrible man, until at last she realized she wanted to please God more than she wanted revenge.

She left the clothes to soak and went to check on Mrs. Foster. The woman was awake and appeared to be a bit stronger.

"Can you eat a little?" Anna asked.

"Maybe, a piece of bread and some milk."

"Do you want me to fix something for the family for supper? What should I cook?"

"I've been sick so long I don't even know what there is. Just fix what you find."

A little distance from the house Anna could see the children working in the garden. She strolled out to talk to them. Five pairs of sad looking eyes turned and stared as she approached. She said, "I'm looking for something to fix for supper. Can you tell me where the food is stored?"

The largest of the girls answered, "There are eggs over there, but we mustn't use very many. Pa takes them to town to sell."

"Is there any meat some place?"

The children shook their heads.

"How much longer do you children have to work? Maybe one of you could help me find something to cook."

"I..." The girl began, but stopped when she saw her Pa storming toward them.

He yelled, "If you brats don't get to work, you'll be working all night." He turned to Anna, "You've no right to be bothering my kids. Don't you have enough to do?"

Anna gritted her teeth and marched back to the house.

"And, Lord, You want me to apologize to him? It was all I could do to keep from knocking him down right then."

Anna found only flour, salt, and cornmeal in the kitchen. She looked outside for a cellar or springhouse, and located a cellar, but it was so dark she hesitated to go down the steps.

All it would take for me to ride out of here would be to find a snake down there. She returned to the house and found a lantern and carried it down into the cellar. After searching the shelves she found some potatoes and a jar of green beans and carried them upstairs.

She peeled the potatoes and put them in a pot and then added the beans, with a little bacon grease. Setting the vegetables on the stove to simmer, she went to check on the washing. After she finished rinsing the clothes, she hung them on a line strung from one tree to the other. She watched as the clothes snapped to and fro in the breeze and knew they would be dry before she left for home.

Anna gave Mrs. Foster her supper and prepared to leave.

"Your pay's over there, on that table. Thank you, Anna. I do hope you'll come back."

"I'll be back next week if you want me."

Anna was untying Bowlegs when Mr. Foster sauntered up close to her. She stepped away and faced him with determination.

"Mr. Foster, I said some things today I shouldn't have. I meant what I said about you not touching me, but I shouldn't have said the rest. Please, forgive me."

The man looked at her in amazement and lowered his head.

"It's me that's been out o' line."

"Well, yes. But, still I must answer God for my behavior. I'll be back to work next Monday, if you agree to the contract I left on the kitchen table. I would like to show your oldest daughter how to do the house work and cook. I don't think your wife's going to get better for a while."

CHAPTER 28

Anna surveyed her garden. It didn't look as organized nor as productive as the Muellers' but still she felt proud of her work. She had managed to provide for herself and her father, as well as caring for and feeding her animals. Mr. Brown had brought the milk cow to her and even her father seemed to be gaining a little weight drinking milk rather than coffee with his meals. She had told the Longs about her experience in the tornado and rather than being angry and demanding payment for their horse, Mr. Long had said, "Anna, let's wait a little while before we decide what to do. The mare may well be dead; still she may show up here or at your house."

June had passed quickly and Anna continued to work for the Browns and the Fosters. She had taught the Foster's oldest daughter how to make bread and cook simple meals. Mrs. Foster was getting stronger and soon Anna would no longer be needed there. Even so, she knew that God would supply her needs. David's words in the Psalms, "I have been young and now I am old but I have never seen the godly go without bread," was a promise that she now believed included her.

Anna felt a warm nose nudge her ankle. She looked down and said, "Survivor, you want some attention?" She had named her puppy Survivor, but Anna felt the name fit her as well. The puppy was growing quite large and would make a good cow dog. She visualized having a herd of her own some day. Maybe then she could bring her ma home. It seemed a ridiculous dream, but with God's help dreams became realities.

She picked up the dog and gave him a squeeze, thankful that her pa had not demanded that she get rid of the puppy. He had already proved to be a true friend and she thought the spunky little guy had almost won over her father as well. Maybe that was more than she should expect, even from the friendly puppy.

Anna gathered the eggs and latched the chicken house door, leaving the fowls inside to roost. She laughed as she remembered thinking that she could never get enough eggs to eat. For several weeks it seemed that she and her father had lived on nothing but eggs. *Moooo!* The sound of Daisy's pitiful call reminded her that she needed to be milked.

Just as Anna finished the milking Pa rode into the yard slumped over on his saddle, his color ashen. She went out to help him off his horse and settled him into a chair in the kitchen. He looked sick. The white of his eyes appeared yellow. What should she do?

"Pa, are you okay?"

He gave her a blank stare and hunched his shoulders.

"Would you like something to eat?"

No reply. She poured him a glass of fresh milk as she dished up the food.

After he had eaten a few bites, his head bobbed as if he were asleep. Anna helped him take off his shoes and socks. She was alarmed to see how puffed-up his feet and legs were.

"Pa, how long have your feet been swollen like this?"

He only shrugged.

"I think Doctor George should check you."

"No doctor," he said and stumbled over to his bed.

As Anna lay on her bed that night, she prayed, "Lord show me what to do about Pa. How can I get the doctor to come see him when I never know when he will be at home?"

Anna felt weighed down with trying to keep things going on her own, trying to live to please God and do things without anyone to give her direction. She wished there were a church nearby. She longed for the support of other Christians. She wanted to see her ma. Was she being taken care of properly?

Why didn't the doctor at Fort Supply write?

Finally, she went to sleep.

Early the next morning, Anna awakened and crept in to check the swelling in her Pa's feet, trying not to wake him. They looked just as bad as they had the night before. Without a word, she saddled Bowlegs and rode to Lucy's.

When Mike and Lucy heard Anna's mule trotting into the farm yard they came out to meet her.

"Anna, what's wrong? Why are you here this early?"

"Pa's feet are so swollen, I wondered if the doctor shouldn't check them. Mike, would you ride to town and ask Doctor George to come?"

"We'll be over just as soon as Mike gets back from town," Lucy said.

Pa was still in bed when Anna returned.

"Pa, you need to stay home today. Mike's gone to get the doctor to check the swelling in your feet."

"Ya aint telling *me* what ta do," he grunted and

pushed himself off the bed and tried to stand up. He began to fall and Anna caught his arm and helped him to a chair.

"Pa, if you try to leave, you won't be able to because I've hidden your shoes."

After a short while Anna could hear Pa snoring and decided she would get her outside duties done while he slept. As Anna worked, she lightened the burden by thinking about how it would be to have her own home and a husband she loved and that loved her. Her thoughts turned to John.

I wonder if he even remembers me. Lord, would you put thoughts of me in John's mind? What a foolish idea. She couldn't leave her pa alone. The Bible said to honor your parents. Who would want to marry her and take on the responsibility of her pa as well? She didn't want to borrow trouble or limit God. Still, her faith could not grasp anything as wonderful as having a loving husband, and being able to honor and care for her parents at the same time.

It was time for dinner and still Mike had not arrived. She fixed Pa a bowl of soup and gave him some fresh bread and butter. He sat up on the side of the bed, took a few sips of soup and then lay back down and turned his back on her. Why couldn't pa show a little gratitude, at least acknowledge that she was there.

Please, Father God. Help me be patient.

Lucy and Mike arrived in late afternoon at about the same time as the doctor.

"Sorry to be so late. I was out at the Johnson's delivering a baby and just returned. What do you hear about your ma, Anna?" Dr. George asked.

"We don't know anything, really. I want to go see her but they still won't allow the family to visit."

"Sorry about that. I hated to send her off to Fort Supply, but she refused to talk and Tom said she wouldn't eat anything. I was concerned that she would starve herself to death here. Well, let me see the patient."

Lucy and Anna went into the kitchen while Mike went with the doctor to see Mr. Ebbessen. After the doctor examined him, he walked the family outside to talk to them.

"Your pa's in bad shape, but I guess you knew this. He's about drunk himself to death. Liver probably about eaten up. You're going to need to taper him off this booze. Give him a little bit at a time and find some that's better than what he's been drinking." The doctor pressed his lips together and looked at them with tired eyes.

"His heart's not working right. That's causing the swelling in his feet and legs. He's got the dropsy. There's a new pill out made from herbs and other stuff that is supposed to help this. I'll leave some and you can give them to him and see if it does any good. Be sure you give them just as I prescribe."

"Yes, I will."

"About this liquor he is going to need; can you take it home with you, Mike, and bring him some three times a day? If Anna keeps it around here, he may need some so bad, he'll get violent. I guess that's nothing new, though."

Anna gripped her hands together. How in the world could she keep Pa away from his liquor?

"I think I know of someone who makes a better

kind than Taylor," Mike said. "I'll keep it, and Howard can bring it if I can't. We'll help you all we can, Anna."

The doctor went back inside to talk with the patient. Mr. Ebbessen sat on the side of the bed and looked up at the doctor with watery eyes.

"I need a drink." Anna brought him a glass of water. He took a drink, and then spit it out.

"I want my booze, Gal." His eyes blazed with rage.

"Mr. Ebbessen, you must stay in bed until this swelling goes down," the doctor said. "Anna's going to give you some medicine every day. Don't give her any trouble about that."

"I want a drink."

"You can't keep drinking like you are or you're going to kill yourself. Mike's taking all your liquor home with him. He'll bring you a little every day."

Mr. Ebbessen glared at the doctor and said, "Give me a drink."

Doctor George reached into his black bag and brought out a bottle and poured about two ounces of liquor into the glass.

"This is the amount you'll be getting at a time."

"Not enough," shouted Mr. Ebbessen.

"But that's all you're getting. Don't pester Anna for your booze. She won't have any to give you."

Mr. Ebbessen narrowed his eyes to slits and turned his face toward the wall.

Mike and Anna walked the doctor out to his buggy. Mike asked, "Doc, do you think Anna's going to be able to handle that old man?"

"Come over here, Mike," the doctor said. Mike followed him to the barn.

"I'll tell you where to go to get some whiskey that isn't rot-gut like he's drinking. Buy two bottles and give one to Anna to hide so if her pa got too obstinate she could give him a little. That girl's got a hard row to hoe with that old codger."

"I don't see how Anna's going to be able to leave him to go to work."

"Well, I guess you better go get that liquor, and I need to be on my way."

A few hours later Mike returned with the liquor. "Anna, Howard or I will come three times a day and give Pa his whisky." He poured out two ounces and took it to Mr. Ebbessen.

"Pa, I'm giving you some booze, but I'm taking the bottle home with me," Mike said. "I'll be back tomorrow with some more, but in the meantime don't bother Anna. She's not going to give you any."

Mike left a bottle in the barn with two ounces of liquor in it, in case Pa became violent. He also gave Anna a club.

"Don't try to reason with him, Anna, because he'll be beyond reasoning. Just get out of the house and take this club with you. If you don't have time to get the club, get yourself out. He may smash up some things. Just let him do it."

After Mike and Lucy left, Anna peeked in to check on her pa and saw that he was asleep. They had propped his feet up with a pillow and she noticed that his toes poked out from the holes in his socks. It was time to do some mending. Trying not to awaken him she removed his socks and picked up his other pair from the laundry box. There were holes in those also.

She went into the kitchen and took the sewing box off the shelf. On the side of the box someone had written Margretha, her Ma's name. Anna drew her fingertips across the inscription and repeated, Margretha. It sounded like music to her. She loved that name.

Ma, I need to see you. I need to tell you how God has changed my life. Anna threaded the needle and put the thimble on her finger. How many times had she watched Ma patch their old clothes? Tears pooled in her eyes until she could hardly see to finish the mending.

"Dear Father God, make a way for me to see my ma. I want to tell her about your love." She felt the whisper of God's presence that covered her with a sense of peace and knew somehow her prayer would soon be answered.

~~~~~~~~

The next morning even before Anna was out of bed, Pa started yelling.

"I need a drink. Git my booze, Gal."

"Pa, Mike's bringing it."

"Git it now! Not waitn' on Mike."

Anna walked out the door without answering him. She was nearly finished with her outside work when Mike rode into the farm yard. He dismounted and asked, "How did things go last night?"

"Quiet enough, but Pa woke up demanding his drink. Fortunately, he ate a little breakfast and that seemed to distract him."

"I'll give him this and then I'll look around and see if there is anything that needs fixing."

"Thanks Mike. The fence is coming down. I'm

afraid the cow will get out and I'm not strong enough to repair it by myself."

Anna was helping Mike tighten up the fence when they heard a loud noise in the front of the barn. They threw down their tools and ran to see the cause of the racket.

"Hi Anna," Matt called. Sitting in an automobile were her brother, Matt, his wife, Katy, with Lucy, her baby, and Danny.

CHAPTER 29

Mike and Anna stared at the vehicle.

"Matt, Katy. What a surprise," Anna said.

"Wow! Matt, what a prize," Mike said.

"It's a Model T Ford. Best car made," Matt said.

Lucy jumped out of the automobile and said, "Guess what, Matt's going to take you and me to see Ma. When can you get away?"

Anna just stared at her. She shuddered remembering her first experience in an automobile. Then she remembered the long wagon ride from the Muellers'. Maybe the automobile ride would be best after all. She turned to Matt and Katy.

"I am so glad to see you both. Come in and see Pa." She hugged them as they got out of the vehicle.

"Anna, Matt brought some mail. I got a letter from Fort Supply and they said we could come see Ma. Can you can go?"

"Oh, yes I'll go, but we'll have to work something out. I don't think Pa can be left alone for very long. What mail did I get?" Lucy handed her a letter from Mrs. Mueller. Anna smiled and tucked it into her pocket. She could hardly wait to read it.

"Let's go inside. Pa will be glad to see someone besides me," Anna said.

"Pa, Matt and Katy came to visit you," Lucy said.

"Humph, 'bout time," Pa grunted, then closed his eyes and ignored them.

The women went into the kitchen. Anna stoked the fire and made coffee.

"Have you had dinner?" Anna asked. When they

shook their heads, she stirred up the coals and pulled the pot of soup over to the front burner to warm.

"I'll go out and get some milk and butter."

Katy said, "I'll go with you." As they walked out to the water tank for the food she said, "Anna, is your pa always like this?"

"He's stubborn and sullen most of the time. Now that he can't get out for his liquor he could get mean."

"How do you stand it?"

"Hum ...Well, I guess mostly I'm relieved when he makes it home safely each night. While I lived with the Muellers they taught me about God; how much He loves me, and how He can help us with our problems. I've found this to be true. That's the only thing that gives me patience to 'stand it'." Anna picked up the milk pail and as they walked back to the soddy.

Katy stopped and pointed to the barn and out buildings.

"You've made amazing changes here. Lucy said Mike had helped you a little, but that you've done most of it by yourself while working as a hired girl at the same time. I don't see how you've managed."

"Working for people who taught me another way to live made the difference. They worked hard, but they took time to show love for each other and me. Still, I worried about Ma and wanted to be with her." Anna rubbed her hands together and frowned.

"Every letter I got from the family said I should have stayed home, but I didn't have a choice. Ma told me to leave and I couldn't talk her out of it." She paused, not sure if she should continue. "What hurt most was that Esther thought I was having a party all the time I was gone."

"A neighbor told Esther she saw you in town and you had new shoes and some new clothes," Katy said. "She thought you were getting above yourself. She doesn't get many new things, but she could do a lot better and help Howard more and maybe she could afford a new dress once in a while."

"We've been gone so long, I hope Lucy stirred the soup," Anna said.

When they returned to the kitchen Lucy had everything ready. Anna took Pa some dinner and he ate a bit of soup with a chunk of bread, and drank a little milk.

"Need a drink," he growled.

Mike walked to his bed and said, "Not time yet, Pa."

Eyes filled with fury he yelled, "Always time for a drink."

Matt took Anna aside and said, "We have it all planned. Katy will bring our children and stay at Lucy's and care for her two, while I take you and Lucy to see Ma. When would you like to go?"

"Today is Friday. Would Sunday be too soon?" Anna asked.

"Sounds fine," Matt said. "Lucy, can you go on Sunday?"

"Yes, if it's okay with Mike."

"I'll go see Tom and tell him he has to come home Saturday to stay with Pa." Matt said.

"Matt, how can I thank you?" Anna asked.

"Tom can stay until early Monday morning. I'll tell his boss, we need him. We'll leave now so we can stop off at Tom's and still get back home before it's too dark. Anna, I've never seen Pa so clean, or the house and farm so well kept. I know it's been hard; I didn't realize how hard until Mike talked to me today." He patted her arm and then hopped into his auto.

Tears of joy streamed down her cheeks as she waved good-bye.

I can't wait to see Ma. Will she have changed much after all this time?

A smile lifted the corners of her mouth as she withdrew Mrs. Mueller's letter from her pocket. When she finished reading the letter she tucked it into the box under her bed. The Muellers were doing well as were the Petersons, but John had not yet returned from Kansas. Might she never see him again? Oh, how could she bear the thought? On a separate sheet Mrs. Mueller had written out the requested verses. Anna now felt ready to see her ma. God's timing was indeed perfect.

Late in the afternoon, Anna heard an automobile driving into the yard. Tom sat in the seat beside his brother; he didn't look excited about being home.

Matt said, "Tom's boss said he could come today and stay until Monday morning since they weren't that busy just now. We have to rush on home: This auto doesn't know the way in the dark like my horse does. See you Sunday, Anna."

Tom got out of the car and they waved good-bye.

"Come on in. You can visit with Pa if he'll talk to you."

"Boy howdy, you sure made a lot of changes around here. Don't know how you did it."

"Mike helped, and don't let him tell you different. He should be here soon to give Pa his ration of liquor. The doctor said Pa could only have two ounces of whiskey three times a day. He's not happy about it, keeps demanding more."

"I'll bet that old .... Sorry, Matt told me to watch my language around you. Sis, what happened to you that I can't swear around you?"

"Tom, I found God, or I guess I should say God found me. He's forgiven my sins, and as hard as it is to believe, He lives in my heart and helps me face each day and its problems. I'm not good explaining, but I know that without God's help I could never have returned and put up with Pa's cantankerous ways. I'll find you something to eat while you go talk to him."

Tom walked over to Pa's bed. The old man opened his eyes and said, "Gi' me a drink."

"Pa, I didn't bring any whiskey with me. You'll have to wait 'til Mike gets here."

"Now, I want a drink *now!*" Mr. Ebbessen hollered.

"Pa, I said I didn't bring any. I quit drinking. Janie's pa said he wouldn't let her marry a drinking man. So I quit. I wanted to marry her real bad."

"Tom, food's ready."

After he had eaten, Anna asked, "Will you take Pa outside? Walk him slowly because his feet are quite swollen."

"What's the matter with him? Matt just said he had to stay in bed."

"Doc said his heart's not beating fast enough to take the water away from his lungs. And it's collecting in his legs. He called it dropsy. Pa's about worn out his heart, maybe his whole body, with his drinking. If we don't get him off the booze, it's going to kill him. I don't think Pa cares. Anyway, he's really sick."

Tom helped Pa to the outhouse and then walked him to the barn and back to the house. All the time he was outside, he demanded that Tom give him his whiskey. He said, "Find my bottle. That dang gal hid my drink. Find it."

"Can't do that, Pa. Doctor's orders."

As soon as they entered the house Pa began yelling.

"Ya aint my boss, boy. Give me my bottle!"

Anna was washing the dishes. He lunged for her, but she darted away and left the house, as Mike had told her to do.

While she was standing outside, Mike rode up.

"Sorry I'm late, Anna. I hope you haven't had any trouble."

"Tom's home and he's with Pa. He's getting the brunt of Pa's anger. I know this is a lot of trouble for you, but if I had some whiskey here I would just give it to him. "Tom didn't bring any whiskey with him. He said that Janie's father told him he couldn't marry his daughter if he was going to drink, so he quit."

Mike went inside and poured a bit of liquor into a glass and added a little water. Mr. Ebbessen grabbed it, gulped it down and then held out the glass. "Give me som' more."

Mike shook his head, "That's all I have."

The old man began to yell and curse.

"Enough of that, or I won't be bringing you any in the morning," Mike said. "Don't make any more trouble." Mike walked out while the old man continued to rant and rave until he finally fell back on his bed, too weak to continue.

Anna walked outside with Mike and asked, "Do

you want to leave the liquor here and let Tom give it to Pa? That would save you some trips."

"I'm afraid Pa would act up if he thought the whisky was here. Tom might let his anger get out of control and hurt him." By then Mike was in the saddle and ready to leave. "Anna, I'm glad Tom's home and can see how things are with you." He waved and left.

The next morning Anna crawled out of bed even before daylight. She hadn't been able to work for several days and with Tom home she planned to go to the Brown's. After she finished milking, she started breakfast. Tom came into the kitchen just as she put the biscuits into the oven.

"Morning, sis. Sorry I slept a little late. Something sure smells good."

"Tom, I need to go to work today. I need you to feed and water the animals and watch over Pa while I'm gone. Will you help Pa take a bath? If he gives you arguments about it threaten to dunk him in the horse tank." Tom looked at her as if he thought she had lost her mind. "Just do it, Tom," she said.

Anna had a song in her heart as she left. Today she would see the Browns again and tomorrow she would see her ma. She could hardly wait.

1909 Model T Ford

CHAPTER 30

Early Sunday morning Matt and Lucy drove into the Ebbessen's lane. Lucy hopped out of the auto and went into the house where Anna was hanging up pans. She said, "I think it's going to be a hot, windy day. Bring something to tie over your hair, Anna, or it might blow right off your head."

Anna walked over to her Pa's bed and said, "Matt's taking Lucy and me to see Ma. Do you want to send her a message?"

He grunted, shook his head then made a fist at Anna.

"Want a drink. Now!"

"Mike will bring it soon. We're leaving, but we'll be back before dark." She and Lucy walked out to the automobile.

"Sit in the front seat with Matt." Lucy said. "That'll give you a chance to visit."

Anna scooted into the front but the noise from the vehicle and the wind made talking difficult. After several attempts at conversation she gave up and pulled some papers from her purse and began to read.

"What are you reading, Anna?" Lucy asked.

"Mrs. Mueller sent some Bible verses to read to Ma. She may not understand, but I feel like I can't pass up an opportunity to let her know how much God loves her."

"When you finish, may I read them?" Lucy asked.

"Of course. Maybe you can help me talk to Ma. Although she may not understand what we say to her, I'm going to try. God can do things we can't."

Anna handed Lucy the papers, praying that she would have a desire to know more. She adjusted her bonnet against the hot, dry wind.

They arrived at Fort Supply Mental Institution around noon. For many years the buildings had served as a military fort and only two years earlier had been converted into a hospital for the insane. Anna stared at the two long, narrow buildings which were joined at the corner by a two story building that had served as a lookout tower for the fort.

The courtyard surrounding the building was enclosed by a tall wooden wall with guard towers at each corner. The area was bare of trees and the dry July heat had turned the few patches of grass crusty brown. Old wagon parts were scattered about. To Anna, the place looked like a prison, not a hospital. Matt pulled the automobile inside the gate and parked.

They walked up the dirt path to the front door located in the corner building. Inside the front door was a large room and in the center was a table with three empty chairs behind it. The only light came from the small windows at each side and above the door. Along the halls that extended on both sides from the entrance room they saw sad, hopeless looking patients in ragged, soiled, green gowns. Several patients were yelling and flinging their arms about. Narrow iron beds lined the halls. Thin gray curtains, which could be drawn around each bed, gave the only means of privacy for the patients. The stench of unwashed bodies and soiled bed linens gagged Anna.

As they searched for an employee, or someone who could help them find their mother, a man with food caked on his chin, hair matted and uncombed, and eyes with a haunted, fearful stare, grabbed Anna's arm and cried, "Get me out of here. Get me out of here." Anna froze, unsure what to do when Matt stepped up and removed the man's hand.

"Where are the employees? I can't believe they call this a hospital," Matt said.

Anna gripped Lucy's hand.

"How will we find Ma in this place?" she said.

"We'll find her," Matt said eyes blazing, hands gripped into a fist.

They continued wandering the halls until they located a woman in a white uniform.

"Can you tell us where to find Mrs. Ebbessen?" Matt asked.

"She's at the end of this here hall," the woman said. "Ya just wasted yer time cumin' ta see 'er. She don't know nuthin' nor nobody."

Heat crept up Anna's neck and face and she had to bite her lip to keep back her angry response to the woman's rude remarks. How could a place like this help her ma get well?

Matt looked at the woman, eyes dark with fury, and said, "Nevertheless, we want to see her. Please, take us there."

They found Ma sitting in a straight backed wooden chair looking off into space. Her dirty, rumpled gown hung on her thin, frame and she smelled appalling. The bed beside her chair was unmade and by the stench and look of the sheets they had not been changed in some time. The siblings gasped and looked at each other in shock. How could this have happened in a hospital? Hospitals were where people went to be healed. Instead, the people here were in a deplorable state.

Anna clamped her teeth together and marched out of the room to find an employee. When she located several workers sitting in a room laughing and talking, she felt like yelling and telling them how lazy they were but rather she said, "We want to clean up our ma, Mrs. Ebbessen. Show me where I can get a clean gown and bed clothes and some soap and water so I can bathe her."

At the tone of Anna's voice, several people jumped up out of their chairs. One woman said, "This ain't her day for a bath."

Anna replied, "Oh, yes it is. Get me the things I need. This place is filthy and I don't see any excuse for it, and certainly no excuse for the patients looking and smelling like they do. I'll see you down in her room."

Anna later learned that the patients received a bath and clean linens only twice a month; however, Ma looked like she had missed her last bath and that it was past time for her next one. When someone brought the linens and water to the bedside, Anna pulled the skimpy, worn curtains around her ma's bed and she and Lucy proceeded to bathe her. When they removed her gown Anna said, "Lucy, look at these bruises. How do you think she got them?"

"This place is terrible. We need to get her out of here." Lucy replied.

As Anna bathed her ma she repeated over and over, "Ma, God loves you and so do I. God loves you and so do Lucy and Matt. We came to see you, because we love you."

Once Ma turned to look at her, but said nothing, still Anna gave thanks for that little response. After finishing the bath, they put a clean, although shabby gown on Ma, and made up the bed with fresh linens.

"Ma, do you want to lie down or sit up?" Anna asked. When Ma didn't respond they left her sitting while they continued their visit.

A little later the employee that had directed them to Ma's room bought in a tray of food. The bean soup had spilled onto the tray and the cornbread looked moldy. The woman said, "She has to be fed and it takes forever. We don't have time to feed 'er much. You want ta do it?" Anna took the tray and began feeding her ma. She gulped down the food.

"Breakfast must have been one of those times they didn't have time to feed her. Ma looks like she's half starved. I don't know how she can eat this; it smells spoiled and looks worse. Next time let's bring her some food."

After Ma had eaten, Anna read the Bible verses from her paper. She began with John 3:16. "For God so loved the world that He gave His only begotten Son, that whosoever believeth on Him should not perish, but have everlasting life."

She said, "Ma, we can talk to God like we talk to another person. God welcomes anyone to come to him. All we have to do is recognize that we are sinners and ask for forgiveness, and He forgives us. We become His child, and when we die, we will go to heaven and live with Him forever. God loves us that much. God loves you, Ma. I love you, too."

Anna read her mother two more verses: "For all have sinned and come short of the glory of God,' and 'Believe on the Lord Jesus Christ and thou shalt be saved." She then tried, in simple words, to tell her Ma the story of redemption. Anna watched her ma as she talked; hoping to see some sort of response, but Mrs. Ebbessen continued to sit silent, with her hands in her lap staring bleakly off into space. Anna sighed and looked at Lucy.

"Do you think she understood anything I said?"

"I don't know Anna, but they were lovely words. I want to hear more about them soon."

"I have been praying for an opportunity to talk to you."

At that moment Matt returned to the room. He had gone to find the director to talk to him about their concerns. He said, "Couldn't find anyone in charge of the place. Only aides and cooks seem to be working today." He looked at Ma. "She looks tired. Guess we better get ready to leave. Sure wish we could take her with us and get her out of this place."

Anna and Lucy lifted their mother out of the chair and helped her walk to the bed.

"Ma, we have to go now. I'm going to leave this paper and I'll ask someone here to read to you. Just remember God loves you, even if it doesn't seem like it." Anna leaned down and kissed her Ma on the cheek, the first time she ever remembered doing this.

"I love you, Ma. I wish we could take you home with us." With tears running down her face, she left to find someone to read the paper to Ma. Anna saw a female employee standing near her ma's room.

"When you have time would you please read this to my ma, Mrs. Ebbessen? It might help her get well faster." She handed her the paper.

The woman quickly read through it and said, "These are fine words. I'm a Christian, but I really don't know how to talk to people about God. I'll read it to your ma every chance I get. Maybe I can read it to some other patients, also."

Words could not express their sorrow as they left the mental institution. Most of the way home they traveled in silence. Finally, Anna said, "That was one of the hardest things I've ever done, walking out of that place and leaving Ma there. Surely when the doctors are on duty things are better. They must be giving her some kind of treatment."

"I'm going to talk to Doctor George. He's the one who told Pa to take her up there," Matt said.

"I don't know if I'm sorry or glad I went. I was happy to see Ma, but not in that place," Lucy said.

Anna said, "I'd like to see her again whenever I can get Tom to come watch Pa, and you can take us, Matt. Thanks for taking us. I have some money I will give you for gasoline."

"Keep your money, Anna. You may need it for something else. I'll check with the doctor and pay his bill for seeing Pa. Do you think Pa's doing any better?"

"My faith isn't very good about getting him off the liquor. The swelling in his legs and feet has gone down some, but not enough for him to walk unassisted. I think he's getting weaker, maybe from being in bed. Or it could be his heart. Doc takes his blood pressure with that machine thing he has and tells me it is still too high."

"Doesn't sound too promising."

"Pa acts like he hates me, but maybe he really hates not having his way."

"It's not you. Pa never has shown love to any of us that I can remember," Lucy said.

By the time they drove up the lane to Lucy's house the sun had dissolved into streaks of golden, red, and orange that stretched across the western sky. Matt said, "Lucy, tell Katy to get ready to leave by the time I'm back from taking Anna home. We'll have to hurry to get home before dark.

On the way to Pa's house, Anna said, "Matt, I was so young that I didn't really get to know you before you left home. I sure didn't learn to appreciate you as I do now. Thank you for taking us. I'll have to quit thinking about what I saw today, and remember we have to do what's best for Ma." Anna left the car crying.

CHAPTER 31

Anna had heard Uncle Chris say that the wind only blows twice a year in Oklahoma. It started on New Year's Day and blew until June second, and then started again on June fourth and blew till the last day of the year. She didn't really believe that they went even one day without wind, but today the heat would have been unbearable without a breeze. It was the dog days of summer, as the old timers called them. August, the hottest month of the year, when the prairie grass looked like a fire had scorched it and you wanted only to sit in the shade and fan, but that wasn't possible for Anna. If they were to have food to eat, she had to keep going. She grabbed her hoe and headed for the dry, weed-filled garden.

"What good does it do to hoe this garden? The weeds grow faster than the plants," she grumbled as she smacked the stubborn red clay with her hoe.

"I need a change of scenery or I'm going to lose my mind." She hadn't been off the place for weeks, nor had she received any mail. Pa wouldn't talk to her and when Mike came, just once a day now, to bring Pa his liquor, he didn't stay long. Self-pity absorbed her every thought.

I've got to stop this. It just makes me feel worse, and makes things seem more difficult. I need to see Lucy, she'll cheer me up.

She put the hoe in the barn and headed for the house. The cool gloom of the soddy felt welcome after working in the strong sunshine. She gave Pa a glass of water and helped him to the outhouse, and then she said, "I'm going to see Lucy. Please stay in bed while I am gone, will you, Pa?" He only grunted.

Lucy met Anna on her front step. She wore a crisp, pink calico dress covered by a spotless white apron. Anna wondered how she managed to look smart and well groomed no matter the time of day.

"Come into the kitchen. It's cooler there," Lucy said. "I'll make some iced tea. Mike brought ice from town yesterday and we might as well enjoy it."

They walked into the well kept kitchen with its cheerful yellow gingham curtains. The shades were pulled down to block out the heat of the sun. A soft breeze blew in from the open windows.

"This room always makes me feel peaceful," Anna said. "Lucy, have you heard from Fort Supply? How soon can we go to see Ma again?"

Lucy shook her head. "I'll let you know if I hear anything"

"I'm tired of waiting on them. I'll write Matt and see when he can take us."

Anna needed to get some air before she exploded with frustration. After all it wasn't Lucy's fault that their ma had been taken to the mental hospital. She said, "While you're fixing the tea I'll give Bowlegs a drink and tie her. She hasn't been anyplace lately and might decide to wander off."

As she waited for the mule to drink from the horse tank, she looked around the tidy, well cared for farm yard. She knew Lucy worked hard in the house and Mike in the fields; still they took time for their children and each other. Would she dare hope for a loving husband and charming home like Lucy has?

The sisters munched on cookies and drank their iced tea while they chatted. Finally Anna said, "Lucy, I feel like I have to run away from home for awhile. My life isn't going anywhere. Pa doesn't talk to me. Sometimes he grunts, but that's mostly when he doesn't like what I say, which is most of the time."

Before long Mike came into the house wiping the sweat and dust from his face with a wet, red bandana. He stopped by Lucy's chair to give her a quick hug.

"Hello, Anna. Wondered where you were. I just stopped by your house and found Pa trying to saddle his horse. He's not strong enough to lift the saddle, but he was able to fight me when I tried to get him back into the house. I wanted to tie him in bed, but didn't. He's so cantankerous. Don't know how you put up with him."

"Like I have a choice. Pa exhausts my patience. And today I'm consumed with self-pity. It seems to sap my strength." Anna pressed her hands together and knitted her brows.

"I don't know what to do. Well, I guess I know what to do; ask God for more patience. Still the Bible says 'tribulation worketh patience.' I hate to ask for more tribulation." Lucy and Mike laughed at that, but Anna didn't feel like laughing.

"Well, guess I had better get back and check on Pa," Anna said. "Thanks Mike. Tell the boys I'm sorry they were asleep, and thanks, Lucy, for the tea and talk." Lucy gave Anna a hug before she left.

When Anna returned home, she found Pa wandering around the yard. When he saw her he bellowed, "I want a drink! Get my bottle or I'm going after my own booze."

"Well, just go on! I'm tired of listening to your complaints. I came home because I thought you needed me and the Bible says to honor your parents."

Pa stopped pacing and stared at Anna. She knew she should stop but she had held her temper until it was ready to explode.

"I can't remember you ever saying a kind word to any of us. All I remember is your meanness to us kids and abuse to Ma. As far as I am concerned, it's your fault she's in that horrible insane asylum. I wish you were there instead of her. You deserve it, she doesn't."

Pa's face was getting red and his eyes looked like they would pop out of their sockets. Anna began to fear he would have a stroke, or maybe he would hit her. She backed away from him and said, "Go on back to bed. I need to milk and feed the animals." She turned her back on him and marched into the barn.

After milking, she fed and watered Daisy, and brushed her down. As she stroked the gentle cow she began to regret her angry words.

I guess I had better check on Pa. Lord, I need more patience and love to deal with him.

Exhaustion and fatigue seeped into her every bone. Her pa's belligerent behavior irritated her more than she could abide. What difference did it make if he went back to his drink and evil friends? Why should she be his keeper anyway? Daisy flicked her tail and turned her placid eyes toward Anna, reminding her of how patient God had been. She put her head in her hands.

"Forgive me Father God. I'm no better than he is. I'm ashamed and sorry for my ugly words." With a sob, she went into the soddy. Before she entered she breathed a prayer.

"Please, help me keep my words kind." Problems seemed to shadow her; still she couldn't escape them by venting her anger on Pa.

She found Pa sitting on the side of the bed, trying to lift his legs up onto the bed. Anna helped him lie down, and then said, "Pa, I'm sorry for talking so harsh. I said some hateful things. Will you forgive me?" Her father just stared, his eyes hard and spiteful.

Anna heard what sounded like a horse and wagon out on the road. To her surprise it turned into their lane. As it came near she saw her brother, Tom sitting on the wagon seat. As he got closer she saw that he was driving a loaded wagon.

What had happened? Was he moving back home? She went out to greet him.

Tom waved and called out, "Hi, Anna. I'm home to stay." He jumped down from the wagon seat, grabbed Anna, and swung her around. "It's good to see you. Do you have anything to eat? That was a long, hot trip."

She stared at her brother. Had he and Janie broken up she wondered but dared not ask.

"It's good to see you, too. Yes, I'll fix you something. What's in the wagon? Come on into the house. Pa will want to see you, but if you give him any liquor, I personally will beat you up."

Tom gave a hearty laugh that cheered her. When the two entered the soddy their Pa looked at them and did his usual, "I want a drink. Now!"

Anna said, "I don't have anything for you except some water. You know that and it's not going to change."

Tom looked at his sister, eyes wide, mouth smiling at her blunt reply to their Pa.

"I'm going to fix Tom something to eat. Do you want anything?" Pa just grunted.

After eating, as they sat around the table, Tom began telling Anna of his plans.

"That's lumber on the wagon. I'm going to start building a house for Janie and me. It ain't gonna be real fancy, but Janie said she don't need nothin' fancy."

"Are you already married?"

"No, I thought we needed a house to come to after we get married. I think things will work out. Janie said she could help take care of Pa. She helped take care of her grandpa, but he wasn't an old rascal like someone we know."

"When do you think you'll have the house ready? What are you going to live on now, and after you are married? In my opinion this place'll never be anything but a dry dirt farm. Nothing grows here but weeds."

Tom walked to the door and looked out. Anna knew he was seeing bare ground or weeds in every spot that she hadn't plowed or built something. He stood looking out to the area where the fields of broom corn had been. Finally, he said, "I thought I would try to raise some broom corn like Pa did, but he had all us kids to help him do the work. Come to think of it, I never saw him do no work. I can hire out to work for other farmers around here like I did before, but I would like to try it on my own. Janie's a hard worker. She learns real fast."

Anna felt a sinking feeling in her stomach. She wondered if God was going to desert her now. After all the work she had put into making this hopeless place a home that would support her and Pa, would Tom just move in and expect her to leave? Where would she go?

"What are your plans for me?" she asked. She was annoyed that her voice trembled a little.

"I thought since I would be here I could see about Pa some and you could work out as a hired girl again. I ain't got much money for food. Mr. Morrison gave me the lumber for the house and he'll give me some more when I need it. He's doing this for our wedding present. He's really a great guy."

"I don't have jobs lined up now since I've not been able to leave Pa."

Tom turned to look at his pa. Anna looked too. He had his swollen, puffy legs propped up on pillows. Since Tom's last visit Pa had lost weight; his gaunt face and lifeless eyes made him look years older than his age.

Liquor did that to him, Anna thought.

"When's Doc coming?" Tom asked. "What's wrong with Pa's legs?"

"Doc hasn't been here for some time. I guess he thinks there isn't anything he can do for Pa. His condition's called *dropsy*. That means his body has water collected in it that his heart isn't strong enough to take away."

Tom sat for a while, eyes thoughtful, head leaning against his arm, and then he headed outside. Anna cleared the table and stacked the dishes in the sink. After she finished, she set out to care for the animals, her mind in turmoil.

What's going to happen to me? Am I going to have

to stay here and be a drudge for Pa, Tom, and Janie?

Tom unloaded the lumber from the wagon and after Anna finished cleaning the kitchen, she walked over to where he worked and leaned against the wagon.

"Tom, how big a house are you going to build?"

"Janie wants three big rooms to start with. I hope I have sense enough to do it."

"As soon as Matt comes again, Lucy and I want to go see Ma. Now would be a good time for us to go since you could stay with Pa."

"I forgot to tell you that on the way here I stopped to see Matt. He'll take you to Fort Supply on Saturday." "I'll tell Mike when he comes in the morning with Pa's liquor."

Tom threw up his hands. "You mean we have to put up with Pa hollering for something to drink that long?"

"Welcome home, big brother. We've got him weaned to one drink a day and I don't have any hope to do better than that."

CHAPTER 32

That night Anna tossed and turned trying to stop her anxious thoughts.

Can Tom really build a house? From the looks of things when I got home, he couldn't even drive a nail. What will I do when Tom marries? Round and round her mind spun, trying to imagine how Tom's return would change things. Prayer and worry, she knew, did not fit together; still her anxious thoughts would not stop.

Where will I go? They won't need me. Won't want me around. What will I do?

As if she were hearing an audible voice, words she had read from the little book of readings spilled into her memory: "Trust is like stepping off a high cliff and knowing God will catch you. The future is no stranger to God. You can run toward it with confidence that He is there and will hold your hand and even carry you when you are too weak to walk."

The sweet voice she had come to recognize as her friend and Savior whispered, "Cast all your cares on Me, for I care for you. I know what is going on in your life. Trust Me, Anna. Trust…" Anna drifted off into peaceful sleep.

The next morning nothing had changed; Tom was still there, Pa was still sick and grumpy, but Anna's heart felt lighter, more hopeful. She had coffee perking and biscuits baking when Tom came into the kitchen.

"Breakfast 'bout ready? I'll look in on Pa and take him to wash up." He rubbed his eyes and ran his fingers through his collar length blond hair. Anna thought her brother was a handsome man. She prayed he didn't turn to drink if things didn't work out on the farm as their pa had. When the men returned, she had breakfast set out.

"Pa, want to sit at the table with us?" Anna asked. Without answering he dropped into a chair and grabbed a cup of coffee. Mike came with Pa's liquor while they were eating.

"Morning, folks. Pa, good to see you up," he said as he handed Pa his drink.

Pa gulped it down, then Anna left Mike and Tom at the table discussing Tom's building project and helped Pa to bed. When the men moved their talk outside, she returned to the kitchen, cleaned up the breakfast things, and began preparing food for that day and the next. What should she take to her ma? Joy, edged with worry, kept her uneasy.

Would Ma be able to talk to them this time? Would she look better? Worse? No matter, in whatever condition they found her, Anna would push to bring Ma home. With Tom home, she felt certain that she could manage both her parents care. Yes, she would insist that the hospital release her ma.

She went outside to tell Mike that Matt was coming the next day to take them to Fort Supply. She waited as the men stepped off some spaces and wrote something on a board, and then she said, "Mike, Matt's coming Saturday to take me and Lucy to see Ma. I'll leave lunch for you men before we leave. Also, let Lucy know I plan to take snacks for Ma."

~~~~~~~~

The trip to Fort Supply seemed shorter this time as the siblings adjusted to the noise of the auto and were able to communicate better. Anna said, "I dread seeing Ma in that terrible place. With Tom getting married and moving back I think I could take care of her at home. Still, I may need to work out to support us. Tom doesn't seem to have any extra money. One more mouth to feed will quickly wipe out what little money I have."

"Does Tom help you with the outside work, or do his own laundry?" Lucy asked.

"You're trying to be funny?" Anna laughed. "He does help me with Pa a little. Pa's getting weaker. I'd like for Doc to look at him again."

Matt said, "Remember, I told you I'd pay for Pa's doctor bills and medicine. Now that harvest's over and I won't have so much to do; I'll try to see Pa more often."

The automobile pulled into the hospital courtyard in Fort Supply. Anna felt as if the sun had disappeared and the sky had turned gray and dreary. She said, "Is it the place or has the weather turned stormy?"

Lucy said, "You don't know how much I dread going back in that place. Well, maybe you do."

The three siblings trudged up the dusty path, anxious to see their ma, but fearful of what they would find. They entered the building and again no one welcomed them at the entrance table. The place smelled no better than the last time. Gloomy, desperate looking patients ambled about the halls, and many called for help.

A man, who looked like he weighed no more than a thirteen year old child, grabbed Matt's arm and pleaded for something to eat. Anna felt guilty not offering him some of the food she had brought for Ma;

nevertheless, she closed her ears and hurried away.

When they arrived at their ma's bed, they found the curtain closed. As they pulled it back, the three stood speechless, shocked at the sight. The sheets were covered with vomit; their ma lay huddled on the bed half naked, gasping for air. Her face, ashen white, was streaked with traces of food and dried blood. Dark purple bruises ran up and down her thin arms. Matt, the first to recover, ran to his ma and knelt, weeping as he wrapped his arms around her.

Anna said, "I'm going into the hall and yell until someone comes." She marched out and did just that.

"WHERE IS EVERYBODY? We need help. *Somebody come help us.*"

Minutes passed, still no one responded, and when she saw a woman dressed in a dingy, white jacket, hair disheveled and falling out of her bun, walking toward her, she wasn't sure if the woman were a patient or an employee. Anna clamped her jaws tight, as she tried to get her temper under control before speaking.

The woman said, "What's going on here? This is a hospital. We must have quiet."

In spite of her anger Anna felt like laughing. This place was anything but *quiet*, with the patients wandering about moaning and yelling, but when she spoke her voice held no mirth.

"Do you take care of Mrs. Ebbessen?"

"No. We don't have time for those in her condition. She's gonna die soon and others more deservin' get our attention."

Anna gasped, and knotted her hands together to keep from slapping the women.

"Who's in charge here?" she asked.

"Well, nobody's in charge today. Doctors only come every other week. In the mean time we just try to keep the inmates fed."

"Inmates! My ma's no inmate. She's a patient!" Anna shook with anger. Struggling to gain control of her emotions, she said through clenched teeth, "Find someone who can tell me why no one notified us of her condition."

"There's just me and two other workers today. Ain't our business to know the condition of your ma."

"Bring me some hot water and soap and towels, *now*. We're taking our ma out of here as soon as I get her cleaned up. And call the police." Anna marched back to her ma's room.

"What did you find out, Anna?" Lucy asked.

"You don't want to know. Matt, can we take Ma home in your auto? We could wrap her in a blanket and carry her out. I don't think anyone would try to stop us."

"I think we should take her home as well, but will you be able to handle both Ma and Pa?"

"I'm not leaving her here. What else can we do?"

By then a worker had brought the water and linens. Anna recognized the woman as the one who had said she would read to their ma.

The woman said, "Miss, I'm sorry you found your ma in this shape. I didn't go along with not giving her more care. I tried to get her to eat, but she wouldn't."

"How long has she been like this?" Anna asked.

"About two days. Doesn't eat or drink anything. I did read the paper to her when I could slip away and come in here. One day when I finished reading, she smiled a bit, and nodded her head. I wanted you to know."

Tears were running down Anna's face. The woman continued, "I also want you to know that I read the paper to my husband and he said it made sense to him. We started going to church."

Anna hugged the woman.

"Thank you. I asked the other woman to call the police. Could you check and see if she did, and if she didn't, would you call them?"

"I don't think I could do that, Miss. I'd get into trouble. Might be best if your brother went to find one."

"That's a good idea. Lucy, would you go with him. Ma needs a gown if we're taking her out of here. See if you can find rubber sheeting and a blanket as well. I'll get her bathed while you're gone."

Anna began to wash her mother and to clear away the dirty linens. Ma's condition did not improve and her labored breathing became harder. When Matt and Lucy returned with the policeman, Anna had her ma bathed. He stood with his hat in his hand, shifting from one foot to the other. He clearly didn't feel comfortable being in that place.

They stepped outside the curtain and Anna said, "We don't want Ma to stay here. She isn't getting any care and while she may die on the way home, at least we'll be with her."

"If she does die, what would we do?" Matt asked.

"Well, this is unusual, indeed." The policeman rubbed his chin. "Get a doctor to check her and if she's dead he'll need to make out a death certificate.

That's about all I know about it. I wouldn't want to be in this place neither."

"Will you inform the authorities in charge of this place? No one should be treated this way," Matt said.

"I'll write up a report. But don't look for much to be done. Seems like the state don't take an interest in what happens up here. Just keeps sending them, even from the prisons, but don't send much money for their keep."

Anna put the new gown on her ma and they wrapped the blanket around her. Matt and Anna carried Ma down to the automobile. Lucy, spread the rubber sheeting on the back seat. Just as they moved her into the auto they heard someone calling, "Here, here, you can't do that. Stop right this minute."

They looked up to see a short, stout man in tight fitting top coat with pinchers perched on his nose running toward them. He clutched a bowler hat in his hand.

"What's the meaning of this? What are you doing with that body?"

Matt said, "Who are you? What does it look like we're doing? We're taking our ma out of this filthy hole."

"I'm the manager here. You have no permission to remove one of our inmates."

"This place isn't fit for human beings. If you did your job you would know that. You must sit in an office all day with the door shut. What's your name? I may want to tell my attorney."

Matt nudged Anna, and motioned her to get in the car. They drove off, leaving the man standing there with his mouth agape.

Anna got into the back seat and eased her ma down into her lap. She rubbed her arm gently and said over and over.

"Ma we love you. Things will be better soon. We're taking you home."

She wished she could remember some of the Danish lullabies Ma had sung to her when she was a little girl. The music might sooth her. She moistened a handkerchief and tried squeezing a few drops of water into Ma's mouth, but she seemed unable to swallow. She sponged her face and tried to keep her lips moist.

It hurt to listen as Ma gasped and wheezed, trying to breathe. Anna prayed that God would spare her Ma. She longed to tell her how God had forgiven her and given her new life in His Son. She wanted to tell her about the Muellers, about John, and her dreams for the future. Anna continued stroking her ma's arms.

"Ma I'm sorry I left. I feel so guilty for leaving you. But I'm going to take care of you now."

"We all should have stepped up when we saw things were getting worse, Anna. Ma always tried to hide how things were from us kids. Guess she just wore out," Lucy said.

Matt said, "I should have gone to see Ma as soon as they put her in Fort Supply, no matter what the doctor said."

Anna bent over and gave her ma a soft kiss.

"I love you Ma. I'm going to take care of you and nobody's going to hurt you again."

At these words, Ma's lips curved into a smile and her breathing became stronger. Anna took her hand. Ma gave it a gentle squeeze.

"Lucy, Matt, Ma's responding. Thank you Father God. Thank you."

"Hold on Ma. We're almost home," Lucy said.

Anna's heart sang with joy at the hope of having her ma well again.

For several minutes Ma's breathing seemed to grow deeper and stronger, but then once again it slowed and became shallow. Her hands and feet began to turn blue. Anna cried, "Ma, we are almost home. Don't let go now."

"Do I need to stop Anna? Maybe if I rolled down the window a little air might help," Matt said.

"Just keep going Matt. Looks like we are getting close to Freedom. We can stop there."

Matt shoved down the gas pedal and sped up.

Anna tried rubbing her ma's hands and arms but the blue color continued creeping upward.

"Ma, we're almost home. Please, breathe."

Ma's eyes opened and she looked up as if she saw something. A light filled them and she opened her mouth as if trying to speak, and then her chest went still and her struggle ended; her face turned pasty white.

Anna cried, "Ma, *no*. We're almost home. *Breathe*. Try! " Nothing changed. "Please, Ma breathe."

Anna placed her head on her mother's chest. No heartbeat.

"Oh, dear Father God, no. No!" She began to weep.

Lucy turned around and said, "What happened?" She stared at her ma's still form and began to sob.

"Oh, no. Ma, please. Don't leave us." Lucy buried

her face in her hands and let her tears flow. "Why didn't we get Ma out of that terrible place the first time we visited? I feel so guilty,"

Matt gripped the wheel and gritted his teeth, mashed his foot on the accelerator and sped into Freedom. He drove straight to the doctor's office and pulled the auto to a stop.

"Maybe the doctor can do something for Ma," he said as he jumped out and ran to his door.

CHAPTER 33

At the entrance of the doctor's office Matt banged on the door and called, "Please, quick. Come check my ma. She's not breathing."

"Hold on young man. What's the trouble?" the doctor asked.

"Come to my auto. Ma's stopped breathing," Matt said.

The doctor followed Matt to the automobile and after examining Ma he said, "She's gone. I'm so sorry. Nothing more can be done. I'll make out some papers declaring her deceased. Take them down the street to Mr. Hardy, the undertaker."

Lucy covered her face and sobbed. Anna caressed her ma's face, hoping for a miracle. Matt, head hanging low and tears pooling in his eyes, left Lucy and Anna in the car with Ma and walked over to the undertaker's.

A tall man, with graying, untamed hair and a bushy beard, answered the door. "What can I do for you young man?"

Matt blurted out, "My ma's dead. She's in my automobile; in the back seat." He pointed across the street where his auto was parked.

"Well, I must say, that's a mite unusual. Do you want me to take care of the body?"

"We don't know the procedures," Matt explained. "We brought her from Fort Supply Mental Institution, where we found her in a deplorable condition. She died just a few miles from here."

Mr. Hardy said, "Bring the body in and I'll see what needs to be done."

"We'd like to do this as simply as possible. We'll bury her out at the farm," Matt said.

"Fetch her and I'll fix her up and bring her to your place sometime tomorrow afternoon. How 'bout a plain pine box to bury her in?"

Matt returned to his automobile and repeated his conversation with Mr. Hardy. Anna handed Matt the dress she had made for her mother when she thought they would be able to bring her home with them.

"Give this to the undertaker to put on Ma. I'd like to know she had a pretty dress for her burial," Anna said.

After they had left their ma in the care of the undertaker, Matt cranked up the automobile and with heavy hearts they started home.

"I blame this on Pa. I don't think I'll ever forgive him," Lucy said.

"I wish I hadn't left. I know Ma told me to go but if I'd stayed Pa wouldn't have taken her off to that horrible place." Anna put her head in her hands.

"Don't blame yourself. Ma may have known she was losing it and didn't want you to end up like her," Matt said. "We need to start digging the grave today. If Mike and Tom help, and maybe Howard, we should get a little done before dark."

"Who's going to tell Pa, Ma died?" Lucy asked. "I don't want to talk to him. Maybe we can wait until morning. Probably won't matter to him, anyway."

"Matt what about the rest of the family?" Anna asked.

"I plumb forgot! I better turn around and go back to Freedom and send them a telegram," Matt said. "You girls make a list with addresses for our brothers and sisters, and Uncle Chris. Write out a brief message, also."

The afternoon sun was low when they drove into Lucy's farmyard. "Lucy, would you ask Mike if he could help dig the grave today? And ask him to stop at Esther's and let them know about Ma. See if Howard will help with the grave," Matt said. "Tell Katy to hurry out, would you?"

When Katy slid into the front seat Matt said, "Anna, I think it's best that Pa be told right away so we don't let something slip. Would you and Katy do that? I'll talk to Tom."

The women agreed.

"I'll take care of Pa." Anna rubbed the back of her neck, trying to relieve the tension.

"I'm afraid Esther will come with Howard and I don't know if I can cope with her."

Matt went to look for Tom and the women went into the house. When Pa heard them come in he began yelling, "Where ya been? I need a drink."

Anna grabbed the bucket to draw fresh water from the windmill. When she offered her pa a drink he threw it at her. Anna bit her lip to hold back her outrage.

"Pa, behave. I'll not tolerate you throwing a fit."

"Git my bottle, Gal."

Anna's legs trembled with weariness.

"Pa, I hate to tell you, but Ma died today. We left her body with the undertaker in Freedom. He'll bring it out tomorrow."

Afraid she would break down in tears she left without waiting for his reaction. When she returned to the kitchen, Katy had already stirred up the coals in the stove and had coffee warming.

"What shall we plan for supper?" Katy asked.

"I can't even think of food right now, but I know we will have to plan for tomorrow. We will have a crowd to feed at the burial."

"Anna you're right. I'll take care of the meal. Just tell me where you keep things."

You'll find whatever you want in the cellar. I'd better take Pa to the necessary."

After Pa got his shoes on, Anna helped him outside. He stumbled along, leaning heavily against her.

"The doctor needs to see you. You're getting weaker."

"Don't need no doctor. I need a drink."

Anna narrowed her lip, and fought to keep her patience as she helped Pa to his bed. When she stepped into the kitchen, Katy had gathered jars of chicken and broth, green beans, pickled beets, and some fruit from the cellar.

"Thanks, Katy."

"I don't know how you raised and canned all this food, and at the same time made this place decent, especially since you were working for other people most of the week."

"God gave me the strength to do what I had to do."

"I don't know much about God, but I know you've changed. Why would somebody way off in heaven care about us? Still you act like He does."

Anna breathed a silent prayer and said, "A Bible verse that helps me says, *'Cast all your care on him for he cares for you.'* These words comfort me. Do you have a Bible, Katy?"

"No. I've hardly ever seen one. When I was little, we may have had a big family Bible, but no one ever read it. I thought it was only for decoration."

"If you can find one, start reading in the New Testament. Ask God to give you understanding as you read. I must get to work. I'll be back soon."

Anna gathered the eggs and milked Daisy. Working seemed to ease her heartache a bit, still tears burned in her eyes.

Ma I know you are better off, but I sure wish I could have had time to tell you I'm sorry I didn't do better by you.

After she had strained the milk and poured it in a clean bucket, she took it to the water tank to cool and brought the older milk and butter back to the house. Katy had everything ready for their supper.

"Anna, Let's take a breather. I know you must be exhausted."

"My feet do need a rest. Pa seems to have dropped off to sleep. Let's walk out to see how the men are getting along. They might need someone to boss them."

"I would rather just sit a spell, Anna." Katy pressed her fingers against her temples. "Okay, maybe we should see how much longer they plan to work."

They found the men ready to quit work. Matt said, "I believe we can finish by midmorning tomorrow."

Tom laid down his shovel and said, "I'm going to clean up at the horse tank and ride over to see Janie and tell her about Ma. I'll be back just after daylight in the morning."

Matt said, "Katy, I need to talk to you for a minute." They walked off to one side and when they returned Matt said, "We decided that if someone will lend us something to wear tomorrow, we had better stay the night. It isn't safe to drive home with such little light as our vehicle has. Mike, can we stay with you?"

"You're welcome to stay. It seems time we quit for the night."

The men agreed and tossed their shovels on the ground.

After eating, everyone left. Anna checked her pa and found him sleeping soundly.

When she lay down every bone screamed with exhaustion, but her deepest pain was the memory of her ma struggling for breath, and then the silence when her battle ended.

It's my fault. I should never have left her here with Pa. She covered her head with her pillow to smother her weeping. *Father God, how can I bear this? How can I say a final good-bye to Ma tomorrow? I'm so weary.*

CHAPTER 34

"Tarnation Gal, git out 'o here," Pa yelled.

"It's time to get up. The men are already here. The grave will be finished soon."

"Git my bottle and leave me be."

"Pa, let me get you washed up and dressed. The undertaker will be here for ma's burying soon." Anna said.

"Git out! I can dress myself." Pa sat up and grabbed the clothes Anna was carrying. As he tried to stand his swollen legs gave way. Anna caught him and helped him to a chair and left him, struggling to get into his overalls on his own, and went into the kitchen where Katy and Lucy waited.

Lucy said, "I brought a cake and a big pot of rabbit stew. We'll have a crowd to feed after the burying."

"Mike fetched the shovels and the men are digging," Katy said.

"Git me out 'o here. I wan'ta see what's goin' on," Pa hollered.

Anna peeked around the quilt that separated pa's bed from the kitchen and said, "It's too far for you to walk but maybe Matt could drive you out."

"I'll go ask if he'll come take Pa," Lucy said.

"We can't stay long." Anna went to the barn to get a stool for Pa to sit on at the grave site, while Matt brought the automobile around.

Matt drove as close to the grave site as possible and they got out. Anna looked around at the bleak, colorless field that would give shelter to her ma's body. The grass, now the color of toast, burned up and lifeless from the August sun, spread before her. Not even an unsightly, twisted scrub oak shaded the grave. Desolate like Ma's life had been. Anna saw a clump of goldenrods, only a weed; still its dazzling gold-color reminded her that Ma now walked on streets of gold, free from tears and suffering. She would pick some for Ma's service.

Pa watched in stoic silence as the men pushed their shovels unto the hard dirt and tossed it out for the wind to catch and carry away. Anna wondered what her pa was thinking. Had he ever loved her ma? Did he feel any regret for the way he treated her? She had not seen him shed a tear nor speak words of grief. How did a person become so coldhearted? Looking at his leathery, deeply lined face and hunched form as he perched on the stool, she fought back bitterness at what could have been, but would never be.

When she saw that his legs were swelling she said, "Pa, we need to get you back to bed." He made no comment, and Matt went over and took his arm and helped him into the automobile.

Anna waited outside the soddy until Matt had Pa settled. When he returned she asked, "Matt, do you think Pa will want to go to the burying? Would you mind asking him? He doesn't like me much today. Mike forgot to bring his drink."

Matt went back into the soddy. When he returned he said, "He wants to go. I need to get back to the digging." He turned to leave then stopped and gazed at Anna.

"I know I'm the oldest, but I'm no good at words. Would you do whatever talking needs to be done at the burying? Now that you got religion, seems to me you know more how to speak about those things than the rest of us."

"I'll do what I can. I appreciate you asking me, Matt."

By late morning all the family members except Esther, were present. Tom hadn't arrived as early as he intended, but then Tom's intentions didn't always work out. Their oldest sister, Pearl and her husband, Harry, with their two nearly grown children, Frank and Mary Sue, pulled their wagon into the farm yard at about the same time as Saul, their brother from across the state line in Kansas. Saul greeted the women and said, "Had to leave the wife behind. She's a little sickly today. Where's Pa? I want to let him know I'm here, and then I'll go and see if the fellows need help."

"I'm just too tuckered out." Harry said. "Think I'll find a shade tree and rest up for dinner."

"Sounds about like Harry. He's so lazy I don't know how he gets a fork into his food and up to his mouth," Lucy whispered to Anna and Katy. Anna had to cover her mouth to keep from laughing out loud.

"Wait up, Uncle Matt," said Frank. "I'll come along and see if I can help."

"What can we do?" Pearl asked.

"Everything's ready here. The men can set up tables outside when they finish," Lucy said. "Let's find some shade and visit a spell."

While the women gossiped, Anna went inside to think about the service. She opened her Bible and looked in the concordance for something about life after death. John 11:25, 26 seemed fitting and she placed a marker at the selection.

Lord, teach me what to say about eternal life so

everyone who hears will understand. This is probably the only time I will ever have to talk to my family about you. She also chose Psalms 23. If Mr. Long came she would ask him to read that. She wished there could be at least one song. Perhaps Mr. Hardy would sing.

By afternoon the farm yard had filled with wagons and horses as neighbors and friends arrived: the Longs, the folk who lived north of Lucy's, the Rueffer's, who had helped Anna out after her terrible experience in the tornado, and others she didn't recognize. News travels fast in a small community. Her brothers and sister in Oregon would not be coming. Esther, with her children and mother-in-law, arrived just as they were serving dinner. Anna felt grateful that most of the neighbors had brought a dish, and along with what Lucy had prepared, there would be plenty.

They had finished eating and the women had cleared away the leftovers when Mr. Hardy arrived with Ma's body. Anna asked him if he would sing.

"I sometimes sing at interment, but only if no one else is available," he said.

When it appeared that everyone who was coming had arrived, they gathered around the grave. Anna took the small bouquet of goldenrods that she had picked earlier and laid it on top of the plain pine box. There were no other flowers or decoration. When she finished she announced that Mr. Hardy would sing.

"I'll sing *Amazing Grace.* Anyone that knows the words, please join me," Mr. Hardy said. Anna knew the song and sang along, softly. A few others joined in occasionally.

"Would anyone like to say something about Ma?"

Anna asked. When no one spoke up, she said. "I want to read the Holy Bible from Saint John, chapter eleven, verses twenty-five and twenty-six. "Jesus said, 'I am the resurrection, and the life: he that believeth in Me, though he were dead, yet shall he live... And whosoever liveth and believeth in Me shall never die.'"

After she finished, she gave a simple interpretation of Jesus words. She then talked about giving the paper with the plan of salvation to a woman employee at Fort Supply to read it to her ma, and that the woman believed Ma had understood the words and had accepted Christ as her Savior.

"I've asked Mr. Long to read the twenty-third Psalm. If you know the words please say them along with him."

When Mr. Long finished reading Anna said, "Please, bow your head and we'll close in prayer. Lord, thank you that you loved the world enough to send your Son to die so that we might be saved and that Ma had a chance to accept you as her Savior. Thank you for your mercy and grace and for your strength to get through this sorrowful time. We pray in the name of Jesus, our Savior. Amen."

A few people thanked Anna for her words; others left without saying anything.

As the men filled in the grave, Anna slipped away. Her shoulders sagged with fatigue and her eyes burned from unshed tears. She rubbed the back of her neck and rolled her shoulders. Never before had she felt such exhaustion, mentally and physically.

Katy moved over beside her and whispered, "Thank you Anna for everything. I'm going to find a Bible and read those verses." She gave her a quick hug.

Matt patted her arm and said, "Thanks, Sis. I appreciate what you've done around here."

"Thank you for taking us to see Ma. I only wish we had gone sooner. Maybe things might have turned out differently."

"Anna, if you get any bills from the doctor or Mr. Hardy, send them to me," Matt said. "If you get into any trouble with Fort Supply, refer them to me. I'd like to have a talk with them or anyone who can do something about that mess." Matt wiped his forehead with a handkerchief.

"We have to go. My neighbor's taking care of things until I get home. He didn't know I would be gone so long. Good-bye, and thanks again."

After Matt and Katy left, Anna had a few minutes to visit with Calvin and Mary Long.

"Thank you for coming. And thank you Mr. Long for reading the Psalms," she said. "Have you heard anything of Sandy?"

"You're welcome, and no, not a word. Still we won't give up hope that the horse will come home or be found."

When Lucy and Mike prepared to leave Anna asked, "Mike, did you bring Pa his drink this morning? He acted like you didn't."

"Anna, I'm sorry. I left it in Matt's car, and I guess he's gone. I'd better bring you some tonight in case he doesn't settle down."

"No, Mike, don't bring it back. We're all so weary, Pa can wait till morning. Maybe he's tired enough to sleep. If he gets mean, I just might sleep in the barn."

Pearl and her family had brought quilts to make pallets in the wagon or wherever else they could. Anna wondered if Esther would take them for the night. She walked over to ask her, but before she could say anything, Esther began to complain.

"Well, it looks like you finally had time ta speak ta me. You put on quite a show. Had people fussin' over you like you was somebody special."

Before she could say anything else, Tom interrupted, "Esther, just shut up. You don't have nothing to gripe about. Anna's hardly had time to draw a breath for the last three days and she certainly doesn't need your bellyaching. What did you do anyhow? Did you even bring food?"

"Tom, ya don't know nothin'. Have you ever taken care of a youngin? Cries all night and I don't feel good no-how." She puckered her lips in a pout and glared at Tom.

To everyone's relief, Howard said, "Git in the wagon, woman. Time to go." He took Esther's arm and marched her out to their wagon and drove off.

"Tom, would you and Frank do chores tonight? Please, and thank you," Anna said.

Tom agreed and Anna, Pearl, Harry, and Mary Sue walked toward the soddy.

"I don't have anything cold to offer anyone to drink, but I can get some fresh water from the pump. Y'all sit down and I'll be right back." No one volunteered to go in her place so Anna grabbed the water bucket and marched to the windmill.

"I guess I'll be back if I have the strength to make it that far and back," She muttered. "Harry's such a trial. How does Pearl put up with him? It takes a lot of nerve to be as lazy as Esther and Harry. Here I go, judging, Lord. Please forgive me."

She arrived at the soddy in time to hear Harry say, "Cut me a piece of pie. I need something to tide me over until supper."

Anna said, "We'll eat when Tom and Frank finish outside. Pearl, why don't you and Mary Sue help me put the food on the table. Should be enough left over from dinner."

After supper was cleared away, Tom took Pa to the necessary and then settled him in bed for the night. By that time it was dark and sleeping arrangements had to be made. Finally, everyone was bedded down and Anna heaved a sigh of thanks that the day had ended.

Alone at last Anna let her tears flow. Ma was in a better place, she knew, but knowing that didn't fill the big hole in her heart. She licked the salty tears from her lips and said, "Ma, I love you and already miss you." How she longed to gather her ma into her arms and give her a hug, but as she thought about it she realized that her ma was now in the arms of Jesus. Ma would never again feel pain or sadness.

"She's yours now Father God. I'll miss her but you know best."

CHAPTER 35

The next morning, Pearl's family, Tom, and Anna gathered in the kitchen for breakfast.

"Did anyone talk to Saul yesterday?" Anna asked. "I hardly had a chance to speak to him before he left."

"I told him I planned to get married and move into my house, shortly" Tom said. "Couldn't give him a date, as we haven't decided yet, but the house will be finished in about a week."

"Will it really be ready that soon?" Anna asked, trying to keep concern out of her voice.

"Mike and Howard are planning to help. If Frank and Harry would stay for a couple days it might be finished before then," Tom answered. "Could you stay, Harry?"

"Well, I don't guess there's anything pressing to do at home, is there, Pearl?"

"Can't think of anything but, Anna, could you put up with us all?"

"I'd be glad to have you. I'm still in shock over Ma's death and the company might do me good. Every time I think about Ma at Fort Supply I feel sick. Lucy and Esther may need someone to talk to about it as well."

The next few days passed in a haze of work. The women cooked and cleaned, did laundry and shared memories, while the men hammered and sawed, getting Tom's house raised and ready for the soon-to-be-wed couple. Pa had been calmer since Ma's burial and the swelling in his legs had gone down some. Saturday morning Pearl said, "Let's ride over to Lucy's today. I haven't seen her house since we've been here."

"Mary Sue, would you let Tom know we're leaving. Pa should be okay if one of them will check on him every once in awhile," Anna said.

"Yes, Aunt Anna." Mary Sue hurried off to give the message to Tom.

Anna readied the wagon and she and her sister and niece left. On the way they stopped to see if Esther wanted to go. She dropped her older boy off at Howard's ma and brought the baby with her. Esther sat on the wagon seat next to Anna. She handed the baby to Mary Sue and said, "Guess, y'all rather visit Lucy than me, seeing as how they have a fancy big house and all." Before anyone could speak she continued, "Pearl, I've been expectin' you ta come over. What, with all I have ta do, you should be helpin' me out, not Anna."

The baby began crying and Mary Sue said, "Aunt Esther I think Jakey's hungry."

"Well, he'll just have ta wait. Can't nurse him the way Anna drives this wagon so rough. Jars a body to death. Howard needs ta get us an automobile like Matt, but he's just too tight fisted."

Anna was relieved when they arrived at Lucy's farm yard. As they stepped from the wagon, Pearl whispered to Anna, "How will we abide an afternoon with Esther and her sour spirit?"

Lucy served dinner and after they had cleaned up she said, "I've been trying to remember the good times we had when we were young, before Pa's drinking got bad. Ma worked hard but she was a great cook and often sang as she worked. Pearl, remember how the family played games and sang together before Pa moved us to Oklahoma Territory?"

The older sisters talked of better times, but Anna had few good memories, and only remembered her pa as angry and abusive. It cheered her to hear her sisters' stories of happier days. Still, Esther grumbled.

"Might hav' seemed good times ta the two of you, but you got ta go ta school while I had ta stay home and help Ma with the work and the babies."

"Esther Marie, what are you saying? You hated school," Pearl said. "I remember you skipping out and hiding because you didn't want to go. After second grade Ma quit making you and let you help out at home."

"Pearl, and I had to stay home plenty of times and work," Lucy said. "None of us but Anna got to go beyond sixth grade."

"I am grateful Ma didn't let Pa keep me from going to school," Anna said. "He always fussed, but she stood up to him on that. I wonder if he took it out on her later."

"Ma never had an education herself. Guess that's why she insisted we have a chance," Pearl said.

The afternoon passed quickly and the pleasant memories helped the ache in Anna's heart, but when she saw the sun setting she said, "We better get back. There's supper to fix and we've left Pa alone quite a spell." She hoped that Tom had remembered to check on him.

When they arrived back at the farm, the men were still working on the house. Anna hurried into the soddy.

"Pa, we're home," she called. No answer.
They found him sprawled across the floor beside his bed.

"He must have tried to get out of bed by himself," Pearl said.

Anna bent close and checked him over. His breathing was shallow; no bones appeared to be broken, but he had a large knot on his head.

"Pa, can you hear me?" Anna said. He made no response.

Pearl said, "Mary Sue, run call your brother and Tom and ask them to help us get Pa back in bed. Then one of them should go for the doctor."

~~~~~~~~

The doctor arrived at twilight. He examined Mr. Ebbessen in the dim light of a lantern as best he could, and when he finished he called the family into the kitchen.

"Looks like your Pa suffered a stroke. His blood pressure's extremely high, and he could have another one anytime. If he does, I don't think he'll survive it. Nothing much to do for him, except get a little fluid down him. Don't give him any liquor, even if he hollers for it." He paused, "Give him water and broth. He may choke on it, but do the best you can. Someone needs to keep an eye on him day and night." He closed his bag. "I'll try to check on him tomorrow. If not, I'll be back as soon as I can."

Pearl said, "We need to go home tomorrow, but Frank could stay. We'll go by and tell Saul and Matt about Pa. Harry can bring me back Monday afternoon. You can't take care of everything by yourself, Anna."

"Thanks, I'll need some help."

"I'll ride over and tell Esther and Lucy about Pa," said Tom, "Sun up in the morning, I'm going to Janie's to get the furniture for our house."

With supper finished and the kitchen straightened, Anna felt she had lived at least three days in one. Pearl stayed up that night and watched Pa. After about four hours, Anna woke up and checked on him.

Pearl said, "He seems to be sleeping but his breathing isn't even. I've given him a little water but I'm not sure he's swallowing." They watched their pa for a few minutes. "Go back to bed, Anna."

"Thanks, Pearl. Tomorrow's going to be a hard day. I'm not sure I'll have any help."

Before dawn the next day Frank helped his pa load their wagon, and Harry, Pearl, and Mary Sue left.

Anna sat beside her pa's bed. Listening to his raspy, shallow breathing, and seeing his emaciated body, broke Anna's heart. She patted his bony arm and was overcome with a longing for a comforting touch or kind word from him; a yearning she knew would never be realized.

Meanwhile, Frank worked outside sweeping the new house and cleaning up scraps of lumber scattered about the yard. He pulled weeds from the garden and watered the plants that were still producing. Survivor followed him about as he worked.

"Poor feller, no one's had time for you." Frank bent over and raked his fingers through Survivor's dirty, tangle of fur and pulled out a few thistles. Survivor waved his tail and shook with delight. "Better check on Aunt Anna. Time someone relieved her," Frank said.

When he went into the soddy, he heard her say, "Pa, why wouldn't you listen to me when I tried to tell you about God? It just breaks my heart to think that you might die without knowing Him. He loves you, Pa. He wants to forgive your sins. Just think His name, *Jesus*. He died for your sins. Just think His name, *Jesus*.

"Please, Lord, give Pa enough consciousness that he can say, or at least think Your name. Oh, Father God, help me bear this." Tears spilled down Anna's cheeks.

"Pa, you can't go to heaven if you don't accept His grace and mercy. His grace is a gift. Just accept it if you will. God loves you and wants you to be His child. Pa, please think the name, *Jesus*." Her pa made no response. "Father God, I commit Pa to you. I don't know anything else to do," she prayed.

Frank backed out the door and went outside to think about what he had heard. His ma and pa never talked about religion. His ma was a good person, but his pa was lazy, and always jawing and criticizing him. Any work to be done, he'd disappeared behind the barn to chew tobacco and whittle, leaving the labor to his family. Only time they saw him was at meals and he sure didn't miss any of those. Wouldn't make Frank any difference if his pa burned in hell.

How could Aunt Anna think God would forgive her pa? How could she forgive him? First chance he got, he would ask her to explain this mystery. When he heard her moving around in the soddy, he went back inside.

"Anyway I can help out, Aunt Anna?"

"Would you help me turn Pa?"

The change eased Pa's raucous breathing and Anna lifted his head and spooned a little water into his mouth. He swallowed it and seemed to want more so she continued, giving him a bit at a time.

"Aunt Anna, don't you want to rest?" Frank said. "I'll watch Grandpa."

"Thank you, I'm really tired. It's hard, thinking each breath might be his last. Call me if you need me."

After a restful nap Anna awakened and fixed a light meal for her and Frank. That afternoon she worked in the soddy and Frank took care of the outside work. She baked cookies so those who watched Pa later would have something to eat with their coffee. Mike and Howard stayed that night. When they left the next morning, Lucy, and then Esther, came.

While Lucy looked after Pa, Anna decided to go for a walk and invited Frank to join her. Survivor ran alongside as they rambled down the dusty road.

"Aunt Anna, I heard some of the things that you said to Grandpa yesterday but I didn't understand," Frank said. "How can you believe God would forgive him? Can you explain that to me?"

"I'll try. I'm a fairly new Christian, but I know God forgave my sins."

"I'll never forgive my pa for the way he treats us kids and Ma. I don't see how you can forgive your pa." Frank stuffed his hands into his pockets.

"None of us deserve forgiveness, but God pardoned me and gave me the grace to forgive Pa. Now I'm a part of His family."

"Who gets to become His family?"

Anna paused and looked at Frank, "God wants every one of us to become his child and be a part of his family."

"Not just good people like you and grandma? I

hate my Pa. I'm leaving home when I can. Maybe God won't forgive me for that." Frank crossed his arms and glowered, eyes narrowed to slits.

Anna put her hand on his shoulder.

"God doesn't judge one sin as greater than another. Father God sent Jesus, the Son, to die for all sin. Everyone who accepts Jesus as Savior becomes God's child."

Anger slid from his face and a tender longing filled his eyes.

"Aunt Anna, I think I would like to become a child of God. Can you help me? What do I have to do?"

"Actually, you don't have to do anything. It's a gift to all those who accept Jesus as the sacrifice for their sins."

Frank smiled.

"Just tell Him you want to know Him and live for Him and believe that He is God and will forgive your sins."

Frank lowered his head, "Dear God, forgive me for my anger at my Pa. I accept Jesus, your gift of love, for my sins. I want to be your child and a part of your family."

Anna's heart pounded. Joy and gladness bubbled in her soul as Frank hugged her.

"Thanks, Aunt Anna, for caring enough to tell me how to become a part of God's family, and how to be forgiven for my sins. I feel like a load of coal has been lifted off my chest."

"I'm so glad we've had this time to visit and get to know each other better. When you go home, write to me anytime you have questions, and I will help you all I can. Try to find a church that teaches the Bible. I think your ma would like that, also. I guess we had better head back. Lucy may be getting tired."

When they returned, Anna said, "Lucy, do you think Pa would be more comfortable if we bathed him and changed his bed?"

"I never thought I would be giving my pa a bath," Lucy's lips twitched with a soft chuckle.

"One never knows what's coming in one's life. I never thought about Ma or Pa getting sick and dying. Honestly, I try not to think about death."

"I didn't either until I met the Muellers. They made me consider where I would spend eternity, a place of everlasting joy with God, or a place of never ending suffering with Satan. I tried to talk to Pa about this, but he wouldn't listen. It breaks my heart."

"Anna, since I read your paper giving the plan of salvation, I've been reading the Bible some. Mike and I have been discussing it but we don't understand much. We wish there was a church nearby."

"I miss church as well. We need the fellowship of other Christians. Let's pray that a preacher will come to our community. Maybe we could talk to the Longs and other neighbors about getting together on Sundays." Pa began to moan. "I guess we better finish up and I'll get some laundry started."

~~~~~~~~~

Pa continued in a state of unconsciousness five more days and left the earth without a hint of regret for his wicked life. On the day of his interment, dark, heavy clouds hung low and a fierce north wind stirred up dust devils across the open field. A spirit of gloom fell over the small group that gathered around the grave. For the service Mr. Long read some Scripture and prayed. Grief, that Pa had resisted the message of God's love, felt like a stab wound in Anna's chest; she had no words of hope to say at his burial.

Would life ever get back to normal? She wasn't even sure if she knew what *normal* was.

CHAPTER 36

Tom and his new bride moved into their home soon after Pa's burial. He and Janie were married in a simple ceremony with only her family present. The couple arrived at the soddy that same afternoon.

"Anna come meet my wife," Tom called as he opened the kitchen door.

Anna didn't want to stir from her bed, not even for a new sister-in-law. Since Pa had died, she had hardly combed her hair or put on a clean dress. She wanted only to sit in a dark room and stare at the wall. She had shed no tears for her pa nor did she wish to.

"Anna," Tom called again. "Are you home?"

"I'll be out in a little while, Tom. Go on to your house and get settled. I'll meet you there later." How would she manage to walk the distance from the soddy to Tom's new house? The thought of meeting her new sister-in-law made her feel dizzy and weak. What had happened to the strong, self-determined woman everyone knew her to be? That woman was gone, lost in a haze of grief, with nothing but an empty future before her.

She stood up and ran a comb through her unruly locks and fastened them in a tight bun at her neck. She pulled a clean dress over her head and laced up her boots. The once fashionable shoes now looked scuffed and shabby, but it didn't matter. Who cared about her or her appearance, anyway?

Tom and Janie met her at the door of their house.

"Come on in, Anna," Tom said, "This is Janie, my wife," his grin was so wide Anna thought his mouth might split.

Janie reached out to give her a hug, but Anna extended her hand and Janie took it, looking a bit baffled.

The smile left her lips as she said, "Please sit down, Anna."

Anna studied the couple. Tom, tall and blond and fair skinned, had chosen a wife the total opposite. Janie had inky, black hair that fell almost to her waist, eyes the color of chocolate and remarkable olive-tan skin. Beside the petite girl, Anna felt like an awkward giant; gauche and plain. She fidgeted with her apron strings, and sat on the edge of her chair, lips drawn tight.

Tom shook his head, mystified at Anna's uncharacteristic behavior.

"Guess I'll get our trunks unloaded while you two get acquainted."

Anna didn't know what to say. She wanted to escape but that would certainly appear rude. Her sister-in-law began to chatter and tell about her family and how they loved Tom, and after a time Anna relaxed and sat back in her chair. She jerked to attention when Janie said, "Anna, Tom tells me you read the Bible and have a personal relationship with God. It means a lot to me to have a sister in Christ. I'm praying that Tom will soon know the peace of being a child of God, also."

"Thank you, Janie. I've been a little lost since Ma and Pa died. We don't have a church or preacher in this community and since I've been home I haven't had anyone to talk to about my faith. I must be going now, but let me know how I can help after you and Tom settle in."

Anna returned to the soddy with a lighter heart and quicker step. Tom had chosen well. She looked forward to knowing Janie better, if she could just get over her tiredness; if she could feel herself again.

Janie was a fit mate for her brother. Her diminutive stature and her winning dark eyes, that held a hint of humor, hid a strong character that put up with no nonsense. Besides, she had an astute mind. She and Tom would without doubt make the farm productive and be able to support their family. Furthermore, Anna found her to be a friend in the Lord. Without Janie she wasn't sure she could have endured the dark, empty days that followed her pa's death. Food turned sour in her stomach and took away her appetite. All she wanted to do was sit in the soddy and stare at the dark, dirt walls. She had disappointed everyone. She let Ma die because she had left her alone. Even when she returned to help care for Pa, she failed to make any difference; he died in his sinful state. And she lost the Long's mare.

She was a failure at everything. Where was God's grace? Where was the comfort of His presence? Her heart felt empty and alone. She needed to get a job, needed the money, but she could hardly force herself to get out of bed to take care of the animals. How would she manage to work for other people?

Before sunup one morning, about a month after Pa died, Survivor began barking and scratching on the kitchen door. Her devoted dog had never before behaved this way. What could be troubling him? Had one of her pa's drinking buddies learned that she lived alone and lurked about in the dark? Anna wished that she had learned to shoot a rifle. Maybe she should ask Tom to teach her.

The barking and scratching became louder. Anna crept out of bed, slipped into her dress and shoes, tiptoed to the front door, and peeked out. In the dark she could see nothing. She opened the door cautiously.

"Survivor, what's wrong? Settle down, fellow," she whispered. The dog wagged his long, shaggy tail wildly and licked her hand. He didn't seem to be warning her of any danger. What could be the trouble?

Only a pale, golden light threaded the eastern horizon. It was still too early to start milking; however, she was already up.

"Come along, buddy, I'm awake. Let's get busy." Anna grabbed the milk pail from under the separator table and started toward the barn when she noticed the outline of a strange animal near the windmill.

"Bowlegs is that you? You silly mule. How did you get out of the stable?" She stepped over to take him back to the barn and realized that the animal wasn't Bowlegs, but an unfamiliar horse. She froze; paralyzed by fear. Where was its rider? *Who* was its rider? Terrified that a thief, or someone wishing her harm, hid on the other side of the water-tank, she began backing away, trying to get a scream past the knot in her throat. The horse moved toward her and began to nuzzle her hand. No strange horse would do that.

"Sandy? Sandy? Is that you?" she whispered. She studied the animal in the predawn light and felt sure it was the lost mare.

"Sandy, come here girl." The horse ducked its

head and shook its mane, whinnied, and followed Anna. Inside the barn she lit the lantern and began rubbing her hand across the animal's neck and side. She felt a jagged scar along its flank. Perhaps in better light she could be sure if this was indeed, Sandy.

Later that morning, Anna brushed and combed the mare, definitely Sandy. By the looks of her coat she had had little care and had probably traveled a long distance.

"Where have you been? I wish horses could talk. I'm sure you would have quite a story. It looks as if you've had some rough times. Thank God, He brought you back to me." She gave Sandy a handful of oats and was rewarded by a nudge on the arm. "You're welcome, I'm sure," she said.

That afternoon Anna took Sandy back to the Longs. As she rode Bowleg, with Sandy tied to the saddle and following along behind, her heart bubbled with anticipation. She could hardly wait to see Mr. Long's face when he saw them coming.

Mr. Long met them as she rode into his land.

"Well, bless my soul. What have we here?" he said a grin stretching across his face.

Anna dismounted and Mr. Long untied Sandy and guided her to the water tank. "Mr. Long I can't tell you how glad I am to be able to return Sandy. I know you hadn't given up, but I thought we would never see this horse again."

"Well, God works in mysterious ways. Truly, I'm thankful how this turned out. Go on inside and visit with the wife. She'll be happy to see you."

Anna left the Longs with a cheerful spirit. Sandy had returned. Still, almost as surprising was Mrs.

Long's news. Sunday services would begin at the school house the first of the month. That was only one week away. After Pa's funeral, several neighbors had talked with Mr. Long and it was agreed to begin Bible study and prayer together. Mr. Long would be their leader until God sent along a preacher. Anna's prayers had been answered. God hadn't forgotten about her after all.

The following days Anna bustled about with a melody in her heart. It seemed as if the sun shone with a new shimmer, the birds sang sweeter, and her heart beat with fresh energy. It was time to do something about her future. Sandy was home. The Sunday attendance was increasing and a circuit rider preacher would soon be visiting them once a month. Mike and Lucy were growing in their faith and Howard had even visited the meetings. It would take a miracle to get Esther to attend, but wasn't God a worker of miracles?

The doctor had recommended Anna to several families as a hired girl but there seemed no reason to stay now that Ma and Pa were gone. She longed to see the Muellers, the Petersons, and *John*. A warm tingle surged through her at the thought of his name. Had he found a wife after she left? Their friendship had been dear to her, and she thought it had meant something to him as well. Still, he could have written. Well, she could have written him, also.

Anna decided to let Mrs. Mueller know she was looking for work and see what happened. A few days later Mike drove into the farm yard.

"Anna, come see what I have for you," he said eyes sparkling with suppressed laughter.

"Mike, is it a letter from Mrs. Mueller? Let me see," Anna could hardly keep from snatching the letter out of his hand.

Mike handed her the letter and said, "I'll get on over and visit Tom. Hope it is good news."

The minute he left, Anna tore open the letter. Survivor began jumping and licking Anna's hand, begging for attention, but all of her attention was on the words she read. When she finished she hugged the letter to her chest and said, "Survivor, they want me to come stay with them while I look for work. They want me to come!"

~~~~~~~~~

Anna sold the cow, chickens, and pigs to Tom and gave them the food in the cellar. She gathered her few belongings, and said good-by to Tom and Janie. As she saddled Bowlegs, Survivor rubbed against her skirt. She bent over and he turned on his back as she scratched his belly. He began switching his tail about, showing his delight, and at the same time struggling to keep from toppling over.

"Survivor, how am I going to leave you behind?" she said, biting back the wave of sadness that pushed to be free. "Take good care of Janie while I'm gone." Anna blinked away her tears and mounted her mule, and rode off to give her farewell to her sisters.

Esther met her in the farm yard. "Goin' back ta them fancy Mueller's that spoiled you," she said. "Think your ta good for the like o' us."

"I came to say good-by, Esther. Don't know when I'll be back. Tell Howard good-by for me." Without another word Anna patted her mule and they trotted out of the yard toward Lucy's.

Mike and Lucy, with Danny stood on their porch watching as Anna dismounted.

"Hi, little cowboy. I came to tell you good-bye."

Danny ran over and clutched her legs. "I don't want you to leave, Aunt Anna."

She bent down and swung him into her arms. "You will always be my favorite feller," she said and gave him a kiss on the cheek.

"Mike, what's the best way to get to the Muellers' house?"

"I think I would ride a little north of Freedom, and take the road east to Alva and then south on to the Muellers'. That's the best route, with more people on the road in case you need help. Are you sure you want to ride Bowlegs?"

"I'm not walking all the way as I did to Uncle Chris's, that's for sure. I don't know how far I can ride at a time. Bowlegs can be stubborn and if she decides she wants to stop and rest, I'll have to oblige her." Anna patted her mule. "I brought some treats to keep her going when she gets obstinate."

"Do you have enough food? I've got some fried chicken you could take," Lucy said.

"Thanks Lucy. I've packed food and water, but your fried chicken sure sounds good."

"Do you think it's safe to sleep out? I heard mountain lions have been spotted around them caves near Freedom," Mike said.

The thought of a mountain lion roaming about gave Anna a shock. Trying not to show her fear, she said, "I'll travel as far as I can away from Freedom before I stop for the night."

Anna said her final good-bye, gave Bowlegs a

nudge in the flanks and rode away. She would miss her family, but was already anticipating the future. She wondered if John ever thought about her as she did him.

Lord, would you put me in his mind? In his heart, too. Help him know that he needs a wife, even if he does think that his handicap would keep a woman from loving him. Not just any wife, Lord, me."

CHAPTER 37

Three days later Anna turned Bowlegs into the lane leading to the Muellers' farm yard. Ben trotted over to greet her, barking and flinging his tail about. She hardly had time to dismount when Martha and Sarah scampered out and threw their arms around her neck.

"Anna, Anna we missed you," the girls chorused.

Anna scooped them close and said.

"I missed you, too." She led Bowlegs over to the water trough.

Mrs. Mueller appeared, carrying Davy.

"Just leave your mule. Sam will take care of him," she said. "Here, let me help you with your baggage."

"Thank you Mrs. Mueller. It has been quite a trip."

Mrs. Mueller gave Anna's hand a squeeze.

"I know you must be tired. Come in and have a cool drink." The women visited, talking nonstop, except when the girls interrupted. It seemed as if she had never left. This place felt more like home than her home had.

The next day Mr. And Mrs. Peterson arrived in their buggy.

"Roy, come out to the barn, I want to show you our new mule," Mr. Mueller said, his mouth twitching with mirth. The new mule he was talking about was Anna's Bowlegs.

The women went into the kitchen. Mrs. Peterson settled her generous frame in a chair and said, "Let me help peel potatoes while we visit, Ellen."

Anna wanted to join them but Martha said, "Anna, help us gather eggs."

The two little girls skipped alongside Anna, chatting about the baby chicks they were raising, how Ben had caught a rabbit, and other childish tales, but Anna wasn't really listening. She was wondering about John. Had he returned from his visit to his grandmother? Had he found a wife? When they opened the gate to the chicken yard, the chickens surrounded them, swanking and flapping their wings. Anna chortled and said, "It's not feeding time. We're just gathering eggs." Laughter felt good, even if her joke had been silly. She must quit fretting about John and start thanking God for friends like the Muellers.

After the eggs had been gathered and placed in a basket in the water trough to cool, Anna went into the kitchen and listened to the women's amiable chatter, hoping to hear news about John. But when Mr. Peterson came to the porch door and said it was time to leave, nothing of John had been mentioned and she felt too shy to ask.

Later that evening Mrs. Mueller said, "I wonder why John didn't come with the Petersons today."

"Ellen, Mr. Peterson told me that they have decided to turn the farm over to him. He will live in their big house and they will move into the smaller one. They're in poor health and just couldn't keep up with it all; besides, John will need the larger place when he gets married."

Gets married! Anna rushed out of the kitchen to the orchard, hoping no one had seen the tears that were filling her eyes. John was engaged. What made her think he might marry a big, unsightly girl like her?

Anna collapsed under an apple tree. Only then did she let herself weep, for what could never be hers.

The next few days Anna settled in while she waited to hear if anyone in the neighborhood needed a hired girl. Mrs. Mueller was teaching her how to sew. She had cut out a dress from the material she bought in Alva and was putting it together using Mrs. Mueller's treadle machine. Learning to move her feet just right to get the treadle to shift up and down had been a little tricky, but after a time she conquered the rhythm.

~~~~~~~~

John sat on the porch stoop of the Petersons' big house. No, it was now his house. His uncle had turned it all over to him, the land, the house, everything, and they had moved to their smaller cottage across the road. He felt grateful that they trusted him, but wondered if he were up to the task of running a large farm and caring for his aunt and uncle.

He looked down through oak trees that lined the drive leading into the farm yard. Scarlet, orange, and gold leaves swayed in the morning wind, their stunning colors singing the glory of autumn. But John didn't feel like singing. Grandma was gone. Her broken hip had healed but then she took a fever. The fever had won and she lost her fight to live. John had watched her struggle and been unable to help. God knew he'd tried, sitting up night and day, sponging her burning skin with cool water. Still as he remembered her last words assuring him that she wanted to go to be with her beloved husband, and to be with Jesus; he knew his grief was selfish.

He must move on with his life. He thought of

Anna. He knew she had returned and was staying with the Muellers. How many times he had thought about her while he was away. He had bragged to his grandma what a fine woman Anna was. His grandma would have loved her. Still he hesitated to go see her. She deserved better than a crippled husband. He looked down at his twisted ankle and heard the gentle voice of his Savior.

"John, you are my child. You are whole in my sight. Love sees no flaws."

"Thank you Father. I know you love me, but can a woman? A woman as perfect as Anna?"

"Trust me," was the reply.

John put his head in his hands.

"Forgive me, Lord. I do trust you."

~~~~~~~~

One afternoon Anna went out to the orchard to gather fruit. She set her stepladder under a tree, climbed up on it and began picking apples and placing them gently into her bucket. A brisk breeze flowed between the branches; the scent of fall teased her senses. A mourning dove cooed from a branch nearby. Anna had begun to hum a melody, remembered from childhood, when she heard someone calling her. She turned cautiously from her perch and saw John looking up at her with a lopsided grin. He extended his hand and said, "Let me help you down, Anna."

Her legs felt like taffy and her heart pounded until she felt a button would burst on her shirtwaist. Her hand trembled so that she was afraid to touch John's. Instead, she gave him her bucket, and climbed down the ladder on her own.

She tried to act nonchalant and to keep her eyes off John, but they acted as if they had a mind of their own. Shyly, she glanced up and their eyes locked. He gave her a glorious smile that turned her bones to jelly and set her stomach churning.

"How have you been?" he asked.

She fought to get her emotions under control before responding.

"These months at home have been the hardest I've ever lived. Seeing Ma in that abysmal Fort Supply Institution was almost more than I could stand. Pa dying without any sign that he called on the name of Jesus was harder yet."

John twisted the loose locks around Anna's face in his fingers.

"I wish I could have been there for you," he said.

At his touch a shiver tiptoed down her spine and she fought to keep from grabbing him and giving him a hug.

"I believe Ma came to the Lord, but I have no hope for Pa. My faith, along with my Bible and the *Book of Readings* you gave me, were my strength." She bit back her tears.

"I'm sorry for your loss, Anna, but I'm glad you had the Lord to uphold you. I wish I could have been there, but I only recently learned of your troubles. When I went home in January, I found my grandma in bad shape and I stayed with her until she died, just a few weeks ago."

"John, I'm sorry. I know how much she meant to you."

As they strolled toward the house John moved closer and linked her fingers in his.

"Did you think of me while you were gone? I thought of you often."

"No, I didn't think of you very much. Just about twenty times a day is all."

John put his arms around Anna and drew her close.

"That was a 'like' hug. Do you mind if I give you a 'love' hug?"

"I wish you would, and do you mind if I hug you back?"

John kissed her, unaware that they were being watched until he heard giggles.

"Mama, John is kissing Anna on the lips," Martha said. "You told us never to kiss that way."

Everyone started laughing, including John and Anna.

Martha said, "I heard Mama and Papa say they thought you and John might get married. Are you going to, Anna?"

"I don't know Martha. John hasn't asked me."

"Are you going to ask her John?"

"Maybe, when we have a little privacy. Anna, would you like to take a little walk with me?"

John put his arm across her waist and they strolled out to her favorite place beside the stream and sat down. John took her hands and traced a line up her arms to her cheeks.

"My aunt and uncle have turned over the farm work and their house to me and moved into the smaller one. The house is too big for one person. I am hoping to share it with someone special." John took Anna's hand and looked into her eyes. "Someone very dear to me." He drew her close and she leaned into his embrace.

"I love you, Anna, and want to marry you. Will you marry me? Soon?"

"Oh, John, I've prayed that you could love me. I do want to be your wife. Still, I would like a little time to get ready. Would two or three weeks be too long?"

CHAPTER 38

Anna slid her hands along the smooth, silk bodice of her wedding dress.

"Stand still. You're shaking the hair pins out," Janie said. She combed her fingers through Anna's thick, wavy locks and swept them up into a loose chignon atop her head, leaving a few wayward tresses cascading into soft zigzags that framed her face and accentuated her velvety neck and shoulders.

"There. That's perfect." Janie studied the up-do then ran her fingertips along the folds of Anna's dress. "This lavender silk certainly becomes you. What would Esther think if she could see you now?" Janie teased.

"I did feel guilty when I bought this fabric." Anna said as she remembered her debate with herself when she stopped in Alva on her way to the Muellers. She truly had needed new garments, but buying silk was extravagant.

"Guess, my weak moment paid off," she said.

Janie tucked a snippet of bittersweet in Anna's hair and said, "All finished. Come along before John thinks you've changed your mind."

They stepped outside into the brisk October afternoon. The cloudless blue sky hung like a canopy overhead. Even the relentless Oklahoma wind had slowed to a gentle breeze, giving its nod to this perfect day. Anna looked across the yard where her family stood chatting as they waited for the ceremony to begin. She smiled with pride as she watched them laughing and talking to the other guests. They had cared enough to come. Only Esther had refused to make the long journey, but she would not let Esther's bitter spirit steal her joy today. Katy and Lucy and Tom and Janie had arrived in Matt's automobile. Uncle Chris, Aunt Nettie, and Betty Lou, traveled on the train. Anna had a swift, stabbing pain of regret that Ma was missing. Still, somehow, she felt a sense of her blessing.

Anna noticed the Hunters visiting with other neighbors. Beside them Carl stood, his face twisted into his usual sulk. What was he doing here? She certainly hadn't invited him. He better not cause trouble or do anything to ruin her special day. Still he was the Hunters' nephew. He must have come with them. As she watched the troublesome intruder, she saw the petite young woman she had envied approach him and tuck her arm into his. Anna stifled a giggle at the thought of the unlikely pair.

Matt's anxious voice broke her reflections.

"Janie, Anna, step on it. The fiddle music's starting."

The women met him in the yard where he stood tapping his boot in the dirt impatiently. Anna drew near and he hooked her arm in his and guided her along the path to meet her groom. Her rich, violet colored gown shimmered in the sunlight as the soft wind tugged at the folds of the skirt. When Anna stepped alongside John, Matt smiled and said, "John you better take care of my sis." He placed Anna's hand into John's and went to join his family.

John whispered, "You take my breath away. You are beautiful."

A thrill shot through her at his words. No one had ever called her *beautiful*.

After they repeated their vows, Rev. Bradford,

the circuit rider preacher, said, "Folks, may I introduce Mr. and Mrs. John Edward Davis." In that moment John gently took her in his arms and kissed her soundly.

After the reception John helped Anna into his buggy and they drove to their home. At the front door he swung Anna up into his arms and said, "Welcome home Anna. We have the rest of our lives to be together. I can hardly wait."

Epilogue:

Several weeks later John said, "Anna, follow me. I want to show you something." They strolled across the yard until they reached the brook. John cupped her face in his hands and turned her toward a pasture of green winter wheat.

"Our first crop," he said.

Anna surveyed the carpet of emerald, surrounded by red dirt and stubby, lifeless prairie grass.

"This meadow reminds me of the song Mr. Mueller sang the first time they took me to church," she said. "Do you remember?"

John shook his head.

Softly, Anna began to sing, *"In shady, green pastures, so rich and so sweet, God leads His dear children along. Where the water's cool flow bathes the weary one's feet, God leads His dear children along. Sometimes on the mount where the sun shines so bright, God leads His dear children along; sometimes in the valley, in darkest of night, God leads His dear children along."*

She paused and John lifted his voice with hers.

"Some thru the waters, some thru the flood, some thru the fire, but all thru the blood. Some thru great sorrow, but God gives a song, in the night season and all the day long."

"John, I feel like I've been through the flood, the fire, and great sorrow; and I know I've been through His blood. Now I'm in His green pastures and my heart is singing a new song."

The throaty sound of a mourning dove nearby crooned, *cooOOoo*.

John gathered her into his arms.

RECIPE OF ANNA'S FAMILY FAVORITE
"Frikadeller" - med kartofler - sovs og surt!
Pork Meatballs

2 lb. lean pork
2 eggs
1 large onion, grated
2 slices white bread, soaked in milk
1/2 tsp. pepper
1/2 cup milk
1 tsp. salt

Grind lean pork in a meat grinder twice, or let the butcher do it. Add soaked bread, grated onion, eggs, mix well with a wooden spoon. Add salt, pepper, and milk. The Frikadelle mixture gets better the more you mix the ingredients together. It is best if you leave the mixture to rest about an hour in the fridge then mix again.

Melt butter (or margarine) in a pan. (May use vegetable oil.) To shape, take a tablespoonful of the mixture, then smooth against the wall of the bowl. When all the meatballs are shaped, fry them at high temperature on both sides and then continue frying at low heat around 5 minutes on each side. The meatballs are served with boiled potatoes, pickled beets, sour, preserved cucumber, and thick brown sauce.

Thick Brown Creamy Sauce

1 1/2 cups milk
3 tablespoons flour
1 tablespoon brown color
1/2 cup cream
1 teaspoon salt

Stir the flour smooth with a little of the milk. Heat the remaining milk and cream to boiling, adding the flour mixture and brown color. Cook until thickened and add salt. Milk instead of cream may be used by adding two tablespoons of butter substitute.

The first mention of Frikadeller is a handwritten cookbook around 1280. In this recipe, minced pork and chicken meat were mixed and formed into meatballs. Frikadeller, was mentioned again in 16th and 17th century cookbooks. The 1837 cookbook of Madam Mangor gives a recipe for Frikadeller listing the same ingredients that are used today.

RECIPE OF ARELINE'S FAMILY FAVORITE
Cinnamon Rolls *

3.4oz pkg. vanilla instant pudding
3 teaspoons salt
3/4 cup sugar
11 cups flour (un-sifted)
2/3 cup shortening
1/2 cup margarine or butter
3 pkg. yeast
6 eggs
1/2 cup warm water
2 cups milk

Mix dry ingredients in a very large mixing bowl. Add shortening and butter. Mix with hands until mixture is crumbly. Mix yeast and ½ cup warm water and set aside. In a small bowl, mix eggs, milk, water, and yeast mixture. Add this to the dry ingredients and mix with dough hook or wooden spoon until well blended. Turn dough out on a floured surface and knead until it no longer sticks to floured surface, but feels a little sticky to your hands. Pour a bit of oil into the very large mixing bowl. Place dough into bowl and swirl around in oil and turn dough upside-down. Cover with towel and place in a warm area to rise until doubled in size.

To make cinnamon rolls:

Take approximately 1/3 of the dough at a time and roll each piece out on a lightly floured surface to a little less than ½ inch thick, in a rectangular shape. Melt ½ cup butter.

Spread dough surface with melted butter. Sprinkle generously with sugar and then lightly with cinnamon. Roll up dough and seal the edge tightly. Cut into about 1 1/2 inches slices and place cut side down in a well-greased pan having 1 - 2 inches high sides. Space rolls so they do not touch. Repeat with the remaining dough until all dough is used. Press down the top of the rolls and let rise until doubled in size. Bake in a 375 degree oven for approxmently 15 - 20 minutes or until golden brown. Do not over bake. Makes approximately 45 to 50 rolls.

Glaze

About 2 cups powdered sugar   3-4 tablespoons milk
½ t vanilla
Mix powder sugar and milk with ½ teaspoon of vanilla. Glaze top of rolls to suit. (Our family likes more rather than less topping.)

*For other recipes see *Something Special Cookbook*, Areline Bolerjack. Cookbooks may be ordered at, www.languagefootprints.com or from bwjbook@yahoo.com

AUTHORS' NOTES

Areline Bolerjack's mother and maternal grandparents homesteaded near Freedom, Oklahoma after the Cherokee Strip was opened to settlers in 1893. In their book, **Anna's Song**, authors Bolerjack and Jones drew from some of their experiences.

However, the book is a work of fiction. All other characters, names, events, and dialogue in the novel are either products of the authors' imagination or are used fictitiously.

Areline had been to a family reunion of her mother's relatives, and while there, she asked if anyone knew anything about her maternal grandparents who were both born in Denmark. At the time she was studying with the Long Ridge Writers Group and her assignment was to write three chapters of a book. She chose to draw from what she had learned about her family, and with the encouragement of her instructor she began writing this book. After working on it off and on for several years, Areline decided to collaborate with her husband's niece, and together, they have woven an inspiring historical novel portraying life in the late 1800s and early 1900s.

Fort Supply is located in the western part of the Cherokee Outlet in present Woodward County, Oklahoma. Originally named Camp Supply, it was established in 1868 as the supply camp for the military campaign against the Southern Plains Indians. When the Cherokee Strip opened on September 16, 1893 to non-Indian homesteaders, the Army troops at Fort Supply oversaw the land-run, and this operation was their last major assignment.

The Army's presence was no longer needed as the frontier filled with white settlers and many native people were relocated to reservations, and in 1894 the Fort was abandoned. On November 16, 1907 Oklahoma Territory became a state, and the Fort was ceded to the new state for use as its first Mental

Institution. When it opened in 1908, two train loads of patients were brought from a private institution that had burned to the ground. This created overcrowding and understaffing at around the same time Anna's mother, Mrs. Ebbessen, became a patient.

The experience of Anna's mother being placed in the Mental Hospital at Fort Supply has been fictionalized; however, our research shows that the story's description is not unrealistic. A common belief of that day was that the mentally ill lost their reason because of exposure to severe stress or shock. Terms such as brain fever and shattered nerves were used to describe this kind of condition. Often **family members were discouraged, or in some cases not allowed, to visit their loved ones**. Patients were seen as needing protection from society for a time so they could recover, and were institutionalized until they either died or somehow got better.

Early treatment of the mentally ill might consist of branding a patient's head with a red hot iron in order to somehow bring him to his senses. As late as the end of the nineteenth century, a mentally ill person might be strapped into a harness and swung around to *calm the nerves*. According to documents taken from the early 1900s overcrowded hospitals, poor food, restraining patients in strait jackets, and in some cases sadistic or unsympathetic employees, were common practices.

Areline Bolerjack grew up in Alva, Oklahoma, near her grandparents' homestead where this story took place. She graduated from the Cadet Nurse Corps and is a retired Registered Nurse. Her husband was a World War II veteran whom she married after a whirlwind courtship of three months. He retired from the U.S. army as a Staff Sergeant and passed away a few years ago.

Due to her husband's military assignments, the couple moved around a great deal but wherever they lived Areline found herself teaching an Adult Bible Study group. For the last few years she served as an assistant Sunday School teacher to fourth grade girls and prepared biweekly dinners for her senior adult group.

She lives in Blackwell, Oklahoma and has two sons, a daughter-in-law, two grandchildren and four great grandchildren. For nearly 15 years she wrote a column for two newspapers under the byline, Something Special. In 1982 she published her first cookbook which was revised and reprinted in 1994.

Barbara Wright Jones is an award winning writer and published author of a biography and several articles and short stories, as well as curriculum books for Spanish language teachers and finger puppet plays. Her most recent book, *Rolling Heads and Other Tales to Tell*, is a medley of stories of Spanish explorers and folk tales of the native people of the Americas. She is also a professional storyteller who has performed story programs in many venues.

Barbara is a native Oklahoman, born on a farm near the homestead her great grandparents received in the land-run of 1889. She and her husband were career missionaries with their denomination and lived in Mexico, Peru, and Paraguay, and traveled extensively in South America for 19 years.

She is a graduate of Southern Nazarene University and has taught elementary school, high school, and adult education. For the last 10 years she has taught adults preparing for ministry. She lives in Meeker, Oklahoma with her husband, Kenneth. They have three married children and five grandchildren.

Made in the USA
Charleston, SC
05 March 2013